> **"Is a night in bed being offered?" Brett asked**

"Are you nuts!" Charlotte exclaimed.

He grinned lazily. "I must be, to be this involved with you."

"Or maybe you're working for the enemy!" Charlotte blurted out. Her newest theory voiced, Charlotte regarded him bluntly. "I don't even think you're really the person you're claiming to be!"

She was getting too close to the truth, Brett thought. He stepped toward her, an irascible gleam in his eyes.

"You've overstepped your bounds, sir," Charlotte warned, watching him come close. He didn't stop until he was right in front of her.

"Lady, from what I know about what you've been up to," Brett drawled, "I haven't even begun."

ABOUT THE AUTHOR

Cathy Gillen Thacker believes that love and laughter go hand in hand, and readers love her warm family stories. A charter member of Romance Writers of America, she is the author of forty novels and numerous nonfiction articles. Four of her books have appeared on the Waldenbooks bestseller list. A native Midwesterner, Cathy lives in Texas with her husband and three children.

Books by Cathy Gillen Thacker

Don't miss any of our special offers. Write to us at the following address for information on our newest releases.

Harlequin Reader Service
U.S.: 3010 Walden Ave., P.O. Box 1325, Buffalo, NY 14269
Canadian: P.O. Box 609, Fort Erie, Ont. L2A 5X3

Cathy Gillen Thacker

MISS CHARLOTTE SURRENDERS

Harlequin Books

TORONTO • NEW YORK • LONDON
AMSTERDAM • PARIS • SYDNEY • HAMBURG
STOCKHOLM • ATHENS • TOKYO • MILAN
MADRID • WARSAW • BUDAPEST • AUCKLAND

ISBN 0-373-16568-4

MISS CHARLOTTE SURRENDERS

Copyright © 1995 by Cathy Gillen Thacker.

Dear Reader,

My writing career began on a rainy autumn afternoon in Texas eighteen years ago, when I sat down at the kitchen table to write a "short story" while my toddlers napped. Writing that first short story proved much more difficult and more involving than I had imagined, but the characters stayed with me, and the more I wrote, the more I wanted to know. By the time I had finished months later, I had given my hero and heroine the happy ending they deserved...and I had a *book-length* work!

That first love story was never published, nor were the six novels that followed as I painstakingly taught myself the writing craft. But with my eighth book I struck gold and *Island of Desire* was published in July, 1982.

The last eighteen years have brought many changes in my writing career. I abandoned writing longhand, in favor of a typewriter, then abandoned that for a computer. I moved from the kitchen table into a sunny skylit office, built *adjacent* to my kitchen. To date, I've published forty novels of romantic suspense, warm family drama and romantic comedy. My novels have been published in over thirty countries, in a dozen different languages. It's very gratifying to have come so far in such a short time, and I enjoy seeing my work in print immensely, as do my husband and three children. But most important of all, are the heartfelt words I receive from readers. I love to hear from you and I can be reached via Harlequin Books, 300 East 42nd Street, New York, New York, 10017.

I hope you enjoy reading my new romantic comedy, *Miss Charlotte Surrenders*, as much as I enjoyed writing it, and I look forward to hearing from you.

Cordially yours,

Cathy Gillen Thacker

Prologue

"I want that woman off my back," Stephen Sterling grumbled to his New York City attorney.

Franklin Dunn, Jr., picked up a gold pen and turned it end over end. "Charlotte Langston has been a pest, hasn't she?"

"And then some." Stephen stroked his gray goatee and sighed, then turned back to Franklin with a relentless scowl. "I'm not going to let that nosy journalist unmask me," he vowed.

"I don't blame you," Franklin said. Waving his pen in lecturing fashion, he continued, "And to that end, I have a suggestion for you."

Stephen's bushy gray brow lifted in speculative interest. "Name it."

"You need a spy in the enemy camp."

Stephen grinned as he casually tucked his silk ascot into the open collar of his shirt. "Someone to keep her from finding out everything she has always wanted to know?"

"Exactly. As long as the person you hire is one step ahead of the indefatigable Miss Langston, keeping her in the dark about you will be easy," Franklin assured him.

Stephen sat back in his chair. He ran his hand thoughtfully over the ivory handle on his cane. "You've got a point," he said slowly. A wicked gleam came into his eyes. "Furthermore, I know just the man for the job."

"Who?" Franklin sat forward expectantly.

"Brett Forrest," Stephen said with a contemplative grin. "He'll keep her so busy and aggravated that poor Miss Langston will never guess an enemy has infiltrated her nest."

Chapter One

Charlotte emerged from her car, stiff from two straight days of driving, and took a good look around. The house where she and her sisters had grown up was just as she remembered it. Twelve tall white columns braced the front of the majestic three-story plantation home. Dark green shutters adorned every window and contrasted nicely against gleaming white wood. Creamy-petaled camellias with evergreen leaves surrounded the veranda on all sides. But there, the tender loving care stopped.

Her heart sinking, Charlotte realized the grounds of the rural Mississippi plantation were in terrible shape. The once beautiful lawn of Camellia Lane was now peppered with crabgrass and dandelions and streamed wetly up past her knees. The flower beds that lined the drive stood empty. Even more disturbing, one of the shutters on a second-floor window had been knocked loose by the wind and hung crooked on one hinge.

Her younger sister, Isabella, had hired a caretaker. What on earth could he be doing with his time?

Charlotte frowned. Having seen the grounds, she wondered what kind of condition the caretaker's cottage was in. Deciding to find out, she marched down the flagstone path to the cottage, which was some distance away, and knocked on the door. Once... twice. There was no answer.

Determining she had better check on things, Charlotte unlocked the door and stormed in. The place was a wreck.

Papers and books were everywhere. A state-of-the-art laptop computer and portable LaserJet printer sat on the table. Charlotte frowned. What caretaker could afford that luxury? Furthermore, what caretaker had ever been this incredibly handsome, even when sprawled on a sofa, apparently fast asleep?

Even in repose, every inch of him was tantalizingly, ruggedly male. He had dark coffee-colored hair that fell away from his face in thick rumpled waves. A full mustache emphasized rather than hid his sensually chiseled lips. High cheekbones and the squareness of his jaw added to the rakish appeal of his straight-blade nose and rectangular face.

He had to be at least six foot four of solid male muscle and was probably in his mid-thirties. He wore faded jeans, a sparkling white T-shirt and a light gray sweatshirt bearing the Yale insignia.

Some caretaker, Charlotte thought irritably, as she ran her hands through her dark curly hair. She could be a robber, ready to steal Camellia Lane blind and he would never know.

She stepped closer, put a hand out to touch his shoulder.

The next thing she knew she was flat on her back, beneath him, one of his hands circling her waist. The other held both her hands above her head.

"You've got two seconds to tell me what you're doing breaking into my cottage," he warned mildly.

Charlotte had thought he was handsome when he was sleeping. It was nothing compared to the way he looked when he was awake. His lashes were long and thick, his eyes a vivid electric blue. His mouth was soft but firm beneath the thick mustache. True, he needed a shave. She could see the eighth-of-an-inch bristles of his beard against the suntanned hue of his skin, but he smelled of Old Spice. Charlotte had always loved that cologne.

"Unhand me this instant!" she demanded, wiggling furiously and feeling every soft, slender inch of her torso and legs brush up against every hard, unyielding inch of his.

Heat started at the base of her throat and swept up into her face.

"Not," he bargained wickedly, settling more comfortably between her thighs, "until you tell me who you are."

The mischievous glint in his eyes indicated he knew his sensual tussling with her was completely unnecessary, if entirely pleasurable. Charlotte glared up at him, fighting the tingles of awareness with every ounce of fortitude she possessed.

At her response, he did everything to suppress a grin. He knew, of course, that he could let her go now that they'd quickly established she was no threat. But the feel of her beneath him, her silky hair spread out on the sofa cushions, the feistiness in her emerald green eyes, was hard to resist. This woman presented a challenge for any man brave enough to take her on. And he never had been able to resist a challenge. Particularly the beautiful, hot-tempered, female kind.

"Your name first," he demanded again and was rewarded with another burning flash of her emerald eyes.

Charlotte's breasts rose and fell with each agitated breath she took. She regarded him imperiously. "I am Charlotte Langston, you fool!"

Finally, it seemed, she had gotten through to him.

"Charlotte Langston," he repeated, stunned. He loosened his grip on her slightly. His electric blue gaze swept the band collar of her starched white shirt and the navy-and-gold tapestry vest before returning to her face. "*You're* Miss Charlotte?"

"Yes, I am Miss Charlotte," she bit out, her face flooding with telltale heat as her formidable temper rose another notch. She couldn't believe she was wrestling on the sofa with the new caretaker, never mind almost enjoying it. "Now let me up before I do something we'll both regret, like punch you in the nose," she snapped.

He grinned at that, as if he were thinking he'd like to see her try. Wordlessly, he stood and offered her a hand.

Aware her trouser legs had hiked up almost to her knees in the struggle and one of her heels had fallen off, Charlotte struggled to get herself together.

Her composure restored, she bent to rummage for her shoe.

He scooped it up first, then knelt in front of her and slipped it on for her. "I apologize for flipping you onto your back like that," he said as he continued to kneel like an errant knight paying homage to his queen. "But you shouldn't sneak up on people."

Charlotte stood. Not surprisingly, after what she had just been through, her knees felt a little wobbly. "I knocked," she defended herself sharply, irritated that their brief tussle on the sofa had left her feeling so unsettled. "You didn't answer."

Again, that slow, sexy grin that wreaked havoc with her insides. "That's 'cause I was asleep."

Charlotte arched a brow. Her dark green eyes glinted with a deep disapproval she made no move to hide. "At two in the afternoon?" she asked.

"Give me a break." Irritated, he pivoted away from her and began to gather up the papers he had strewn across the table. He shoved them all in a brown accordian envelope and secured them with a string. "I was up all night working," he continued with a beleaguered frown.

"On Camellia Lane?" she asked in patent disbelief.

He shook his head and corrected her. "My dissertation. Didn't your sister Isabella tell you? Guess not, from that scowl on your face. I'm a doctoral student. I've been working on my dissertation for several years now—"

"You're a little old to be a student, aren't you?" Charlotte interrupted suspiciously. She couldn't put her finger on it, but something about this guy just didn't ring quite true to her.

"I'm thirty-five." His glance skimmed her wickedly from head to toe. His lips curved in a teasing smile. "How old are you?"

Thirty-three, Charlotte thought, but she had no intention of telling him that!

"Uh-oh. That look means you're over thirty for sure. But not to worry," he drawled with an exaggerated Southern accent as his bold glance slid over her heart-shaped face. He was standing so close she could feel the warmth of his body, but she didn't move away as he whispered in her ear. "You still look damn fine to me, Miss Charlotte. Damn fine!"

Irritated to find herself secretly pleased at his approval, Charlotte planted both her hands on her hips and glared at him wordlessly.

His roguish grin widened, as if he knew he had annoyed her every bit as much as he meant to. "Besides," he continued lazily, rubbing the underside of his chiseled jaw, "no one's too old for an education."

"Oh, I don't know about that," Charlotte shot back. She looked him up and down in the same manner he had just surveyed her, taking in his ruggedly handsome face. Ignoring the rapid pounding of her heart, she said, "By the time you've hit your mid-thirties, if you don't have a real job..." She let her words trail off sarcastically.

To her frustration, he looked not the least bit offended by her tone. Eyes twinkling with unstinting humor, he said lazily, "Being a caretaker is a real job, Miss Charlotte."

Charlotte thought of the condition of the grounds, and rolled her eyes in a demonstration of exasperation. "You'd never know it, by the way you take care of this place." She grasped his arm above the elbow and dragged him over to the window. Promptly dropping her hand from the tantalizing sinew of his bicep, she pointed to the outside. "The grounds are a wreck. The grass hasn't been cut, the camellias around the main house weeded or the honeysuckle around the cottage cut back."

He pivoted toward her, legs brushing hers slightly. Towering over her by a good ten inches, he held up a palm to halt the flow of her criticism. "Isabella hired me to watch over the place during the day while she and Paige are gone," he announced flatly. Still watching her face, he crossed his arms in front of him implacably. "To get me to do repairs and cut grass, you'd have to pay me a salary, and I'm not getting money to stay here."

Charlotte blinked, the wind temporarily taken from her sails. "That's all?" If what he said was true and she guessed from his expression it was, then Isabella had really dropped the ball on this one.

"That's all," he confirmed matter-of-factly, keeping his sober glance on Charlotte's upturned face. "Otherwise, I never would have agreed to stay here."

It figured, she thought. Every time she left something to her softhearted sisters, it got screwed up. Isabella, in particular, needed to learn how to drive a harder bargain. "Where'd you meet my sister, anyway?" she asked, backing away from him casually and returning to the center of the room. She didn't know if it was the sheer size of him, but every time she was close to him her heart beat a little too fast for comfort.

"I met Isabella at the Poplar Springs Public Library. I was doing some research on farming methods in Mississippi. But enough about me and my work." Hand on her shoulder, he propelled her into the adjacent kitchen, which to Charlotte's surprise was extremely neat and tidy. He picked up a pot and poured coffee into a stoneware mug. Wordlessly, he offered it to her. Although she was dying for a cup after her long drive, she declined. No way was she drinking that noxious brew.

"So. What do you do for a living, Miss Charlotte?"

She wondered why he was asking. Deciding she'd better try to find out why he was so curious about her, Charlotte played along cautiously. "I'm a reporter for *Personalities,* the gossip magazine."

"Gossip, huh?" He lounged against the counter. Seemingly unable to take his eyes from her face, he asked innocently enough, "What happens if you don't find any dirt on a person? Do you make something up?"

"No, of course not," Charlotte snapped indignantly. Beginning to feel a little too attracted to him again, she prowled the kitchen restlessly. Had it always been this small? She hadn't noticed before. "Besides, there's always something to find," she continued with an airy wave of her hand.

He quaffed some of the awful coffee, grimaced as it hit his taste buds, then wiped his mouth with the back of his hand. "So how come you aren't working on a story now?" he asked curiously.

"I *am* working on a story," Charlotte explained, wishing he didn't look and smell quite so good. Having someone this handsome and mischievous underfoot could prove quite distracting. "As a matter of fact, I'm hunting someone down as we speak," she finished, telling herself she could handle being temporarily cooped up in here together if he could.

His blue eyes focused on hers contemplatively. "Well, now, that sounds ominous," he drawled.

Charlotte did not consider either her work or her conversation with the hunky new caretaker inconsequential. Her shoulders tensed as her defenses slid back into place. "It often is for my quarry," she admitted seriously. "Remember the treasury secretary scandal and the Bel Air madam? Those were both my stories, and I broke them." She was unable to keep the pride from her voice. There was nothing like the satisfaction she felt when she exposed corruption or deceit of any kind.

Evidently deciding he'd had enough of the poison he'd been drinking, he tossed the remains in the sink and began washing out the pot. Charlotte watched as he set about efficiently making a fresh pot, using vanilla-almond beans.

He had great hands, she thought absently. Large, square, capable ones with nimble fingers and neatly trimmed nails.

"So…who is this person you're hunting down?" he asked conversationally.

He certainly was presumptuous. Charlotte tossed her head. Dark, silky hair flew in every direction as she narrowed her eyes at him suspiciously. "Why are you asking all these questions? Are you trying to steal my story?" she prompted, only half kidding. There were a lot of gossip reporters tracking down Sterling. It was possible their hand-some new caretaker was one of them.

He grinned. "Why do you ask?" he bantered back lazily as the dimples on either side of his mouth deepened sexily. "Are you afraid I will?"

Charlotte lounged against the opposite counter and folded her arms in front of her as the delicious aroma of coffee filled the room. "Not at all," she said with a confident lift of her pretty chin. Her eyes zeroed in on his, letting him know she meant every word. "No one beats me to a story."

"Ah, I see. And what happens when you catch up with this person you're trying to interview?" he challenged bluntly.

Charlotte shrugged, all too aware he was watching her every movement. "Then I find out what the person is hiding and write the story," she said.

He regarded her tolerantly. "How do you know this person you are currently chasing is hiding anything?" he asked in a deep, faintly amused voice.

Charlotte pursed her lips together in aggravation. "Call it instinct."

"And that's all you have to go on?" he asked incredulously.

Charlotte had learned the hard way how to sniff out a fraud. "This person I'm hunting down is a celebrity who has worked hard to achieve his fame and yet he doesn't want any publicity, period," she explained. "In fact, he's downright paranoid about it. That strikes me as odd and tells me there is a story there."

Seeing the coffee had finished brewing, he reached for two mugs and filled them. "I see your point."

Their hands brushed as he handed her a mug, and again, she tingled when they came in contact.

"On the other hand, if this guy wants to preserve his privacy, he ought to be able to do so, celebrity status or not, don't you think?" he said reasonably.

Charlotte could see the sinewy imprint of his shoulders and the tautness of his chest beneath the soft cotton of his sweatshirt. "Only if he's not involved in something fraudulent," she stipulated firmly. And that had yet to be determined. "Have you read any of the work of Stephen Sterling?"

He rummaged around in the cupboard and brought out a tin of butter cookies. He opened it and Charlotte took two. He took one himself, set the box on the small kitchen table and motioned her to a chair. "Has he written anything on dirt farming in the western hemisphere?"

Charlotte sat down opposite him only because she was tired of standing. As their knees touched accidentally, she felt goose bumps break out. "No. And why would you ask that?"

He shrugged. "Because dirt farming is what I'm doing my dissertation on, and books on farming are about all I've read recently."

Somehow, Charlotte just didn't buy that, either. But she had no chance to pursue it, as he was already asking another question.

"Back to Sterling. What kind of books does he write?" he asked.

Charlotte helped herself to another cookie and sat stiffly in her chair. No way was she letting their knees come into contact again. "He writes adventure novels. So far he's only published three, but all have been on the *New York Times* Best Sellers List."

Noticing he'd nearly drained his cup, he got up to retrieve the coffeepot. He brought it back to the table and retopped both their mugs. "Lots of authors make the bestseller lists. What's so special about this guy that you have to hunt him down?" he asked, his eyes lasering in on hers.

"It's not just his readers who don't know who he is. No one in the entire publishing world knows, either. His real identity is so hush-hush that not even his publisher knows who he is. All his manuscripts come through an attorney, Franklin Dunn, Jr., and *he* isn't talking."

She had even hired on as a temp in Dunn's office, but didn't have any luck finding anything. She still had hopes, though, of getting the information from Dunn's personal secretary, Marcie Shackleford.

"So you're getting discouraged?"

Ha! Charlotte thought. "Not on your life," she said with a determined scowl. "There's a mystery here and I'm determined to get to the bottom of it."

He shook his head. "Why are you so hell-bent on doing something that clearly looks impossible?" he asked.

"Because finding Sterling and unmasking him to the world would be a real coup."

He savored that for a moment. Then apparently discarded her motivation as unsound. "What about the poor schmuck who writes the books?" he asked argumentatively, his dark brow furrowed in concern. "Doesn't he have a right to privacy?"

Charlotte sighed and leaned forward urgently. "Look, if Stephen Sterling wanted privacy, he shouldn't have written three bestsellers and earned millions of dollars. He's the one who wanted people to buy his books, and now they're understandably curious about him."

Charlotte could tell by the look on his face that he didn't agree with her. His disapproval made her more determined. "Sterling's readers have a right to know who he is," she argued passionately. "If he's even a *him,*" she finished cautiously. Noting the time, she drained her cup and got up to go. Her sisters would be home soon, and she wanted to talk to them. They had a lot to go over.

He put the lid on the cookies and walked with her back into the living room. "What makes you think Sterling's not a guy?" he asked casually.

"Nothing." Charlotte stepped outside and breathed in the honeysuckle-scented air. The afternoon sun shone brightly down on them. Although the grass was not cut, it was thick and beautiful and rolled out around them like a pastoral blanket of green. Just looking at the grounds filled her with the sense of coming home.

"Do the Sterling books read like they were written by a woman?" he asked.

"No, they read like they were written by a very romantic, adventurous, exciting man," Charlotte replied. Which was, of course, why they were on the bestseller lists.

"I don't get it." He looked at her blankly.

Charlotte shoved her hands in the pockets of her navy blazer. She tilted her head back to better see up into his face. "It's just that readers *expect* adventure novels to be written by a man," she explained. "And that could be the reason why the author is trying so hard to keep his—or her—identity a secret. Haven't you ever heard of the famous mystery novelist P. D. James? She was a woman, but they didn't think men would read her books, so she went by her initials instead."

He shook his head as if she were making no sense at all, then stroked the edges of his mustache thoughtfully. "What happens if you actually find this Sterling, and he—or she—is not all that exciting a person? Won't that be a turnoff to people?" He leaned closer and his voice dropped to an urgent rumble. "What if you wreck this person's career by exposing him or her? Have you thought of that?"

Charlotte's first rule of thumb was never to allow herself to think negatively. The second was to never let anyone else's agenda become her own. She knew what she had to do to save Camellia Lane. "First of all," she announced confidently, aware this was none of their caretaker's business, anyway, "I've read the Sterling books. You haven't. He could be a nun in Bolivia and people would still want to read all about him. In fact, that would probably make his public persona all the more interesting."

He shook his head in disagreement. "You're taking an awful lot for granted. I certainly wouldn't want to know a little old lady was really writing adventure books."

"Writing gossip is my business. And I know what I'm talking about," Charlotte continued stubbornly, even as she wondered why she was allowing this man to get under her skin. She faced him hotly. "I know people will be interested in finding out the truth about Sterling, whatever it is."

He shrugged his broad shoulders in dissent. "If you say so, but I still think you ought to think twice about destroying someone else's career."

This was ridiculous! He was making her feel guilty about doing her job! "I want that story on Sterling." Even more importantly, she had been promised a big bonus if she landed it. She regarded him with annoyance. He looked equally exasperated and unhappy with her.

Finally he nodded, understanding her decision, though not approving. He turned back toward the cottage. "Well, as nice as this chat has been, Miss Charlotte," he said with a certain weary reluctance, "I better get back to my research."

She watched as he ambled slowly away from her, his steps long and lazy and undeniably male. Even his walk was sexy!

Charlotte frowned. She just couldn't see a flirtatious rogue like this man contentedly leading the life of a bookish scholar. And that made her wonder what he was really doing there. Was it simple coincidence that had landed this man at Camellia Lane? Or did his past bear looking into, too?

He turned to look at her when he reached the front door, as if wondering what she was doing still standing there, watching him. She paused, her heart pounding as their eyes clashed once again. Belatedly, she realized that although he knew plenty about her, she still knew nothing about him. But that, she promised herself resolutely, would soon change. "By the way, what did you say your name was?" she asked with deceptive casualness.

"Brett." His teeth flashed white against the suntanned skin of his face in another wicked, bad-boy grin. "Brett Forrest."

Chapter Two

Brett crept soundlessly up to the open kitchen windows and took cover in the bushes that rimmed the veranda. A glance inside the wide bay windows showed the three Langston sisters making dinner. His timing was perfect.

"What do you really know about Brett Forrest?" Charlotte asked Isabella as she took the makings for a salad out of the refrigerator and carried them to the long chef's table in the center of the room.

"He's working on a Ph.D. And he's very nice." Isabella slid breaded chicken into the frying pan, wiped her hands on the apron around her waist and then turned to Charlotte. "What else is there to know? Why are you so suspicious?"

'Atta girl, Isabella, Brett thought. Defend me to that snoopy older sister of yours. Throw her off the scent.

"I am suspicious," Charlotte answered as she began to slice carrots with a vengeance, "because Brett Forrest is no nerd. Yet he wants us to think he's one."

"I don't know about that," Paige interrupted. "Anyone who would seriously devote his life to studying what kind of crops can be grown in the dirt sounds like a nerd to me."

"Exactly!" Charlotte crowed triumphantly. "But aside from the books cluttering the cottage, have either of you seen any hard evidence that he is interested in farming? There was no dirt under his fingernails, no calluses on his palms. The guy had muscles, but they weren't the kind you get from toting bags of fertilizer around on your shoulder.

They were the fluid kind you get from jogging six miles a day or playing tennis.''

Paige whistled. ''Sounds like you noticed quite a bit about our new caretaker, Charlotte,'' she teased.

Brett had noticed quite a bit about Charlotte, too. He had never seen a more fiery Southern beauty, with her dark curly hair, sassy mouth and flashing green eyes. All the Langston women were beautiful. But it was Charlotte who caught his eye. He couldn't stop thinking about her, and that, unfortunately, had nothing to do with the mission he'd been sent here to do.

''These days a man doesn't have to dress in overalls and a straw hat to farm,'' Isabella chided, adding more chicken to the sizzling skillet on the stove. ''Maybe Brett wants to be a gentleman farmer.''

Actually, Brett thought, all the reading he'd been doing so he could be conversant on farming *was* leading him in that very direction, to his great surprise.

''Ha! There's nothing gentlemanly about him!'' Charlotte claimed.

No doubt she was thinking of the way he had pinned her to the sofa now, Brett thought. Okay, so that had been uncalled for. He admitted it. But she had deserved it for storming his cottage without invitation while he was trying to nap.

''Exactly what happened between the two of you during your first meeting, Charlotte?'' Paige persisted with an impish grin as she emptied a package of frozen corn into a saucepan.

Brett peeked around the bushes and saw Charlotte's slender shoulders stiffen. ''Nothing I would care to recount,'' she told Paige tersely.

Brett knew he shouldn't recount it, either. But memories like that were hard to resist. The feel of Charlotte beneath him, her silky hair spread out on the sofa cushion. The fire in her eyes as she gazed hotly up at him. The passion in her low, throaty voice as she talked about her work as an investigative reporter.

"Furthermore, I really think you should fire him, Isabella!" Charlotte continued stubbornly.

Brett frowned and stepped a little farther back into the bushes.

"I can't do that, Charlotte!" Isabella replied hotly.

"Why the devil not?" she demanded as she finished with the carrots and began tearing lettuce into bite-size pieces.

"Because—" Isabella used a long-handled fork to turn the sizzling pieces of chicken in the skillet on the stove "—I promised Brett he could stay at Camellia Lane until he had finished his dissertation. And we need someone out here during the day to keep an eye on the place."

To Brett's disappointment, Charlotte wasn't the least bit mollified by sweet Isabella's logic.

"We also need a decent caretaker. Look at the grounds, you two." Charlotte lifted both slender arms. "They're a wreck!"

"Well, that's as much your fault as ours," Paige interjected calmly, sloshing fizzy diet soda over the ice in her glass. She paused to take a dainty drink. "With all of us working, Isabella and me locally, and you out-of-state, Charlotte, none of us has time to cut grass. Frankly, I think we should just sell the plantation and be done with it."

"Over my dead body!" Charlotte said, and Brett frowned. From what he could tell, if the sisters would just agree to sell their money-absorbing ancestral home, then all of his and Stephen Sterling's problems would be solved.

"Father would never have wanted us to sell Camellia Lane," Isabella concurred solemnly, to Brett's disappointment. "Not if we could possibly avoid it."

"Oh, we'll avoid it all right, because there is no way I'm going to allow Camellia Lane to be sold," Charlotte told her sisters flatly.

"Then how, pray tell, are we going to come up with the fifty thousand dollars we owe the bank?" Paige retorted.

Fifty thousand! Brett thought. What kind of trouble were these ladies in?

"We don't have that kind of money," Paige continued. "Nor are we liable to get it from Isabella's work as a librarian, mine as a cosmetics sales rep, or your work as a magazine writer, Charlotte."

"Face it," Isabella said, looking sadder than Brett had yet seen her, "we all love our work and adore this place, but we can't afford to keep up Camellia Lane on our salaries, even with two of us living here full-time."

"Look, I feel bad that my work is in New York," Charlotte said, looking at her sisters apologetically. "I know I haven't been doing my share, in the physical sense, the last ten years. But I plan to make that up to you both by getting the fifty thousand we need."

"Oh, really?" Paige pulled a package of rolls out of the freezer and set them on the counter to defrost. "And how are you going to do that? By selling off one or both of us to white slavers?" Paige shot back.

Catfight! Brett thought.

Charlotte glared at Paige. "I am going to do an exposé on Stephen Sterling," Charlotte announced, moving closer to the blue, beige and white floral priscilla curtains. "And when I do, the magazine has agreed to pay me a bonus of fifty thousand dollars. Voilà! All our problems will be solved."

No wonder she wanted to go all out to find Sterling, Brett thought. The money from the article would allow her to save her beloved Camellia Lane.

"Now back to our situation with that worthless caretaker you hired," Charlotte continued autocratically.

Brett decided this was his cue. He bounded up the back steps, rapped on the kitchen door and stepped inside, before Charlotte had the chance to talk the other two into kicking him off the property.

"Hi," he said cheerfully, stepping inside.

He had been in the spacious plantation kitchen many times, but tonight the cozy square room seemed filled with life. Charlotte especially seemed right at home.

"Oh, hello, Brett! You're just in time," Isabella said, looking pleased to see him. She moved gracefully across the terra-cotta tile floor and sent him a welcoming smile. "Dinner is almost ready."

"What do you mean dinner is almost ready?" Charlotte asked suspiciously. She glared at Brett, then her sisters.

"Brett eats dinner with us every evening," Isabella said, using a sponge to wipe a splatter from the beige ceramic tile above the stove.

"Didn't we tell you?" Paige asked innocently as she began to unload the dishwasher.

"No," Charlotte said, still looking at both her sisters meaningfully. *"You didn't."*

"Want me to set the table as usual?" Brett asked. If he didn't want to be kicked out by Miss Charlotte, he knew he'd better make himself useful.

"Please." Isabella smiled.

"I don't know if this is such a good idea," Charlotte said slowly. She looked at both her sisters pointedly. "We have pressing financial matters to discuss. I was hoping we could do it over dinner."

"Brett knows we're having some problems on that score," Isabella said delicately.

"What?" Charlotte did a double take.

"I had to tell him," she explained with an airy wave of her hand. "So he'd understand why there was no salary with the job."

Charlotte glanced at her watch and frowned. She appeared deep in thought. "How long before the chicken is done, Isabella?"

Isabella shrugged. "Another thirty minutes."

"If you all will excuse me, I've got some work to do in the library," Charlotte said. She pivoted on her heel and brushed past Brett without a word.

What was she up to now? he wondered, drinking in the lilac fragrance of her perfume. And did it have anything to do with Stephen Sterling?

Paige hurried after her sister. Brett heard them murmuring in apparent disagreement, and then Charlotte saying, "I don't care if he is a funny and charming dinner companion or how big a help he is in the kitchen! I'm telling you, there's something about that man that just isn't right!"

Her instincts were right on target about that, Brett thought, as he continued to set the table while Isabella looked for something in the pantry. He wasn't here to study farming or complete a dissertation. He was here for one reason and one reason only—to prevent Charlotte from following through on her mission to unmask Stephen Sterling.

HER DISCUSSION with Paige finished, Charlotte hurried toward the library. It was six o'clock. Dunn's law office was closing down for the day. If she wanted to make a call, she'd have to do it now.

She went swiftly to her desk, sat down and picked up the phone. "Marcie Shackleford, please."

Seconds later, a melodious voice came on the phone. "Marcie Shackleford."

"Hi. This is Charlotte Langston—"

"The nosy reporter who tried to break into the firm's computer?"

"I see you remember me," Charlotte said carefully.

"I certainly do. And I have no intention of talking to you!" Marcie Shackleford retorted.

"Wait—" Charlotte said. But it was too late. Marcie had already hung up.

Scowling, Charlotte replaced the antique black-and-gold phone in its cradle and saw Brett Forrest hovering just inside the library door. She hated not getting what she wanted...especially when someone was there to see her fail. Although Brett was doing his best to pretend he hadn't overheard anything of importance.

And again, it hit her like gangbusters. Something about him just wasn't right. He was too handsome, too sexy, too stealthy and too nosy.

In fact, he reminded her of herself. Was it really possible that he was another reporter, tracking her because he wanted to steal her story? And if that was the case, how was she going to get him to back off? Charlotte sensed he was every inch as tenacious as she was.

Brett stayed where he was, looking impossibly at home among the polished black walnut doors. His boldly assessing glance covered the wide floor-to-ceiling bookcases that held thousands of her father's books on the Civil War. It drifted across the plush emerald green sofa, matching side chairs and slightly darker green carpet, before moving lazily to the huge black walnut desk and matching typewriter stand. Behind that was a twelve-rung ladder used to gather books from the uppermost shelves. Charlotte was well aware there were cobwebs hanging from some of the rungs, as it hadn't been used in ages.

Finally, his glance made it to the desk she sat behind. He grinned. "Okay to come in now?" he asked lazily.

Like he wasn't already halfway in the room, anyway, Charlotte thought. "What are you doing here?" she demanded.

He continued to lounge against the doorframe, hands stuck in the pockets of his jeans. "Isabella sent me to ask you if you wanted to open a bottle of wine with dinner since it's your first night home."

"I don't care."

"I'll tell her to open one, then." He paused, but didn't say anything.

Charlotte knew he wanted to ask her something. Her irritation grew. She barely knew this man, and already it seemed he wouldn't give her any peace. "Was there something else?" she snapped.

"Yes." Looking like he was immensely glad she had asked, Brett came back into the room. He turned and shut the door quietly behind him. "There's a rumor in town that you and your sisters are going to lose this place. Is it true?"

It was against Charlotte's principles to discuss private family matters with outsiders. But in this case, it might help

Brett cut her some slack, particularly if he were, as she half suspected, a reporter competing on the same story as she.

"Unfortunately, yes. Unless we can come up with fifty thousand dollars, we will lose this place."

Brett glanced at the shelves that lined three sides of the large library. "It may be presumptuous of me to ask," Brett said as he came around to take a seat in one of the armchairs on the other side of the desk, "but have you and your sisters ever considered growing cotton again? I understand your family did quite well once."

Charlotte sighed. She only wished that farming were as easy or profitable as it looked. "That was years ago, when my mother was still alive. She had the green thumb and all the know-how in the family. Plus, at that time we had a much better cash flow and the money to hire a crew to do the actual farming."

"What happened to change all that?" he asked.

His question was outrageously personal, considering it was coming from the hired help. But when Charlotte looked into Brett's eyes, she saw a heartfelt sympathy that worked like a balm on her weary heart and soul. She had been carrying the weight of the family's losses for so long, she needed to unburden herself to someone. He was an unlikely confidant, yet it might be easier to talk to a stranger. Besides, Charlotte reasoned pragmatically, this was a good chance for her to test his knowledge about farming. "You're apparently an expert on the subject. Do you think we should grow G. herbaceum?"

Brett shook his head, his expression serious. He hooked his thumbs in the belt loops of his jeans. "Too coarse. I'd recommend G. barbadense."

Charlotte propped her chin on her hand and tried to give the impression she was genuinely interested in farming herself. "How far apart should the hills be planted?"

Half of his mouth crooked up in a faint smile. "Thirty centimeters."

Swallowing around the growing knot of tension in her throat, Charlotte kept her eyes on his as she asked, "What should we do about weeds?"

He stared at her for a moment. "You can use a herbicide or the rows can be flamed. Either method will work."

He knows I'm testing him. But determined to find out the truth about him, anyway, she plunged on. "What pests do we have to watch out for these days?"

He shrugged. Smiled again. Almost mischievously. "Same as always. The boll weevil and the pink bollworm."

Damn. He did know his stuff, Charlotte thought, stifling a sigh. She tossed down the pen she'd been gripping. So much for her theory. Only the most devoted agriculturalist would know all that. Unless, of course, he had just memorized all this as part of his cover. Or had once lived on or near a cotton plantation himself.

"So, who took over the farming when your mother died?" Brett asked.

"My father." Charlotte picked up her pen again. She sat back in her chair, wishing Brett would look at something else besides her face. "Unfortunately, he had no talent for it and we lost money on every crop."

"And so he just quit?" Brett asked gently.

Charlotte closed her fingers around her pen. These memories were even more painful for her. "Actually, he became ill," she said softly. "Cancer."

Brett drew an audible breath. "I'm sorry. That must have been rough on you and your sisters."

Charlotte nodded and once again met Brett's eyes. His look was so compassionate and understanding she found herself telling him even more. "It was. Paige was still in high school at the time. Isabella and I were in college." Charlotte stood and began to roam the length of the library restlessly. She touched the spines of the books that had once belonged to her father.

"We came home to be with him, and over the course of the next two years he tried every treatment available and then some." Charlotte swallowed. "A couple of times we thought he was going to go into remission, but he never did. When he died, our debts were substantial, so we did what the family had always done—talked to Hiram Henderson at the local bank. He gave us two alternatives—sell Camellia Lane, or take out a mortgage on the property, with a balloon payment at the end of ten years. We opted for the mortgage and used the money to pay off our debt, and to help us finish our studies. I graduated first and went to New York. I wasn't making much money initially, but I paid a portion of the mortgage and set aside everything I could for the balloon payment. Isabella and Paige both did the same."

"So how come you don't have that money to make the payment, then?" Brett asked, his brow furrowing.

Charlotte returned to sit behind the desk. "Because this house—which happens to be nearly one hundred and fifty years old, by the way—is a money pit."

"So why not sell it?"

"Because it's our home." Charlotte smiled, unable to help the sentimental note in her low voice. "We grew up here. And we love it. Besides," she added, shrugging, "this property has been owned by the Langston family since 1842, and we promised our parents we would keep it in the family."

"So back to cotton farming," Brett said casually. "Why not try that again, if money is such a problem for you?"

Charlotte bit her lip. "My sisters and I looked into it," she admitted.

"And?"

"Have you ever priced a piece of farm equipment? We don't have the capital nor the know-how to get back into it."

"If you did, would you?" Brett persisted.

Charlotte didn't have to think very long about that. "Probably."

"That being the case, would you mind if I took some soil samples of your fields and sent them off to be analyzed?"

"For what purpose?" Charlotte regarded Brett suspiciously. He suddenly seemed awfully eager to help her.

He shrugged his broad shoulders, as if it were no big deal. "I could tell you how much it would cost for you to get back into farming again. Maybe project some future earnings for you," he suggested mildly.

Charlotte wasn't sure she would trust any estimate he gave her, but she decided to play along with him. If nothing else, taking soil samples would keep him busy and out of her hair. "All right."

"So what next, in the meantime?" Brett asked.

Charlotte sighed, looking down at her calendar. "I've got an appointment with Hiram Henderson tomorrow. I'm going to try and talk him into giving us an extension on that balloon payment."

"Are your sisters going with you?"

Charlotte hedged. "They want me to try and talk to him alone."

"How come?"

"They think I can be charming, in the way that he expects," Charlotte said with a beleaguered sigh.

"Which is . . . ?"

"You know, the typical old-fashioned Southern-lady thing. Soft and pretty and delicate on the outside, hard as driven steel on the inside."

"Hmm," Brett said.

Charlotte didn't like the sound of that *hmm*. She glanced at the clock.

She had spent almost fifteen minutes talking to him. She had also told him far more than she had intended. Worse, he seemed to empathize with everything she and her sisters had been through.

"Hadn't you better go back and tell Isabella to open that bottle of wine?" she asked.

"Oh, yeah." Brett lazily unfolded himself from the chair and shoved a hand through the dark, rumpled waves of his hair. "I almost forgot why I came in here."

I'll bet, Charlotte thought as she scrutinized him silently. She waited until he had left, then picked up the phone and dialed one of her reporter friends. "Listen—ever heard of a reporter named Brett Forrest?"

CHARLOTTE WAS IN a bad mood as she got out of her car the next afternoon and headed for the bank. No one had heard of Brett at any of the magazines. Nor had he worked for any of the wire services. Nor, as far as she could discover, published anything at all. Therefore, if he was a reporter, he hadn't made a name for himself yet. But that didn't mean he couldn't be trying to do so at this very minute, Charlotte told herself firmly. After all, there had to be some reason he was so intent on nosing into her business. He had to be trying to scoop her out of her story on Sterling! Well, she would not allow him to steal the information she had uncovered so far. She might, however, send him on a wild-goose chase if he continued to prove meddlesome.

Hiram Henderson met her at the door and escorted Charlotte into his private office at the rear of the bank. "My, don't you look lovely today," he said.

"Thank you, Hiram," Charlotte said. She hated playing the part of the sugary Southern belle. It seemed like such a waste of time and energy. But in this part of Mississippi, it was also the best way to get what she wanted. And right now the stakes were huge.

Hiram adjusted his clip-on bow tie as he sat behind his desk. "Now, what can I do for you?"

Charlotte smiled at him as she tugged off first one lacy glove, and then the other. Slowly, she dropped both into her lap and offered him her most winning smile. "I'd like to ask for an extension on our loan."

"Charlotte, that balloon payment is due in ten days," Hiram reminded her. He steepled his long, bony fingertips in front of him and regarded her over the rim of his bifocals.

This was going to be harder than she had thought; Hiram didn't look as if he were going to budge. Telling herself to be as fiercely determined on the inside and soft on the outside as her mother had always been, Charlotte crossed her legs demurely at the knee. She tossed her head flirtatiously and offered him another smile. "I can trust you to be discreet, can't I, Hiram?"

"Absolutely, Charlotte."

"My sisters and I are a little short on cash at the moment."

Hiram disengaged his fingertips and dropped his forearms to his desk. He leaned forward, his expression regretful. "As much as we here at First Unity Bank would like to help you, Charlotte, we can't give you an extension on the balloon payment."

She kept the smile plastered on her face with a great deal of effort. She was not going to give up until she got her way. "Why not?" she asked, summoning up the sweetness that came so naturally to her sister Isabella. "You gave us a loan the last time we were in financial trouble."

"And at that time, we financed the maximum amount available to you and your sisters," Hiram explained sternly. "Since then, you've paid down nothing of the principal. That's why the balloon payment is due now."

"What about a second mortgage?" Charlotte asked.

"Against what? You've already borrowed against ninety-nine percent of what the property is worth. If I might be so bold," Hiram said as he picked up a pen and doodled aimlessly on the notepad in front of him, "there is a solution here. There's an auto plant going in here in the next few months. It's expected to be operational within a year."

Charlotte toyed with the strand of fake pearls around her neck. "What does that have to do with us?"

"Six thousand people will be moving to the area, looking for homes. Homes that we don't currently have."

"I'm not a home builder, Hiram."

"I know that. But Heritage Homes is, and they want to purchase Camellia Lane, Charlotte, and turn it into a subdivision of affordable tract homes. Frankly, I think the three of you would be fools to refuse the offer," he continued. "With the money you and your sisters earned from the sale of Camellia Lane, you could pay off the mortgage on the property and be out of debt completely.''

''Forget it. There's no way we're selling Camellia Lane,'' Charlotte said firmly. It was their home. It was all they had left of her parents.

''Perhaps you need time to consider,'' Hiram suggested kindly.

''I don't think so.'' Charlotte got up and started for the door.

''There's something you should know, Charlotte,'' Hiram said, his voice hardening. ''If you don't pay the fifty-thousand-dollar balloon payment, the bank will have no choice but to foreclose on the property.''

''I bet that would just break your heart, wouldn't it?'' Charlotte said, whirling to face him.

Hiram removed his bifocals and set them ever so slowly on his desk. ''I know you're upset, Charlotte dear. But First Unity didn't get you and your sisters into this mess. The bank and I are only trying to help.''

Trying to force them into a corner so the bank could make a profit was more like it, Charlotte thought. ''Tell me, Hiram, who is representing Heritage Homes?''

He didn't answer. But then, Charlotte thought bitterly, he didn't have to.

BRETT WAITED UNTIL all three Langston sisters were gone, then let himself into the house and headed straight for the library.

He frowned when he saw the top of the desk. Last night it had been covered with Charlotte's papers and notes. Now it was clean as a whistle. He had been hoping to get some idea how far along she was in her investigation of Sterling.

Brett tried the desk drawers. Locked. Cursing, he picked up the phone and punched in his credit-card number. Seconds later, Franklin came on the line.

''Brett? What have you got?''

Not as much as I'd like so far, he thought. ''Charlotte Langston called your secretary last night.''

"Yeah, I know. Marcie told me this morning. She also said she hung up on Charlotte. I suppose it's too much to hope Miss Langston won't try again?"

"Way too much," Brett concurred grimly.

"Have you learned anything else?" Franklin asked.

"Just that Charlotte Langston and her sisters are in desperate need of money." Briefly, Brett explained what Charlotte had told him. "She's meeting with the bank this morning to see about a loan," Brett finished.

"You think that's why she's so hell-bent on unmasking Sterling?" Franklin asked.

"That's part of it," Brett said.

"And the rest?"

"She sees it as a challenge." And Charlotte Langston was not a woman to turn away from a challenge, Brett had discovered.

"Any chance she's onto you?" Franklin asked.

That, Brett thought, remembering the three-way conversation he had eavesdropped on the evening before, was a difficult question. "She doesn't trust me."

"Why not?"

"Because she doesn't see me as a farmer, despite the fact I passed her quiz on cotton with flying colors." Brett hoped the dirt samples he had taken and sent out to the lab this morning would help bolster his image as agriculturalist extraordinaire.

Franklin harrumphed his displeasure. "You want me to put someone else on the job?" he asked gruffly.

"Nope," Brett said quickly. This wasn't a job he would trust to anyone else. Charlotte Langston needed special handling. "I'm staying."

Brett heard a car pull up in front of the house. None of the sisters was due back for hours! "Gotta go," Brett whispered into the phone, as he heard a car door slam. He dove for cover behind the long leather sofa, stretching out along the cushions just as a key turned in the lock. Because the sofa faced the fireplace, with its back to double doors leading into the library, he wouldn't be seen by whoever had arrived unless she actually came into the library.

Someone slammed into the house. Brett inhaled the faint scent of lilacs. Charlotte, he thought. Her high heels clicking on the parquet floor, she bypassed the library and headed straight for the kitchen.

Brett breathed a sigh of relief. He was about to get up from the sofa when another car pulled up out front. Cursing his ill fortune, he stayed where he was and continued to feign sleep in case anyone spotted him. In the meantime, he thought, he was in a pretty good position to listen to all that went on, at least at the front of the house.

"I GOT HERE AS SOON as I could," Jared Fontaine said, his straight blond hair gleaming in the sunshine as he took the steps leading up to the house.

"You must've left your office the moment I telephoned," Charlotte said, ushering Jared into the parlor. With its Georgian paneling, milled moldings and soaring white ceiling complete with two crystal chandeliers, the room was the most elegant in the entire mansion. Moving soundlessly across the oriental rugs, Charlotte opened the blue velvet drapes that covered the double French doors, letting sunlight spill into the long, rectangular room. She glanced around quickly, checking to see if everything was in order. "I barely had time to put water on for tea."

"I didn't come for tea, Charlotte. I came to see you." Jared took both her hands in his and held them away from her body. "Honey, you look as if you haven't changed a bit."

That was true, she thought uncomfortably, but at the moment it was correct for all the wrong reasons. Normally, she wore slacks and blazers and clipped her long hair back at the nape of her neck. But that wouldn't work in the conservative Poplar Springs business community, so she had rummaged through the back of her closet for something appropriate to court a hopelessly old-fashioned banker in, and come up with a demure pink business suit. She'd added a strand of costume pearls and clip-on earrings, and combed the heavy waves of her shoulder-length hair in the loose, girlish style of her youth.

Unfortunately, the Southern-belle ensemble that was charming Jared Fontaine now hadn't made a dent in Hiram's stony resolve, Charlotte thought. But that was where Jared came in. An attorney and old family friend, he could advise her on what to do.

Jared dropped his grip on her, thrust his hands in the pockets of his trousers and stepped back. In a white double-breasted suit, he looked dapper and successful.

They exchanged smiles. "Please make yourself at home in the parlor, Jared, while I run back to the kitchen and get our tea," Charlotte said.

When she returned, Jared was seated in one of the two wing chairs in the alcove in front of the French windows. It was the coziest, most intimate spot in the room.

Trying not to attach any special significance to that, Charlotte set the silver tea service down on the table between them as Jared's sherry-colored eyes lasered into hers.

"So what has you so upset?" he asked gently.

"First Unity Bank is trying to force us to sell Camellia Lane because we can't pay the balloon note on the first mortgage."

Jared's expression remained impassive. "How much do you owe?" he asked.

"Fifty thousand," Charlotte replied, as she poured steaming tea into two bone-china cups.

He whistled, his eyes focused on the movements of her hands. "That's not exactly penny change."

"No, it isn't," Charlotte agreed, sitting back in her chair. "Which is why we need your help. I've already talked to Hiram, to no avail. But I thought perhaps if you intervened—"

Jared held up a hand. "I'll be honest with you, Charlotte. The likelihood of you and your sisters getting an extension from the bank is slim. You owe the money. The bank has every right to collect."

Charlotte's expression fell. Jared and his family were very well connected; she had been counting on him to help her. "Couldn't we even get a couple more weeks?" Enough time for her to find Sterling?

"It's doubtful. Life here is changing. With the new auto plant coming in next year, Poplar Springs will no longer be the sleepy little burg we both grew up in. The price of land in this part of Mississippi is already shooting up."

"All the more reason why my sisters and I should hold on to Camellia Lane," Charlotte said stubbornly.

He shook his head. "Don't be a fool. Now is your chance to get out of debt and in on the ground floor of something really big."

With effort, Charlotte kept her voice Southern-lady-pleasant. "You're not listening to me. I don't want to sell, and neither do my sisters."

Jared settled his broad shoulders more comfortably against the back of the chair and balanced the saucer on the flat of one hand. "It doesn't work that way, Charlotte. If you don't sell your land, then someone else here will sell theirs. A year from now, if other subdivisions do pop up in the meantime, then there'll be no demand for your land."

"So much the better," Charlotte said with a shrug.

Jared studied her. "You really want to fight Hiram, don't you?"

"And the Heritage Homes developers. Camellia Lane is one of the few antebellum mansions left in this part of Mississippi. It should be preserved. The question is, will you help me?"

Jared studied her as if a great deal were at stake for him, too. "If I do...does that mean you'll stay on?"

"In Mississippi?"

"Yes." Jared kept his eyes on hers.

Charlotte shrugged, feeling uneasy at the suddenly intimate nature of his gaze. "The magazine I work for is located in New York."

The corners of his mouth lifted slightly. "You couldn't give it up?"

Charlotte drew a deep, enervating breath. "For what?"

"A life here at Camellia Lane."

Again, his gaze was a little too intense for comfort. Surely he couldn't be saying... Charlotte backed off. She raised a hand in a cautionary manner. "I can't think about that today, Jared." And she meant it.

He set his cup and saucer aside and leaned toward her. "Then when?"

Charlotte drew another breath. "I'll think about it tomorrow," she said.

CHARLOTTE SHUT THE DOOR after Jared and leaned against it wearily. She had tried to make it clear from the outset that she had called him because he was an old family friend—not a potential love interest. Unfortunately, he was thinking of her amorously.

She was going to have to think up some way to let him down gently. She didn't want to hurt his feelings.

In the meantime, she had to think of a way to make the balloon payment if she couldn't locate Stephen Sterling in time. With that purpose in mind, Charlotte marched across the front hall to the library. She was halfway across the room when she caught a flash of movement on the sofa and let out a startled scream.

"Lady, what is it with you?" Brett drawled as he lazily sat up. "Must you always scream people awake?"

Charlotte resisted the urge to slug him for scaring her half to death. "What are you doing here?" she demanded.

"I thought you wanted me to do more caretaking."

Charlotte braced her fists on her hips and stood her ground. "What does that have to do with you sleeping on the library sofa?" And why did he have to look so sexy, with his dark hair all rumpled, his blue eyes so vibrant and filled with mischief?

"I came in to see what needed to be done, couldn't decide and lay down to think about it." Brett propped his clasped hands beneath his head and made no move to sit up. "Next thing I knew I fell asleep."

Thank goodness he hadn't overheard her conversation with Jared, Charlotte thought. It was embarrassing to be on the receiving end of a subtle pass from Jared. "Well, I want you to stop it immediately," Charlotte said hotly.

"Stop what? Sleeping? Or eavesdropping?" he prodded as he stretched and got lazily to his feet.

Charlotte swore beneath her breath as he towered over her, his broad shoulders blocking out the sun, dwarfing her. She gasped as he took a step nearer. "You didn't—"

Brett flashed her a crocodile grin. Bracing a palm on the sofa back beside her, he leaned close, the tantalizing scent of Old Spice and soap engulfing her. "I did."

She knew he expected her to back away. Instead, she clamped her arms in front of her and fumed. "You had no right listening in on what was a very private conversation."

His glance moved over the soft swell of her breasts before roving impertinently back to her face. Again, the wicked grin. "It was either that or interrupt the tête-à-tête," he admitted roguishly. "Given the rather...um, shall we say *delicate* nature of your conversation, I figured you'd prefer me to stay put and stay quiet." He leaned close. His dark blue eyes glittered with laughter as he reached up to finger a lock of her hair. Sifting the silky strands through his fingers, he pinned her to the spot with a knowing look. "Or was I wrong?" he speculated brashly.

Charlotte was so aware of him she could barely draw a breath. Gathering her wits, she pointed to the front door. "You, sir, are always wrong! Now get out of my house!"

"Why, I'm hurt, Miss Charlotte." He plastered both hands against the solid wall of his chest and grinned disarmingly. "You didn't even give me a chance to help you and your beautiful sisters out of your predicament."

Charlotte was not amused by his clowning around. She regarded him patiently and uttered a long-suffering sigh. "There's nothing you can do for us."

"I could offer you a piece of advice."

"Which is . . . ?" She offered up a sweet smile, totally ignoring the way he looked in those soft, faded, snug-fitting jeans.

"I think you'd best be advised to find yourself another lawyer—someone who is truly on your side," Brett counseled solemnly.

Charlotte drew a bolstering breath. "Jared is on my side."

"Is he now?" Brett said in a put-on Southern drawl. "Funny, I didn't hear him offer up any options except for you to sell out. Unless of course, you count that veiled proposal to start up something with him. Which leads us to the next question. Just how far would you go, Miss Charlotte, to save your beloved Camellia Lane?"

It was a good question, and one Charlotte really didn't want to think about. She also knew Brett wasn't about to leave without an answer. "I'll do whatever I have to do," she vowed flatly. She would even get down on her hands and knees and beg, if it came to that. Anything to save Camellia Lane.

"That's what I thought," Brett said, his disapproval evident.

Charlotte didn't need Brett or anyone else acting as her conscience. She had enough to deal with as it was.

She put a hand on his sweatshirt-covered chest, intending to shove him out the door if necessary. Big mistake. Beneath the soft cotton, she could feel the swell of solid male muscle. Lots of it. And it was all braced for . . . Well, she didn't want to think about that, Charlotte decided as frissons of desire swept through her in undulating waves.

"Find something you like?" he teased softly. Grinning, he stepped closer, until their legs were touching in one long electric line.

His head was dipping toward hers, and she could feel the closeness of his chest and, lower still, the heat from . . . No! She was not going to let him do this to her, even if he *was* the sexiest man she had come across in a very long time.

Deciding the sooner she got rid of him, the better, she gave a push. "Out."

To her surprise, he merely shrugged and began to move in the direction she'd pointed. He sauntered toward the door. No sooner had he gotten to the front hall, however, than he came back to the portal where she was standing.

This time, when she flattened a palm against his chest he didn't budge. Instead, he covered her hand with his own and tightened his grasp.

"You're not going to do it, are you?" he persisted, searching her face. "Fire Jared and hire another attorney?"

Charlotte extricated her hand from his. She shook off his touch, trying without success to get rid of the tingles. "I have no reason to consult another attorney," she insisted stubbornly.

"If you say so," Brett muttered darkly.

Charlotte stepped past him, opened the front door as wide as it would go and practically shoved him out the portal. "You're wrong about Jared. He's noble." Unfortunately, he also had a misdirected crush on her.

"I see." The corners of Brett's dark mustache quirked up wickedly as he smiled. His blue eyes grew dark and intense. He anchored an arm about her waist and hauled her close. "Too noble to do this, I presume?"

Charlotte had no time to react. One minute she was standing in front of Brett. The next thing she knew she was swept up in his arms, bent backward from the waist. She gasped in astonishment as he slowly...slowly...lowered his mouth to hers. "Brett, don't!" she gasped, feeling both mesmerized and aroused. And then his lips touched hers and the world fell away as he kissed her like she had never been kissed before.

She felt the tickle of his mustache and the warm, insistent pressure of his mouth. The hardness of his chest, the muscular brace of his legs and the iron command in his arms. Desire raced through her in a heartbeat, warming her outside and in. Her tummy was weightless, her knees made of jelly. And still he kissed her, taking everything she had to give.

Feeling as if every romantic fantasy she'd ever had was about to come true, Charlotte started to surrender to the conquering nature of his embrace, then brought herself up short. What was she thinking? Dear heaven, she didn't have time for this!

Temper raging, she tore her mouth from his and pushed at his chest. He laughed softly, his hand still tangled in her hair; then, as gallantly as any Southern gentleman, he slowly righted her and, just as deliberately, released her.

Charlotte was so disoriented and filled with overwhelming pleasure she could barely stand up, let alone think of anything appropriate to say. Brett knew it. Acting strictly on impulse, she slapped his face.

Brett grinned and rubbed his jaw. "Liked my kiss that much?" he drawled smugly, just as Charlotte's two sisters drove up.

Chapter Three

"What's going on here, Charlotte?" Isabella demanded in a shocked tone.

"Don't tell me you're trying to seduce the hired help," Paige drawled, a hand splayed dramatically across her chest.

"Very funny." Charlotte glared at Paige before turning back to Brett. She gave him her most lethal look.

He smiled back at her, pleased at the unprecedentedly passionate response he had wrung from her, without even half trying. Charlotte's cheeks grew even warmer, but she continued to regard him stonily.

Finally, Brett got her message. "I think this is my cue to leave, ladies," he announced to Paige and Isabella. His expression was both rueful and full of mirth.

Paige and Isabella both chuckled, despite Charlotte's silent admonition not to do so.

"Don't be a stranger," Paige called airily after Brett.

Arms crossed defiantly in front of her, Charlotte watched Brett strut down the walk to the caretaker's cottage. She was still tingling all over. And all because of a stupid little kiss. "Don't encourage him," she warned her sisters with a scowl as they retreated to the kitchen.

"Why not?" Paige teased as she flicked on the lights and brought out a pitcher of ice tea. "*You* apparently were."

"All right, you two, don't start!" Isabella ordered, halting the free-for-all. Then she looked at Charlotte, her expression serious. "How did the meeting at the bank go?" she asked as she brought out the glasses.

"Not good." Charlotte sat down at the table with a sigh and began slicing up the lemons. "Hiram Henderson refused to give us an extension on the balloon payment. It's pay up, as scheduled, or they'll foreclose."

"Well, that doesn't leave us in a very good position," Paige said, as she poured ice tea. "Together, we only have four thousand dollars."

"Which leaves us forty-six thousand short of what we need," Isabella said with a worried frown. She went to a drawer and brought out a calculator. "Maybe if we talked to a lawyer—"

"I already spoke with Jared Fontaine," Charlotte said. "He says, legally, there's nothing we can do. The bank has every right to demand we pay up as scheduled."

They stared at one another in glum silence. "This is just impossible," Paige said, looking near tears.

It wouldn't be, Charlotte thought, if Marcie Shackleford would agree to help her locate Stephen Sterling. But since that wasn't likely to happen, she would have to employ a back-up plan for saving Camellia Lane. She looked at her sisters. "I have an idea how we can raise money quickly." It had come to her on the drive home.

"How?" Paige and Isabella asked in unison.

"By holding an antebellum-period costume ball and buffet dinner here."

"Kind of like a charity thing?" Paige asked, beginning to smile again.

Charlotte nodded. "We can call every historical society and women's club in the state. We can't charge admission, of course—that would be illegal. But we can have a party here, because it's a private residence, and we can *suggest* gifts of two hundred and fifty dollars a plate to help us save Camellia Lane."

Charlotte picked up the calculator and did some quick calculations. "As long as we have two hundred and fifty people or so attend, we should be able to carry it off."

WHILE PAIGE AND ISABELLA began making phone calls, Charlotte walked into the kitchen to start dinner. To her surprise, Brett was already there. In jeans and the usual sweatshirt, he looked casual and relaxed.

Trying not to notice the way the late afternoon sunlight spilling in through the open windows brought out the highlights in his tousled brown hair, Charlotte walked by him and peeked in the skillet on the stove.

"Breast of chicken florentine," he explained.

It smelled delicious, Charlotte thought. Brett came up behind her. Placing one hand on her shoulder, he reached past her and took the lid off a saucepan. "The spinach is cooking in here. And here—" he closed in on her slightly, the fronts of his thighs brushing the backs of hers as he lifted yet another lid "—we have some rice."

Warming everywhere they touched, and even places they didn't, Charlotte said, "It looks wonderful." Turning slightly, she slipped out from under his hand, so they were no longer touching.

Brett grinned down at her, his eyes twinkling. "Well, I aim to please you, Miss Charlotte. I surely do."

Again, warmth swept through Charlotte in undulating waves. She knew he was not talking about the dinner he was cooking. He was thinking about that outrageous kiss he had pressed upon her. The one she was still reeling from.

Aware her lips were tingling, she marched past him and went back over to the counter, where he had been slicing the tops off strawberries. "What's all this?" she asked briskly.

Brett trailed after her lazily. "Strawberry shortcake and whipped cream. Isabella told me it was your favorite. So I figured we'd have it for dessert."

He was probably trying to get back in her good graces, Charlotte thought. Well, it wasn't going to work.

Brett dipped the end of a plump, juicy strawberry into the fluffy mound of real whipped cream in the mixing bowl. "Looks good, doesn't it?" he said.

Mouth-watering, Charlotte thought, recalling that it had been hours since she had eaten.

"Here. Have a bite." He lifted the strawberry to her mouth. Her eyes locked with his, Charlotte bit down on the berry. It was luscious and sweet. She didn't know what he had done to that whipped cream, but it was heaven!

Brett smiled down at her, intensifying her sensual awareness of him until she nearly lost her breath. "Good, huh?" he whispered.

Charlotte nodded as she savored the ripe berry with sinful relish, letting its sweetness melt on her tongue. Reluctantly tearing her eyes from his, she looked around for a napkin to wipe the excess cream from her lips. Before she could find one, Brett volunteered to help out once again. "Here, I'll take care of that," he said softly. Before she could react, he dabbed her lip with his fingertip, gently wiping it clean, then sucked the whipped cream off his fingertip. "Want some more?"

For a second, Charlotte was unsure whether he meant the whipped cream and strawberries or another kiss. Telling herself she had to stop thinking like that, she shook off the sensuous aura that seemed to surround her whenever she was with him. "No thanks," she said hoarsely.

Face flaming, she whirled away from him and went to get a glass of water from the tap.

"Sure now?" Brett asked. "There's no law that says you have to have your dessert last, you know."

If there had been a law, he would have broken it, Charlotte fumed. She drank thirstily. And could still taste the salty tang of his skin, and the whipped-cream-drenched berry on her lips.

Brett watched her drain the glass.

"How about just one more?" he asked.

Even one more would be too much, Charlotte thought. "I didn't come in here to indulge myself in sweet treats!" she said hotly, and again Brett grinned wickedly. "I came in here to start dinner," Charlotte continued archly. "Since you have already done that, I'll use the time to talk to you about the plans my sisters and I are making." Briefly, she explained about the party, adding, "I know the deal was you didn't have to do any of the physical labor on Camellia Lane, but in view of the party we're having, that stipulation has now changed. You'll either have to help us get ready for the ball, or move out immediately. Today.''

Personally, Charlotte was hoping Brett would decide to vacate. But, as she could have predicted, she had no such luck. "Normally, I would have to say no to such a request. My dissertation and all. But since you and your sisters have gone all out to make sure I feel at home here at Camellia Lane, of course I'll put aside my own work for a week or so, to help you out.''

No one had to tell Charlotte how cozily at home Brett had made himself there, she grumbled silently to herself, suppressing a sigh. In fact, it was his sheer accessibility that bothered her. He was up to something, and now she was more determined to check him out, to find if he really was writing a dissertation on dirt farming.

The only way she knew to do that was to get a look at the files in his portable computer's hard drive.

DECIDING THERE WAS no better time to investigate Brett than when he was still busy in the kitchen, Charlotte slipped out of the house. Taking care to go the long way and stay out of sight of the kitchen windows, she headed for the cottage. After making sure no one was there, she used her key and let herself in.

Her heart racing, she began to look around. As before, his papers and books were scattered everywhere. She flipped through them quickly. All were on farming. Scowling in disappointment, she sat down at his desk and switched on his laptop computer. Aware of the need to hurry, she called up the directory and took a look at the files. Again, everything pertained to agriculture. Sure she must be missing something, Charlotte utilized the Search function on the computer and began scrolling through the documents. To her frustration, all were exactly as they were labeled.

Finding nothing incriminating or remotely connected to Stephen Sterling, she looked for an alternate directory on the computer. But there was only the one.

Lips pursed, she stared at the screen. Her heart was still racing and she had that prickly, about-to-get-caught-at-any-minute sensation on the back of her neck. Yet she had to find the truth, so she couldn't leave just yet. Was it possible that Brett was exactly as he seemed? she wondered frantically. A lazy, flirtatious scholar and nothing more? Was it possible she had misjudged him?

Without warning, the door opened behind her. Knowing her best defense was a good offense, Charlotte remained where she was and played it cool.

Ever so slowly, she swiveled around in her chair. Brett stood in the doorway, legs braced apart, arms folded in front of him. His expression was very grim indeed.

"Oh, there you are, Brett. I've been looking for you," Charlotte said.

"Really?" he retorted glibly, his blue eyes glittering with an emotion Charlotte wasn't sure she wanted to define. "I was under the impression you knew damn well I was in the kitchen preparing dinner."

"Obviously I thought you'd stepped out for a moment," she replied, using haughtiness as her main defense, "or I wouldn't have come down here."

He nodded, not buying her explanation for one second. His glance flicked over her face, returned to her eyes. "That doesn't explain what you were doing on my computer," he said very, very softly.

Charlotte searched for something to tell him as she switched off his computer, closed the lid and stood. "I noticed it was a newer model than my laptop. I wanted to try it out and see if it was any faster." She flashed him an apologetic smile, then followed that with a demure look as she pushed in the chair. She couldn't help but notice his thighs were girded as if for battle beneath the soft, snug fabric of his jeans. So were the brawny muscles of his shoulders and chest. She returned her eyes to his face and swallowed to ease the ache of tension in her throat. She moved slightly to the left of him. "I know I should have asked permission first—"

"Damn right about that." Brett's expression remained grim as he moved to the left, too, barring any hope of easy exit.

"Sorry. Next time I'll ask first," Charlotte promised.

He glowered down at her. He seemed in no mood to let her pass—yet. "Sure there's nothing else you want to tell me?" he prodded, his mouth taking on a rapacious tilt. He looked as if he were prepared to kiss the information out of her, if all else failed. Drawing a shaky breath, she decided to change the subject back to the business at hand.

Charlotte went back to the table and picked up the notepad and pen she had brought into the cottage with her. "Actually, I did want to tell you what needs to be done on the grounds before the party."

"Isabella and Paige said you went off by yourself to make a list. Funny—" Brett glanced down at her notepad "—there doesn't seem to be anything written on that list of yours, Miss Charlotte."

She shrugged, refusing to let the warmth of his breath in her hair or his knowing expression throw her. "Yes, well, I got sidetracked," she explained.

"Sidetracked spying on me?" he elaborated sarcastically.

"Sidetracked stopping in to see if you were here," Charlotte corrected, her cheeks flooding with warmth. "I wanted to arrange a time for us to get together tomorrow morning." It was all she could do to keep her eyes on his.

Brett continued to regard her steadily. He was close enough for her to see how closely he had shaved. "What's wrong with tonight?" he asked huskily.

"Nothing." Charlotte adapted her most innocent look. "I just thought you might be busy."

Brett said nothing in response and continued to look at her warily. He knew she was suspicious of him, and that she hadn't found what she was looking for. Like her, he had been smart enough to lock his secret documents away. "Well, I'm not busy," he said, mimicking her light, easy tone, "so what did you want, boss lady?"

"I have landscapers coming in tomorrow to plant flowers and trim the shrubs, but I want you to resurrect our lawn mower and mow the grass on the estate."

"Are you going to help me?"

"No."

"There are two hundred acres on the estate. That's a big job."

Yes, it was, but Charlotte had no intention of working side by side with him. Just thinking about the possibility conjured up visions of Brett, muscles rippling, working bare-chested in the sun. No. She did *not* want to see that.

"Just find a way to do it," she advised, exasperated both with him and the unprecedentedly sexual nature of her thoughts. "After that, I don't care what you do!"

Brett knew she didn't care. That was what made his own response to her so curious. It shouldn't have mattered to him how far Charlotte would go to save her beloved Camellia Lane, as long as he kept her distracted enough that she didn't discover Sterling's true identity. It also shouldn't have mattered to him that she was ridiculously naive when it came to Jared Fontaine. After all, it wasn't as if he were *involved* with her. He was merely spying on her.

So what if Charlotte labeled Brett a cad and looked at Jared as her rescuer? He shouldn't have been provoked into kissing her, but he had been. The desire he'd felt as he held her in his arms and experienced the sweetness of her surrender was overwhelming. He wanted Miss Charlotte. And he was going to get her any way he could.

"What if I tell you I won't do this new work assignment without your help?" Brett asked in an insolent way he knew would annoy her.

Hands on her hips, Charlotte regarded him without flinching. "Then I'll ask you to pack your bags and vacate the premises immediately," she said coolly.

He couldn't stop her from unmasking Sterling from afar, Brett thought. He sighed. In for a penny, in for a pound, and he was in this up to his neck. "All right, all right. Starting tomorrow, I'll get the mower up and running and cut the darn grass, but when I'm done," he warned silkily, "I'll expect to be amply compensated."

"With what?" Charlotte asked with an impertinent toss of her dark hair. "Another kiss?"

So, Brett thought with satisfaction, she hadn't forgotten their embrace, either. "Maybe," he said.

"Dream on," she retorted haughtily. "You caught me by surprise once. Not ever again."

Brett grinned. He'd felt her response to his embrace. She had to be yearning for another kiss every bit as much as he was. "Should we bet on that?"

"I DON'T SEE WHY I have to wear the chemise, the corset and the petticoat for the fitting," Charlotte grumbled the following afternoon. She held on to the bedpost with both hands, as Paige laced her up so tight her breasts spilled from the top of the lacy white linen chemise.

"It's the only efficient way to measure you." Paige frowned and gave the strings on the corset another tug. "Can you still breathe?"

"No!"

"Good, then that's probably tight enough," Paige decided. She stepped back to admire her handiwork as Charlotte let go of the bedpost. "You know, I think we whittled a good two inches off your waist with that corset."

"It feels like it, too," Charlotte grumbled. "Now loosen those strings, Paige."

Paige propped both her manicured hands on her hips. She was dressed in street clothes, since she had already had her fitting. "Do you want to look like an authentic antebellum Southern belle or not?" Paige demanded.

"I'd rather be comfortable," Charlotte admitted matter-of-factly. When Paige refused to help her, she reached around and tried to get at the double-knotted laces herself.

Paige slapped her hand away. "Stop that, Charlotte, and quit your complaining! I went to a great deal of trouble to find and borrow these corsets for us."

"Maybe it would help if the person you borrowed the corsets from had been a size or two larger." And her chemise cut a little more modestly, Charlotte thought.

Paige went to the mirror and primped, needlessly adjusting her perfectly coiffed hair. "You look fine."

Charlotte stepped up to the mirror, next to Paige. Layers of lacy petticoat fell from her waist to just above her ankles. Her corset was wrapped snugly around her midriff, to just below her breasts. The chemise was above that. She looked ridiculous, like Scarlett O'Hara getting ready for the barbecue and ball at Twelve Oaks.

"You look wonderful," Paige said, smiling encouragement at Charlotte.

"Primed to seduce someone, you mean," Charlotte corrected. And with that thought, the only person who came to mind was Brett Forrest.

Just because he had kissed her once, fed her strawberries drenched in whipped cream and went out of his way to annoy her did not mean Brett was interested in her, or vice versa. Sure, there was plenty of chemistry between them, but that did not change the fact that he wasn't her type. She liked men who knew exactly what they wanted out of life and had no qualms about going after it. Not men who napped on sofas, played at writing a thesis on farming and skulked around eavesdropping on other people's private conversations.

As for the way she had responded to his kiss, well, that had been due to the surprise of his embrace, Charlotte told herself firmly. And the fact she hadn't been kissed like that in a long time. Actually, she had *never* been kissed quite like that, which was another reason to stay as far away from Brett as possible.

The sound of a car broke the silence of the spring afternoon. Paige rushed to the window. "There's the seamstress now. I'll go down and get her." She pointed a finger at

Charlotte. "Don't you go anywhere. And don't unlace those stays!"

BRETT STOPPED in the doorway of Charlotte's bedroom, stunned by what he saw. She was standing in a chemise, corset and petticoats. Her dark hair tumbled down around her shoulders in wild, tousled curls. Her breasts spilled from the lacy top in very alluring fashion.

Green eyes flashing, she whirled to face him. Blushing, she reached for a stack of midnight-blue damask curtains on the bed and held one in front of her like a shield. "What are you doing in here?"

Pretending a nonchalance he couldn't begin to feel, Brett smiled and sauntered closer. He didn't know what it was about this place, but it was damn near magical. And so was Charlotte. "You know, you look like you stepped right out of another time," he said softly. Having closed the distance between them, he twined a lock of her silky hair around his fingertip.

"It's the clothes," she said stubbornly as their eyes met and held.

"No," Brett disagreed wickedly. "It's not even the lack of them, Miss Charlotte. It's you, plain and simple."

Charlotte shook her head at him. Hand on his chest, she pushed him away. "You're sinful, Brett Forrest."

Her petticoat made soft swishing noises as she glided away from him. Brett followed. "Want to find out just how much?" he taunted playfully, only half kidding.

Charlotte whirled toward him in a drift of lilac perfume. "No, thank you," she said haughtily.

Just as he had suspected. Brett grinned, not the least bit anxious to leave. He glanced at the four tall windows that illuminated the corner bedroom. "Why did you tear all the curtains down in here?" he asked. The only thing she'd left were the translucent white sheers.

Charlotte blushed. "That is none of your business!"

Uh-huh, Brett thought, taking in her increasingly guilty expression. She was definitely up to something. What ex-

actly, he couldn't quite imagine. Unless she was going to
stand in front of those sheer white curtains at night and
drive him crazy with the silhouette of her undressing piece
by piece. . . .

"Why are you looking at me like that?" Charlotte demanded, beginning to panic as she darted around the end of
the four-poster bed.

"No reason," Brett fibbed, making absolutely no effort
to erase the mischievous grin from his face as he lazily traced
her path. It had been a long time since he had chased a girl
at recess. It pleased him to realize he hadn't forgotten how,
because Charlotte was one delectable Southern belle who
absolutely begged to be chased, even if she didn't know it!

"Well, then, why did you come up here?" Having gotten
herself stuck in a corner next to the bureau, Charlotte
turned and regarded him impatiently. Tapping one ballet-
slippered foot all the while, she continued to glare at him
and hold the blue damask curtain to her breasts. "What do
you want?"

Oh, sweetheart, if you only knew. "Just one more thing,"
Brett said lazily. Ignoring Charlotte's soft gasp of dismay,
he grabbed her around the waist and, with a determined tug,
brought her close so only the curtains were between them.
Then he yanked the curtains from her grasp and tossed them
onto the bed, so that nothing was keeping him from feeling
every inch of her against every inch of him. "You know,"
he speculated in a way he knew would absolutely incense
her, "I bet beneath that sweet porcelain skin of yours beats
a heart of fire."

Charlotte's emerald green eyes widened with a mixture of
temper and passion Brett found unbearably exciting. She
splayed her hands across his chest as he slowly lowered his
lips to hers. She exerted even more force with her hands; he
ignored it. "I mean it, Brett Forrest. Don't even think it!"
she warned, her thick dark eyelashes already beginning to
close.

"Then I won't think it," he said softly. "I'll do it."

Her lips were hot and soft, her kiss sensual. He knew she didn't mean to kiss him back, any more than he could help himself kissing her, and somehow that made the culmination of their desire all the sweeter. Groaning, he deepened the kiss, sweeping her mouth with his tongue, leaving not a millimeter unexplored. He had never felt anything like this in his life. Never wanted any one woman so much, never been possessed so thoroughly and so swiftly. And that was when he knew it had to end, before they both suffered the consequences. With difficulty, Brett lifted his mouth from hers. Charlotte's mouth was damp and pink. She was gasping for breath as she slowly opened her eyes. To Brett's further astonishment, she looked dazed and completely besotted. She was still clinging to his neck, looking like she wanted very much for him to start up the kisses again.

It was all Brett could do not to groan again. He wanted more than anything to take her over to her big four-poster bed and lie down with her on it. He couldn't think of anything sweeter or more exciting. He wanted to feel her against him, without all these damnable layers of petticoats and clothes. He wanted to have her against him, all soft and surrendering.

But it wasn't going to be today, not with Paige and that seamstress due back in the room at any moment.

"I'd sure like to be the man to bring you to life, sweetheart," he drawled. To his chagrin, Charlotte looked like she wanted that, too. With all the strength he could muster, Brett released her abruptly and said, "Unfortunately for both of us, I don't have time for this. I have to mow the lawn."

"What?" Charlotte sputtered, looking as if she couldn't believe he had gotten her all fired up and then just let her go!

Brett grinned. It did his heart good to know she was as reluctant to end the steamy embrace as he was. "You should know better than to play with the hired help, Miss Charlotte," he teased. "But perhaps this will teach you a lesson," he added with mock seriousness.

Charlotte flew at him with both fists. He caught her wrists before they could connect with his chest. "You are a dead man," Charlotte said irately, struggling unsuccessfully to free herself. "Do you hear me, Brett Forrest?" she shouted. "A dead man!"

Brett laughed, enjoying more than ever the feel of her in his arms. "You sure are pretty when you're in a temper, Miss Charlotte," he drawled. *And I sure would like to kiss you again.*

From behind them came two soft, feminine *ahem*s.

Face flaming, Charlotte stopped struggling abruptly and turned, as did Brett. Paige stood in the doorway beside a middle-aged woman with a sewing basket. It was obvious from the amused looks on their faces they'd seen just about everything. Brett didn't mind, but Charlotte sure did.

"Are we interrupting anything?" Paige asked.

He took another look at Charlotte in the old-fashioned chemise and petticoats, her tousled hair and pink cheeks. "Nothing that can't be continued later," he promised with a sexy grin.

"So how is it going so far?" Franklin asked Brett, long minutes later.

Brett held the phone to his ear as he paced the cottage. He knew he rubbed Charlotte the wrong way, and he was working hard on heightening her feelings of both apprehension and distaste. Adding desire to the mix had confused her even more, and that was good. The more he could distract her from thinking about Sterling, the better. "I don't think the indefatigable Miss Langston is any closer to finding out who the real Stephen Sterling is yet," he admitted. "But I also know she's not about to give up. So maybe a preemptive strike is in order."

Franklin chuckled. Brett could be *very* creative when it came to taking care of business. "Got anything specific in mind?"

"Aside from spying on her every chance I get?" Brett drawled, tongue-in-cheek.

"Yes."

Brett frowned and tried not to think how pretty Charlotte had looked in the old-fashioned ladies' underwear. He had come here to do a job and couldn't leave until it had been accomplished. In the meantime, he would have a little fun with Miss Charlotte. "Maybe it's time we set up a wild-goose chase for her," Brett suggested finally. Something that would really get her going . . . in the wrong direction, of course.

"Sounds good," Franklin said. "And in the meantime?"

"I'll stay one step ahead of and behind her," Brett promised.

"Won't Miss Langston get suspicious if you're always underfoot?" Franklin asked.

"Not if I sweep her off her feet." Brett grinned, remembering their last kiss. "Besides, she thinks the nature of my interest in her is largely romantic."

There was a pause at the other end of the line. "*Are* you romantically interested in Charlotte Langston?" Franklin asked bluntly.

Brett scoffed at the mere suggestion. "Hell, no. Nosy, spoiled Southern belles are not my type, you know that."

"Mmm. Well, you just watch yourself, Brett. And remember who is investigating whom here. There's a lot at stake and not just for Stephen Sterling."

Brett didn't have to be reminded of that. His future was riding on this, too. He smiled grimly. "Don't worry, Franklin. I've got everything well under control. No matter how much it irritates her to have me around, Miss Charlotte Langston won't make a move without me knowing about it."

Chapter Four

This was no time to be getting an attack of conscience, Charlotte told herself firmly as she dialed the warehouse number for Stephen Sterling's publisher. She had every right as a member of the press corps to investigate him. Furthermore, she was only doing what someone else would eventually do, anyway. Therefore, she might as well be the one to get the credit for discovering who Stephen Sterling really was, and why he was so hell-bent on hiding from the world.

Her mind made up to see this assignment through to the end, Charlotte finished punching in the long-distance number.

"Author sales," a chirpy voice on the other end of the line said.

Charlotte hated this part of her job, but it was necessary to be a little dishonest. So she crossed her fingers and began the ruse she hoped would lead her directly to Sterling. "This is Stephen Sterling's private secretary. I'm calling because he has not received his author copies of the book that was published last month."

"Those copies were shipped over two months ago," the shipping clerk said, puzzled.

A guilty flush climbed from Charlotte's chest to her neck as she pretended confusion. "Are you sure about that?"

"Yes. It says right here that the books were shipped to Joe Smith, Post Office Box 94332, Arlington, Virginia, 22210."

"Well, that's the address all right," Charlotte said after she had finished copying it down.

"And you say the copies did not arrive?" the clerk on the other end persisted.

"No, they didn't," Charlotte fibbed. "Nor did Mr. Sterling get a phone call telling him the books had been sent as requested. Listen," Charlotte said, injecting a harried note into her voice, "I have another call coming through, one I'm going to have to take. So if you want to look into this further, see what you can find out on your end and then call me back, that would be fine."

"I'd be happy to do that."

"You've got my name and phone number?" Charlotte persisted.

"Why don't you give it to me again?" the clerk asked.

"Actually, this might be a good time to check what you've got on file in this area, too, just to make sure it's correct," Charlotte said. "So if you'd just read what you have on file—"

"No," the clerk said firmly, sounding suddenly suspicious. "I think *you* had better tell me what your name and phone number is."

There was no way she could do that. Disappointed her ploy hadn't worked, Charlotte hung up the phone. Her dismay heightened as she glanced up and saw Brett lounging in the doorway to the library. His arms were crossed in front of him in a way that only drew attention to the broad musculature of his chest. From the way he was scowling at her, she knew he had heard enough of her conversation to realize she had lied in order to unearth more information on Sterling.

"There's a place for little girls who tell lies to get their jobs done," he drawled.

Charlotte had no defense for what she had done, so she took the offense, hoping to curb some of the embarrassment she felt at having been caught red-handed. "Why aren't you out cutting grass?" she demanded.

Brett straightened and moved toward her. The look he gave her was direct and uncompromising. His teeth flashed in a knowing smile, and he offered lazily, "I decided I didn't want to cut the grass, after all."

Charlotte regarded him with resentment. "*Want* doesn't come into this, Brett."

He looked at her as if to say, *Doesn't it?*

Charlotte felt another flash of discomfort. She knew there were some who would say there was no justification for the way she had just pried. Under any other circumstances, she might even agree with them. But what she had done was neither here nor there when it came to dealing with their lackadaisical caretaker. "When I assign you a task, as your employer, I expect it to be done," Charlotte advised.

Brett leaned across her desk and braced his hands on either side of her. Their glances met. For a second, Charlotte found it hard to get her breath. Warm color flooded her cheeks.

Brett grinned. "Don't get your knickers in a knot, Miss Charlotte." Without warning, his glance dropped to the notepad she'd been writing on. Charlotte promptly covered it with another notebook. She was unable to tell how much of the address Brett had been able to read.

"I arranged to have the grass cut by a poker-playing buddy of mine who also happens to own a tractor with a grass-cutting attachment," Brett continued, taking a seat on the edge of the grand old desk. He propped his wrists on his spread thighs. "He's going to cut the entire property, starting tomorrow. In return, I'm going to let him off the hook for a poker debt he owes me."

Leave it to Brett to have a good explanation for his laziness, too. "How generous of you," she said sweetly.

He leaned toward her sexily. "Considering how much he owes me, I thought so."

Her pulse racing, Charlotte gave him wide berth and stalked to the window. She opened the floor-to-ceiling drapes. Sunshine poured into the room. "Has anyone ever told you that you're a master at getting out of work?" She whirled back to face him and found to her dismay the distance had done nothing to dim her awareness of him.

Brett took her in from head to toe, his glance lingering on the softness of her breasts before returning to the flushed contours of her face. "I don't want to get out of *all* work," he assured her cheerfully, pushing away from the desk. "In fact, that's why I came in to see you." He strode toward her, not stopping until they were mere inches apart. "I want to repair the shutter out front, but I don't know where the tools or ladders are."

Charlotte drew a deep breath and caught a tantalizing whiff of his cologne. She folded her arms in front of her. "They're in the storage room in the garage."

His glance drifted over the ivory silk blouse she had tucked into her pleated trousers. "There's no storage room in the garage."

"Yes, there is."

"Well, I've never seen it," Brett said.

He was standing so close to her she had to tilt her head back to see into his face. Charlotte sighed. "I suppose you want me to show you?"

He shrugged. His blue eyes were dancing as he looked down at her. "Only if you want the shutter fixed," he allowed.

Right. Frowning, Charlotte picked her keys up off the desk with a snap of her wrist and marched out into the hall.

Brett lengthened his strides to keep up with her. He reached ahead to hold the front door open for her, and she had to run sideways to scoot past him. "Are you mad at me or the person you were lying to on the phone?" Brett asked innocently, as he followed her out onto the porch.

Charlotte turned around so swiftly she almost crashed headlong into his chest. He reached out to steady her, his grip on her arm warm and solid. She leaned into him momentarily. "You need to forget what you overheard when you walked in," Charlotte advised him sternly.

His mustache twitched with an emotion she couldn't quite pinpoint. His hand stayed on her arm, growing warmer and more possessive with every second that passed. "Why?"

Telling herself he had no right holding her that way, Charlotte shook off his grip and glared at him. "Because what I was saying was none of your business, that's why," she snapped.

Brett's dark brows rose. "Just like Sterling's private secretary's phone number is none of your business?" he chided innocently.

Charlotte pivoted sharply and marched down the front steps and around the side of the house, to the back lawn. Brett kept pace with her easily. No matter how much she tried, she couldn't outdistance him. "I refuse to discuss that with you," she said.

"I don't wonder." Brett picked a camellia from an overgrown bush at a juncture of the flagstone path. "After all, it can't be very comfortable trying to benefit yourself at someone else's expense."

Charlotte kept her gaze on the detached garage. The intimate nature of his questions didn't bother her half so much as her desire to answer them fully. Why did she have this gnawing wish to defend herself to him? she wondered.

Charlotte paused outside the garage. She looked over at Brett. He was standing close enough for her to see the half-inch spot of beard on the underside of his jaw he'd missed when he had last shaved. "Why does it matter to you what I do?" Charlotte asked as she put her key in the lock and opened the garage.

Brett held the camellia blossom to his nose, inhaling the delicate fragrance. "It's a long story."

Charlotte paused just inside the shadowy garage. "I've got time."

Their eyes met. This once, Charlotte couldn't look away.

"While I was at Yale, I got engaged. Deidre's family was very wealthy and, because of that, I suppose, extremely overprotective." Brett handed her the camellia. "One day I walked in and found a private investigator going through my things. I know what it's like to have your privacy invaded by a stranger. It's not a pleasant experience, Charlotte.''

Charlotte lifted the white blossom to her face, drinking deeply of the delicate fragrance. ''What happened to Deidre?'' she asked hoarsely, aware she didn't really want to imagine Brett with a woman other than herself.

Brett hooked his thumbs in his belt loops and stood looking down at her. ''We broke up.''

''Why?''

Brett grimaced unhappily. ''Because Deidre thought what her father did, in hiring that investigator to check me out, was okay. I disagreed.''

A shiver went through Charlotte at the unforgiving note in his low voice.

''And on that same score—'' Brett pointed a finger at Charlotte ''—what you journalists do to people to sell magazines is wrong.''

''Now wait just a minute.'' She held up a lecturing finger, then poked it at his chest. ''I've done some darn good work, and you would know that if you had read any of my profiles, particularly the ones on politicians.''

Brett's mouth tightened into a censuring line. ''The bottom line is that you shouldn't have to lie to get a story on someone, Charlotte. If you do, there's something wrong with the way you're going about things. And I would think by now you'd be wondering if you should even be going about this mission to find Sterling at all.''

His words struck a nerve. ''Look, I feel for what you went through while you were at Yale,'' Charlotte said with an indignant toss of her head, ''but that has no bearing on what I am doing now.''

''Doesn't it?'' Brett asked softly. He plucked the flower she still held in her hand and tucked it behind her ear. ''Seems like the exact same thing to me.''

Charlotte turned and flounced toward the storeroom. They never should have started this conversation in the first place, she thought resentfully. ''I intend to write such a good and thorough profile of Stephen Sterling that all people's questions about him will be answered once and for all. Once that happens, everyone else will stop looking for him, and his life will end up being easier," Charlotte said over her shoulder as she hunted for the right key.

Brett towered over her, his tall form temporarily blocking out the dust motes dancing in the pale sunlight. "Never mind the fact Stephen Sterling doesn't want to see a reporter's version of his life in print," he drawled contemptuously. "Right, Charlotte?"

Ignoring what she couldn't answer, and anxious to get away from Brett, Charlotte unlocked the storeroom. Filled with an intense desire to escape his relentless scrutiny, she pointed at the dusty, paraphernalia-filled room. "The ladder is against the wall," she said briskly. "The hammers and nails are in here, somewhere. It's up to you to find them. I don't have the time to help you look."

His cynical expression said he knew she was running. He moved to bar her way. "What's your hurry? Conscience bothering you?" he taunted.

Her heart was racing. Her throat was parched. Charlotte glared at Brett but didn't deign to dignify his comment with a reply. Squaring her shoulders, she spun on her heel, circled around him and stalked off.

She was still fuming when she reached the house, but her resolve to get the story on Sterling was unabated. Particularly since she knew she was just doing what someone else would eventually do, anyway. People were curious about Sterling, particularly his fans. Sooner or later, someone would track him down and expose him, someone perhaps not so determined to reveal Sterling as truthfully as Charlotte would.

She walked into the library, picked up the phone and dialed. "Confidential Investigations? Yes. I have a post-office box in Arlington, Virginia, I'd like to have staked out—immediately." She sighed, recalling her mistake with the clerk at the warehouse. "I have a feeling someone may be in directly to empty any mail out of it and then forfeit the box."

"ARE YOU SURE YOU WANT to do this, Miss Langston?" the pawnshop dealer said as he looked over her mother's antique jade-and-gold pendant and matching earrings. "These are obviously family heirlooms."

Heirlooms that had been entrusted to Charlotte because she was the eldest of the Langston sisters. It wasn't easy for her to hand them over, even for a few days. But what choice did she have? She had to save Camellia Lane!

"I'm in a bit of a pinch at the moment," Charlotte said. "I hope I can buy them back in a few weeks."

"So you'd rather I not sell them?"

"If you can avoid it, yes."

"I'll try. But if I get a good offer on them ..." the shop owner said.

"I know. You'll sell them," Charlotte said. *Mother would understand,* Charlotte told herself firmly. *She would want me to save Camellia Lane before the jewelry.*

Nevertheless, Charlotte left the pawnshop, her spirits dwindling. She walked down to the bank, deposited into her checking account the cash the pawnshop dealer had given her, and then express-mailed a retainer to Confidential Investigations. This post-office box better pay off, she thought firmly. Otherwise, she was in deep trouble.

Her spirits lower than ever, Charlotte returned to Camellia Lane. To her dismay, the shutter on the front of the house was still hanging crookedly. Brett was nowhere in sight, and neither was his banged-up old car. Why did this not surprise her?

"CHARLOTTE, HOW COULD you?" Paige demanded several hours later.

Charlotte looked up from the guest list she'd been compiling. "How could I *what,* Paige?"

"Pawn mother's pendant and earrings!"

Charlotte sighed. "Oh, that."

"Yes, that. You know those were never supposed to leave the family!"

"Hopefully they won't have to leave the family," Charlotte said. "I'll buy them back after we save Camellia Lane."

"How can you be sure the jewelry will still be there to purchase?" Paige asked.

That was the problem. She couldn't be sure of much of anything at this point. Nor did she have much choice. She had to take risks and gamble that everything would work out. It was either that or give up, and Charlotte had never given up on anything in her life.

Charlotte sat back in her chair and dropped her pen onto the desk in front of her. Resigned to reassuring her younger sister, she said soothingly, "Poplar Springs is a small town. Not many people have three thousand in ready cash to buy jewelry. It should still be there."

Paige sat down on the library sofa. "When is the cleaning service supposed to come out?"

Charlotte took a sip of orange juice. "Friday morning."

"Aren't you kind of waiting until the last moment?"

"I don't want the dust to have any time to gather," Charlotte explained. Sensing Paige's continuing anxiety, Charlotte said, "Don't worry, they've already been out to size the job. They're sending a full crew. We'll get it done right and on time."

Paige opened her purse and took out a small navy leather appointment book. "Well, the dresses are coming along fine. However, you may be needed for another fitting."

Charlotte made a face; she hated standing still.

"Sorry to interrupt," Brett said from the doorway. "But I need someone to hold the ladder while I nail the shutter back into place."

Grateful for the excuse to shorten Paige's recital of worries and complaints, Charlotte pushed away from the desk and said, "I'll help."

"How many guests have phoned that they're coming so far?" Brett asked as Charlotte followed him out onto the front porch.

She looked at the ladder, nails and hammer Brett had assembled. It certainly looked as if he were ready to get down to business, she realized with relief. "About half as many as we need. But don't worry," Charlotte said with a great deal more confidence than she felt. "We'll get there."

"Right," Brett said dryly.

She watched as he concentrated on extending the ladder and adjusting it to the proper height. Aware he was getting under her skin again, she said, "And you were supposed to have fixed that shutter hours ago."

Brett propped the extension ladder against the side of the house and made sure it was firmly in place. He turned to her with a winning smile that did things it shouldn't have to Charlotte's pulse. "I couldn't find any nails," he explained. "I had to go into town to get some." Wordlessly, he took her wrist and placed it on the ladder where he wanted her to hold it. Her skin tingled at his touch. "Then I stopped by the library to get a book on home repair, just to make sure I was doing it right." Brett rubbed his thumb across her wrist sensuously. "And I got to talking to Isabella, and she told me the sheriff had been looking for me. They needed a fifth in a game of lunch-hour poker, so I mosied on over to the Red Garter Saloon and played a little cards."

Charlotte rolled her eyes. How was it possible she could be attracted to a man who was so hopelessly lazy and unreliable? But she was. There was no denying her heart beat a little faster whenever he was close, no denying the way she had felt when he had swept her into his arms for an ardent kiss, or the fact that she still couldn't get that mad, impetuous embrace in her bedroom out of her mind. She went to bed at night dreaming that she was Scarlett O'Hara and he was her Rhett. "You have more excuses," Charlotte complained.

Brett grinned wickedly but didn't dispute her comment. He bent to pick up several nails. "Don't you want to know what juicy gossip I heard while I was at the Red Garter?" he taunted mildly.

Charlotte could only imagine. It seemed these days the town did nothing but talk about her and her sisters and the financial troubles they were having.

She looked down her nose at Brett, which wasn't easy, considering the fact that he was a good ten inches taller than she was. "Not particularly, no."

Brett grinned at her. He examined the nails carefully and then put them into a pocket of the tool belt he had tied around his waist. Charlotte watched him bend over to pick up the hammer. She tried her best not to notice how nicely he filled out his jeans, but it was a losing battle. Brett Forrest might not be her type, but he was a very attractive man. A woman would have to be half-dead not to notice, Charlotte thought, and she was very much alive.

"Sure about that now?" Brett offered in a put-on version of a Southern drawl. "The juicy gossip was about *you*, Miss Charlotte," he said, studying her upturned face.

The warmth of her embarrassment climbed from Charlotte's chest up her neck. "Great."

Brett gave his hammer a leisurely examination before he returned his gaze to her face. "And how you just hocked your mother's jade pendant and earrings, presumably to pay for the party here."

Charlotte's jaw dropped. She slammed her hands on her waist. "Honestly, is nothing I do here private?"

"Hmm. Interesting a reporter like you would say that. I thought you were the one who wanted all the facts out in the open."

"Oh, be still."

"Besides, Poplar Springs is a small town, Charlotte." Brett waggled his eyebrows at her playfully. "It's next to impossible to keep anything secret in a small town."

"You're telling me," she grumbled. "You can't sneeze here without everyone knowing about it." Besides, the story about her was all wrong. She had hocked the jewelry to pay Confidential Investigations, not to pay for the party.

Brett climbed the ladder with purposeful steps. Hooking the hammer into the tool belt at his waist, he reached over to right the crooked shutter. He fit the nail into the groove and began to hammer it in. Charlotte watched as he swiftly hammered in the second and third nails, securing the shutter in its rightful place. As he descended the ladder to her side, a landscape truck pulled up in the drive. It was loaded with flats of flowers.

Several workers got out. Charlotte went down to talk to them. By the time she had finished showing them what she wanted done, Brett had put his tools away. He joined her on the veranda at the rear of the house, overlooking the formal gardens. "It'll be pretty when they finish," he remarked.

Charlotte nodded. She gestured at the elaborate maze of overgrown shrubs and empty flower beds surrounding the pretty flagstone walk. In the center was a large three-tier fountain, surrounded by several elaborately crafted stone benches.

"You'd never know it now, but these gardens were the showplace of the whole property years ago." Charlotte watched as uniformed workers carried flats of golden marigolds, red, white and pink impatiens, and purple verbena into the garden area. They set them down and returned to the trucks for flats of white alyssum, red and pink roses, and vibrant begonias.

"I used to play hide-and-seek with my sisters out here." Charlotte pointed to the trees that bordered the perimeter of the two-acre garden. "We were always climbing those apple trees, because the branches were so low and scuffing up our shoes."

Brett grinned as if imagining Charlotte as a rambunctious child. "I bet you were a handful when you were younger."

Charlotte laughed, admitting fondly, "We all were. My mother probably mended more ripped pinafores and Sunday dresses than she would've ever cared to admit."

Brett studied the rolling acres of lawn and garden. "You know, this is still a great place to raise a family," he said thoughtfully.

Charlotte nodded, her expression dreamy as she leaned out over the rail. "I think so, too." In fact, it was one of her secret dreams to find her own knight in shining armor and settle here and raise a family with him. Aware Brett was still studying her carefully, she continued softly, "I certainly had a wonderful time here in my youth."

Brett grinned and gently brushed a windswept lock of her hair back out of her eyes. "I hadn't realized you were so sentimental at heart, Charlotte," he teased, trying to get a rise out of her, and succeeding. He arched a brow in comically exaggerated surprise. "I might have to alter my opinion of you yet."

"I'm not looking for your approval, Brett Forrest," Charlotte murmured with a feisty toss of her dark hair. "I couldn't care less what you think of me." But even as she threw the words back at him, she knew it wasn't true. She did care very much what he thought of her.

Chapter Five

"Isabella wants to know if you found the other punch bowls yet," Brett reported hours later, as he climbed the attic steps.

"One, not the other," Charlotte replied. She was seated on an old-fashioned steamer trunk, dust clinging to her clothes. Her dark brown hair had been wound into a careless chignon on the back of her head. Errant tendrils framed her face and curled down her neck, giving her a pleasantly disheveled look.

"Need some help?" Brett asked as he strode across the attic to her side. The low beams overhead gave a cozy feel to the three thousand square feet of space. Dormer windows on all four sides let in streamers of pale gold sunlight. Faded area rugs that were visibly thin in places covered the floor.

"If you don't mind hunting through about a thousand old boxes," Charlotte replied with a weary sigh. "It seems like I've been up here forever."

Wanting only to help her, Brett sidestepped a stack of worn bed linens and a hat rack to take a place opposite her, on a ripped velvet footstool. Charlotte was surrounded by boxes of papers, all handwritten, many yellowed with age. "What are all these old papers?" he asked curiously.

She smiled proudly. "Early drafts of my father's manuscripts."

Brett pulled the stool up a little closer so they were sitting face-to-face. He welcomed the intimacy of meeting with her this way. "I didn't know he was a writer," Brett said softly.

"Oh, yes." Charlotte smiled happily. "He was an authority on the Civil War. He wrote books and lectured at small historical societies all over the South. There wasn't a lot of money in it, but he loved what he did," she finished affectionately. She stood and looked around a little bit. "Now where is that extra punch bowl?" She opened yet another box and paused.

"What did you find?" he asked. Glancing over her shoulder, he noted she was looking down at a framed photo of two men. One bore a familiar resemblance to Charlotte and must have been her father, Brett deducted. The other was J. H. McMillan, a financier who had quickly risen to fame and then burned out like a comet nearly a decade before.

"I didn't know this was up here," Charlotte murmured quietly, some of the happiness fading from her eyes.

Brett moved in closer, until their shoulders were touching, and took another look at the photo. The two men were standing with their arms locked. McMillan had autographed the photo with the words, *To my newest convert: Life is short. The sooner a man begins to multiply his wealth, the better.*

"Your father knew J. H. McMillan," Brett said.

Charlotte nodded as she sat down again. "My father took one of his You Can Get Rich, Too seminars."

Brett sat down opposite Charlotte, on an old steamer trunk. "Bad idea, huh?"

Charlotte inclined her head slightly to the side. "It didn't seem so at first, while everything was going great, but all that changed when the limited partnerships J.H. had talked my father into joining went bankrupt and J.H. and his theories were declared a fraud, shortly after my father's death."

Brett guessed the family had a lot of money. "I can see where that would be upsetting," he said slowly.

"More so, because I was taken in by J.H., too." Charlotte lifted her eyes to Brett's. "I'd had occasion to meet him on one of his counseling sessions with my father and I was really impressed." Charlotte sighed and propped her chin on her fist. "In retrospect, of course, what ticked me off the most was the thought that if just one journalist had looked beyond his charming, knowledgeable veneer, they would have known that he was a crook."

Brett paused, absorbing all she had told him. Although Charlotte was doing her best to hide it, he could see the hurt and disillusionment in her eyes. "Where does someone like Stephen Sterling come into this?" he asked gently. "I can understand you going after a con artist like McMillan, but Sterling's a novelist."

Charlotte frowned at his rebuke. "I admit Sterling isn't the sort of quarry I normally stalk," she said as she picked up another box and peered inside.

Charlotte looked abruptly weary to the bone, and worried. Brett's heart went out to her. She might be on the wrong path, but she was doing her best to save the family home. He admired her determination, if not her methods. "If there wasn't such a price on Sterling's head, would you still be going after him?" Brett asked, hoping against all reason Charlotte would give him an unequivocal no.

Charlotte shrugged as she rescued two mismatched china serving platters and added them to the pile of party paraphernalia she was taking back downstairs. "What I don't understand is why what I do should matter this much to you, Brett."

Their eyes clashed and held, and much to Brett's chagrin, he couldn't look away.

It matters because I don't want to play games with you, Charlotte, Brett thought. *I want to get to know you, no holds barred. It matters because I've never had trouble doing my job before. I don't like the feeling that my personal life is negatively impacting my professional.*

And Brett knew if he kept on with Charlotte, his own agenda and integrity just might be compromised. "I just don't want to see you make a mistake that could very well end in a lawsuit against you or the magazine you work for," Brett explained casually.

"Well, not to worry," Charlotte reassured him airily, already heading for another box of treasures. "I'm not in any danger of being sued for either libel or slander as long as what I write is the absolute truth and I always make darn certain that whatever I write is one-hundred-percent factual. *What* is this doing up here?" Charlotte plucked a framed photo out of the dust. "I didn't know my grandparents' wedding portrait was up here."

Brett perused the framed black-and-white photo she handed him. The bride wore white. The groom wore tails. They were surrounded by a wedding party of at least twenty. Everyone in the photo looked incredibly happy and well-to-do. "Looks like they had a really nice wedding," Brett said.

"Doesn't it," Charlotte murmured.

Her fingers brushed his lightly as he handed her the photo. Her skin was soft as silk, warm as fire. The combination and the contact made his pulse race.

Charlotte continued to gaze wistfully at the photo. "Wishing you could have a wedding, too?" Brett teased.

Charlotte pressed her lips together in a moue of regret. "Not much chance of that," she admitted with a delicate sigh, looking oddly vulnerable again. She added the frame to the stack of things she planned to take downstairs.

"Why not?" Brett asked, moving closer yet.

She moved her shoulders dismissively, as if the answer were simple—and obvious. "Because there is no romance left in the world today."

Brett was surprised to find himself filled with curiosity. "So you don't want to marry?" he asked, not sure he wanted to believe that.

"No." Charlotte tipped her chin up to his. Her face was luminous in the soft twilight. "I do *want* to marry. I just won't do so without romance. And a lot of other women my age feel the same way. And that, Brett Forrest," Charlotte finished emphatically, "is why Stephen Sterling's novels are so popular."

Brett wasn't sure he followed her logic. "What do you know about his novels?" He watched her carry a stack of threadbare damask tablecloths to the head of the stairs, then return to the boxes.

Charlotte pulled another punch bowl out of the dust and stood again. "A lot," she said.

She met his eyes as she glided by in a drift of lilac perfume. Brett wanted to gather her in his arms and kiss her until she forgot all about Sterling. Instead, he stifled a sigh and followed her to the box of mismatched china serving platters. He beat her to them and hefted them into his arms. "You've read Sterling's books then, I presume."

She pointed to the stairs. "All three novels."

Brett carried the china to where she had directed, and came back for the box of tarnished silver. "So you're a fan," he said grimly.

"Oh, yes," Charlotte affirmed.

Damn, Brett thought, carrying the silver over and returning to her side. *This situation gets more complicated all the time.*

"How come?" Brett asked, working to keep his tone matter-of-fact. He didn't want Charlotte to know that this bothered him at all. He didn't want to feel jealous of Sterling and whatever she felt for Sterling's work.

Charlotte reached behind Brett to pluck a crystal fruit bowl from the pile of old dishes. Her hips swayed provocatively beneath her slacks as she carried it over to the stairs and added it to the stack of items she had rescued. "For one thing, Sterling writes like someone who has seen and done everything. His work literally exudes excitement."

Brett shrugged, tearing his eyes from the slender lines of her thighs and the fluid way her legs moved beneath the loose fabric of her trousers. "I can't speak to that," he said gruffly. And it was true, he couldn't—not without giving away what he knew about Sterling.

"Well, I can, and I'll tell you something else. No one writes a love scene with as much passion and fire as Sterling," Charlotte advised with a toss of her head.

To his own surprise, Brett realized her reaction both irritated and disappointed him. He didn't want Charlotte dreaming about Stephen Sterling. He wanted her dreaming about *him!*

Brett shook his head in exasperation. She really thought she had this all figured out. And although she was close to the truth in some areas, she was way off the mark in others. "You know what I think?" he said.

"No," Charlotte retorted dryly, "but I suppose you're going to tell me."

"I think you're the one with the vivid imagination, not Sterling," Brett said. He watched her peruse the attic slowly, looking for other treasures. "Sterling is probably hiding because he wants refuge from overzealous fans."

Charlotte shook her head in mute disagreement. She bent to look at a rocking chair. "There's more to Sterling's secrecy than that," she insisted tartly as she sank into the chair and tried it out. "Like maybe he really was a spy at one time. He certainly seems to know the business!" She bounded out of her chair.

Brett rolled his eyes, annoyed to find her so far off the mark. Unable to tear his gaze for her, he gave her a faint, unreadable smile. "You're dreaming now, babe. I know a few writers. They lead very dull lives."

"Writers on what?" Charlotte advanced on him, her expression impatient. "Dirt farming?"

"And other things," Brett said, not about to admit to her that he knew Stephen Sterling better than she could imagine.

Charlotte halted just short of him. Every inch of her was vibrant, alive. "You know what your problem is? You just don't want to think that the real Stephen Sterling might be every bit as exciting and sexy as the books he writes."

"And why, my darling Charlotte, would I not want to think that?" Brett drawled, not sure whether to be annoyed or amused at her know-it-all attitude.

"Because you, sir, don't have a romantic bone in your body!" Charlotte retorted, her green eyes flashing with challenge.

Now *that* rankled, Brett thought. To be compared with Sterling and come out on the losing end, especially when Charlotte had just announced that she found his books incredibly sexy and exciting.

"Oh, I don't, do I?" Brett drawled.

"No, you don't!"

Deciding the lady needed to feel as shaken up as he did, he took Charlotte in his arms. She trembled immediately, in a way that told him just how sensitive she was to his touch.

Brett tunneled his hands through her hair and brought her mouth up to his. Desire flowed through him in hot waves, even before their lips touched.

He was beginning to see their lovemaking as inevitable, and judging by the free rein she gave the kiss, so was she.

Their tongues twining intimately, her hands cupped his shoulders, slipping upward to touch his face. She rose on tiptoe, the softness of her body giving new heat to his. He anchored an arm about her waist and pulled her closer still. Feelings poured from his heart, followed swiftly by a need that was soul-deep. No woman had ever touched his heart this way. No woman had ever made him want with such tenderness and desperation. If this wasn't heaven, Brett thought, he didn't know what was.

Charlotte moaned as Brett unbuttoned her blouse, the warmth of his hand slipping inside to cup her breast. She had never been touched like this, so tenderly and evocatively. Arrows of fire shot through her, weakening her knees, making her cling to him as if he were a life ring in a raging sea.

This wasn't supposed to happen now, she thought, as her nipple crowned against the flat of his palm. She wasn't supposed to act on instinct and think later, but with Brett, she did, and she didn't know how to fight it—wasn't sure she *wanted* to fight it.

It was so much simpler just to follow the hidden wellspring of emotion he had discovered deep within her. So much easier just to let herself be carried away on a sweet tidal wave of passion . . . so much easier to simply continue to kiss . . . to let their passion for each other lead where it might. . . .

Brett felt the sweet resignation in her embrace. Too caught up in what was happening between them to care that it might be a mistake, he looked for a place for them to lie down. Finding none, he rained kisses down her neck even as he rebuttoned her blouse. Gathering her close, he felt her heart beating in urgent rhythm with his. "Let's go down to the cottage," he whispered in her ear. His hand ghosted over her spine, fitting her against him, man to woman. "Let's do this the way it should be done." *Slowly and with inordinate care.*

His coolheaded approach was like a bucket of ice water on her tender feelings. Charlotte came back to her senses quickly. Hands splayed on his chest, she ducked his light, possessive grip. She trembled, realizing how close she had come to surrendering to his ardor and making love to Brett. "There's a difference between sex and romance, Brett," she said shakily. She wanted love. Until she was sure he could give her that, there would be no making love.

TORTUROUS, LONELY HOURS later, Brett saved the file he had been working on and shut off the laptop computer. Stretching, he got up from the table and paced the confines of the caretaker's cottage, too keyed up to try and sleep, too worried about what Charlotte might be thinking or doing now to indulge in a solitary pastime like reading or watching television.

Thinking a walk around the estate might relax him, Brett slipped outside. Moonlight washed the grounds in luminous light. Across the lawn, past the shadows of the formal gardens, the main house rose like a fortress, solid and secure. And oh so inviting.

Only one window was lit from within. As if driven by a primal force, Brett moved toward Charlotte's bedroom. Through the sheer white curtains, he could see her moving restlessly about her room. The fact that she, too, was unable to sleep made him feel closer to her. He smiled.

She was wearing something long and flowing and all one color. Maybe a robe? She was brushing her hair, almost absently as she moved.

Knowing she couldn't see him lingering in the shadows below, Brett felt free to look his fill, studying the lush curves of her body in silhouette, the delicate shape of her profile, the beautiful dark hair flowing over her slender shoulders.

His own body tightening in remembrance, he wondered if she, too, was thinking about the passionate embrace they had shared in the attic that afternoon. He knew he was.

He had not come here expecting to fall in love. Far from it. Nor had he ever had any trouble staying away from feisty, hot-blooded Southern belles who were used to having their own way, especially with the men who adored them.

But Charlotte... she was different.

And like Rhett, he couldn't stay away from his Scarlett.

For all her flaws and mystery, for all her stubbornness, Charlotte was the woman who'd captured his imagination and his heart. The more he was with her, the more he wanted to be with her—and the more he wanted to make long, beautiful, passionate love with her.

But would she surrender to him, and soon? Would she allow him into her heart, too?

Brett watched with undeniable yearning as she dropped her robe, climbed into bed and switched off her light. As much as he wanted to join her now, he knew he couldn't.

Morning would be here soon enough. And then he would find out exactly where he stood with her and take it from there. Because one way or another, he was going to make her his. And his alone.

BRETT WALKED INTO the kitchen the next morning just as Charlotte checked on the cinnamon rolls in the oven. Satisfied they were doing okay, she closed the oven door and turned to face him.

To Brett's consternation, she wasn't dressed in the usual silk shirt and dressy slacks, but was instead wearing some sort of frilly mint green sundress, with a full skirt that swirled around her when she moved and a tight bodice that emphasized her feminine curves. She had tied a white organdy blouse over the dress. It was worn open and knotted at the waist.

Charlotte looked like she was ready for more than just breakfast. He was instantly suspicious, wondering what she was up to now. Was this a ploy to turn him on, turn him down and teach *him* a lesson *he* would never forget?

Adopting a casual stance, Brett lounged against the counter and watched as Charlotte stuffed a paper filter into the coffeemaker. "Anything I can do to help you today?" he asked.

He had come here this morning hoping to find some way to get back in her good graces again. Judging from the stubborn set of her pretty chin, that was going to take some doing.

To his surprise, Charlotte turned to him with a winning smile. "Actually, Brett, I think you've earned some time off. I think you ought to drive into Poplar Springs and see a movie or play poker with your buddies."

Brett noticed she wasn't meeting his eyes. Another sign she was up to something. "Careful, or I'll think you want to get rid of me," he said, only half teasing.

Charlotte laughed nervously. She blushed like a Southern belle with too many dates for the same evening. "Don't be ridiculous. I'm just trying to repay some of your kindness. So scoot. Have a wonderful day."

"Just don't spend it here," Brett guessed, his expression deadpan.

To his surprise, the tart retort he was expecting from her never came. Charlotte only smiled as she guided him in the direction of the door. "Goodbye," she said sweetly.

Brett knew there was only one way to find out what she was up to.

Aware she was watching, Brett got in his car and drove off. Unbeknownst to her, however, he pulled off the road half a mile down the lane and waited.

It didn't take long to find out what was going on. Jared Fontaine's white Porsche roared down the road and turned into Camellia Lane. Brett left his car where it was and raced through the woods. Charlotte was on the back porch with Jared. They were sitting at a white wrought-iron table.

Brett could see she had gone all out to entertain Jared. She had put out a pink linen tablecloth and cloth napkins. Real china and silver. Laid out the cinnamon rolls she had baked, the coffee she had just brewed and a carafe of juice. There was even a vase filled with camellias in the center of the table.

He had missed the first ten minutes of their conversation. But it was easy to see what was happening, he thought, as Jared reached over and took the hand of a visibly uncomfortable Charlotte.

"Of course I can get you more guests for the party," Jared was saying as he rubbed the back of her hand with long, sensual strokes. "With my social and political contacts, it would be easy. The problem is, I don't think you and your sisters should be throwing this party at all."

"We have no choice, Jared," Charlotte said in a flirty Southern-belle tone. She gently withdrew her hand from his and dropped it into her lap. She sat back, away from the table. "It's our only chance to raise the money to pay off the balloon note in time."

"I think you're wrong about that," Jared said softly. Without warning, he stood and circled around behind Charlotte.

Brett's fists clenched as he watched Jared put his hands on Charlotte's shoulders.

"If you'd consent to marry me, Charlotte," Jared continued, sliding his hands across her shoulders, down her upper arms, "you wouldn't have to throw the party or worry about saving Camellia Lane."

Charlotte was motionless.

"Jared, you know I consider you my friend and I always have," she said coolly, extricating herself from his grip. She stood and turned around to face him. Her body language definitely said hands-off, but it was a warning Jared ignored.

"I want to be more than your friend, Charlotte," Jared admitted. He lifted his hand to her chin, looking as if he were going to lower his head and kiss her at any moment. "And if you search your heart, you'll know I always have," he continued softly. "Why do you think I never married anyone else? Because I never gave up on the hope that one day you would come back to Poplar Springs, where you belong."

Unable to bear seeing Charlotte in the arms of another man, Brett was considering ways to break up the cozy scene himself when Charlotte pushed Jared away. She marched to the other side of the table.

"I can't marry you. Not feeling the way I do." Brett watched as she looked Jared straight in the eye.

"Not even to save Camellia Lane?" Jared asked.

"What are you talking about?" Charlotte said, aggrieved.

Jared shrugged. He began to show his true colors. "I don't really want this old mansion—I think it's already outlived its time—but for you, Charlotte, for you," he confessed on a seductive whisper, "I might be convinced to do almost anything."

Brett knew the feeling—Charlotte drove *him* to distraction, too. And that irritated him immensely. He wasn't used to being led around by a woman. Never mind one he was trying to spy on!

To Brett's relief, Charlotte turned her head before Jared could kiss her. "I don't know what to think," she said in a coquettish drawl that would have done Scarlett O'Hara proud.

Brett watched, curious to see where all this would lead. He knew how much Charlotte cherished the plantation home where she had grown up. Would she sell her soul to save her beloved Camellia Lane? He had thought she valued herself—and her family name—more than that. But he also knew she would do almost anything to save Camellia Lane from being foreclosed on by the bank. It was beginning to look as if agreeing to marry Jared might accomplish that!

Don't do it, Charlotte, Brett urged silently. *You'll regret it the rest of your life if you let yourself be coerced into this.*

"I might even be convinced," Jared continued, "to float you a loan for the fifty thousand you owe the bank, Charlotte."

To Brett's dismay, he could see Charlotte was tempted by the offer, if not inclined to cooperate sexually. "I don't think it's wise to borrow money from friends," she said firmly. She braced her arms between herself and Jared, successfully, firmly, holding him at bay. "My parents felt the same way, so I . . . couldn't possibly accept a loan from you."

But she would ask for Jared's help in procuring paying guests for her fund-raising party Saturday night, Brett thought, when even a fool could see that *any* help Jared gave her was bound to have strings attached. Brett wondered again at the convoluted nature of Charlotte's thoughts.

"Not even," Jared asked slyly, "if the two of us were married, Charlotte?"

That was it, Brett thought. He'd seen enough. He was going to step in to help Miss Charlotte. It was the only gallant thing to do.

He strolled out into the open. Charlotte started at the sight of him. She stepped out of the circle of Jared Fontaine's arms with a small gasp.

"Brett!" She looked shocked and embarrassed all at once.

As she should be, Brett thought angrily.

And just a tiny bit grateful.

"Good morning again, Charlotte." Brett looked at her old family friend and offered a curt nod. "Jared."

"Brett." Jared nodded at him.

"What are you doing here? I thought I gave you the morning off," Charlotte said.

I thought you might need me, Brett thought. What a crazy idea that had been. Like Scarlett O'Hara, Charlotte could certainly take care of herself. "Had a slight problem with my car," he said with a shrug. "I think I need a little water for the radiator."

Brett looked at the competition and bared his teeth in a falsely congenial smile. "Maybe Jared here could give me a lift back to my car. It's up the road a piece."

Jared exchanged a look with Brett. Brett could see that Jared was suspicious of his sudden appearance at such an inopportune time, just as Charlotte was, and not at all happy about being asked to render aid.

"Sure," Jared said with an affability Brett knew was all for Charlotte's benefit. Jared turned to Charlotte. "About our lunch date later—" he began.

"I can't today after all, Jared," she said firmly, holding Jared's eyes.

"If you change your mind," he said heavily, meeting Charlotte's gaze with equal determination and patience, "you know where to find me."

"WHAT HAPPENED TO the getup?" Brett drawled when he returned half an hour later. Charlotte had cleared off the back porch. Dressed in chinos that cupped her rounded derriere and a silk shirt that did equally delicious things for the rest of her, she was busy cleaning up the kitchen.

"What getup?" Charlotte asked, blushing slightly.

"The gotta-catch-me-a-man getup. You know, the gossamer blouse, the sundress, the heels." The outfit that had conjured up images of moonlight and roses and had him aching to hold her in his arms ever since.

Charlotte evaded Brett's waiting gaze as she covered the cinnamon rolls with plastic wrap and put them in the refrigerator. "I was cold and I decided to change."

The corners of Brett's mustache lifted as his lips formed a sardonic smile. "Sure you didn't just have an attack of conscience?" he taunted, doing his best to get a rise out of her.

And succeeding.

Charlotte whirled on him. "You were the one hiding in the gardens!" She glared at him, her eyes flashing. "Don't you have any scruples?"

Because she looked as if she might flee at any minute, Brett captured her wrists and pulled her against him. "You're a fine one to be talking about scruples," he countered softly, unable to help but notice the way her breasts rose and fell with every quickly indrawn breath. "Valuing Camellia Lane above your own integrity." She'd had no business dressing the way she had, even if it was part and parcel of a Southern belle's charm.

Guilty color flooded Charlotte's face. "That is not true!" She disagreed hotly as she disengaged her wrists from his grip. "I told Jared exactly how I feel!"

Brett folded his arms in front of him. He would have much preferred that her foolhardy conversation with Jared had never happened, but now that it had, he had to make her deal with the consequences. "You also played along with him," Brett reminded her.

Charlotte tossed her head. Silky mahogany hair flew in every direction. "Only to a point and only because I was trying to get Jared to help us save Camellia Lane!"

"But at what cost?" Brett demanded. Changing positions abruptly, he planted a hand on the counter on either side of her and leaned in close. Camellia Lane might engender fantasies of a more chivalrous age, but this was not that time and men did not act *only* gallantly these days.

Charlotte tried to sidle past Brett, to avoid the lecture she knew was coming. But he refused to budge, and her ribs connected with the flexed muscles in his forearm. With a sigh of frustration, she moved back so they were no longer touching. "Fine. You can keep me here if you wish, but I refuse to listen to any more of your pointless lecturing!" Charlotte clamped her hands over her ears.

Refusing to listen would not keep Jared from making another move on Charlotte. The only difference was that next time Brett might not be around to stop the sleazy lawyer from making a play for her.

The need to protect Charlotte surfaced, stronger than ever. Brett lifted his hands from the counter and pried her hands from her head. He flattened his palms over hers and cupped them warmly against the ungiving wall of his chest. "I know you're upset over the prospect of losing Camellia Lane and because you're so distressed you're not thinking straight. But you better get a handle on your feelings," Brett warned, his protective feeling for her magnifying tenfold at the vulnerability he saw in her eyes.

"Or what?" Charlotte said as Brett tenderly caressed the backs of her hands with his fingertips.

"Or before you know it, you're going to find yourself in a position that you'll regret the rest of your life," he said softly. A position where her back was against the wall and she had no choice but to marry Jared. And that he just didn't want to see.

Chapter Six

Brett stood in the doorway to the third-floor ballroom, unable to believe his eyes. Charlotte had a broom in her arms and was waltzing around, her eyes half-closed in what he presumed was ecstasy.

For a second, he stayed where he was, wondering what it would be like to have her in his arms. And he wondered why he found the notion of dancing with Miss Charlotte so exciting. It wasn't just her beauty that aroused him, it was her passion. She never seemed to do anything halfway. He suspected that penchant of hers also applied to making love.

Maybe she did belong in another time.

But right now, she was not wearing a ball gown. And she looked very much like a very modern woman acting out her own private fantasy.

Deciding it would be criminal to interrupt, he stayed where he was, appreciating the way the snug jeans hugged her legs, and the oversize man's shirt emphasized the slenderness of her tall form as she swayed and dipped and waltzed her way around the ballroom. Her mahogany hair had been caught up in a red bandanna and she was humming slightly off-key. Brett noted this was the third time today she had changed clothes. Maybe she was more of a Southern belle than she knew.

Without warning, her eyes flew open, and she gasped as she saw him. Her lithe steps came to an abrupt halt. Hot color filled her cheeks as she glared at him resentfully.

Brett wasn't surprised that Charlotte was still royally ticked off at him. He'd had no business telling her to beware of Jared Fontaine this morning. He also knew that as long as she was mad enough to keep avoiding him, he would never be able to find out what she was up to regarding Stephen Sterling, so he'd come here with the express purpose of making peace with her. His second objective was to enact the ruse that he and Franklin Dunn had set up. So, putting duty above his own feelings, he'd tracked her down again. He wanted to be friends with Charlotte, because when this was all over, she was going to need him.

"What are you doing here?" she demanded with asperity.

"Why, I'm watching you, of course," Brett drawled. Charlotte's green eyes flashed fire and he grinned again. Damned if she wasn't the prettiest woman he'd ever met. And the most enticing.

"Well, stop watching me!" Charlotte ordered as she threw the broom down and marched over to get a dustpan.

Brett rested a shoulder against the frame. "Why?"

"Because I'm busy and you're annoying me!"

Brett glanced at the dusty trail of prints her dancing feet had left from one end of the ballroom to the other. "Oh, I can see how busy you are," he said.

And how annoyed. Even when the two of them weren't arguing about Charlotte's plans to go after Sterling or her naiveté where Jared was concerned, Brett knew he really got under her skin. The funny thing was, he enjoyed their sparring and that was very unusual.

Usually Brett steered clear of women he didn't get along with. But not this one. This one, he couldn't stay away from...his secret mission here aside. Charlotte Langston was constantly on his mind, in ways that had little to do with Stephen Sterling. Brett knew it was dangerous, getting involved with an unscrupulous woman like her, yet he couldn't seem to stop himself. He saw her headed for trouble. He had to act to save her.

"I mean it." Charlotte continued to glare at him. "I want to get some of this dust cleaned up before the cleaning crew arrives tomorrow morning."

At last, she was doing something he couldn't object to.

Brett crossed closely to her side. He might as well use this opportunity to find out more about what she was up to. "Then by all means, let me help you clear some of the dust away," he offered gallantly. But not with a mop or broom, he thought. Her way had looked like so much more fun.

While she gaped at him in astonishment, he took her into his arms and began to hum the same song she'd been singing.

Charlotte gasped as he waltzed her slowly, lovingly, around the dance floor. She knew she should stop him, but she couldn't seem to stop looking into his eyes. It had been so long since anyone had held her with such tenderness. And, she admitted, she had been wondering just now what it would be like to dance with Brett.

Now she knew. It was heaven. And it was becoming all too clear that he was just rogue enough and gentleman enough to hold the key to her heart. But was it wise to get involved with him right now?

Surely, she thought, as she saw his blue eyes darken with a distinctly sexual intent, and his head lower to hers, it would be so much wiser to wait. To be sure before they...

"Brett—" Charlotte said.

He grinned, choosing to misunderstand what she was trying to tell him. "I know," he said immodestly, as he possessively tightened his grip on her. "I'm a wonderful dancer."

"That's *not* what I was going to say."

Charlotte wrested herself from his arms and stumbled to a halt. She was trembling in response to his touch, and agitated color filled her cheeks. Brett thought she looked even prettier.

"What I was going to say," she enunciated breathlessly, "was that I have to finish here."

Brett didn't have to pretend to be disappointed. He had really enjoyed holding her in his arms and spinning her around the ballroom. "You sure know how to take the fun out of an afternoon," he teased.

"Yes, well, those are the breaks," Charlotte murmured dispiritedly, wishing for once she did not have to be the responsible one in the family. But there was no helping it—at least, not today. Paige and Isabella were counting on her. And so, in a crazy way, was Brett.

She shoved her hand through her hair, forgetting the red bandanna. It slid halfway off. With a frown, she removed it completely.

Brett watched her stuff it in her back pocket. He knew Charlotte felt overwhelmed by the party preparations, the search for Sterling, the pressure to save Camellia Lane. He had come up here to see what he could do to help. Now, watching as she stomped over to the vacuum cleaner she had brought up with her, he was glad he had.

"Here, let me do that for you," he said.

Hands on her hips, Charlotte regarded Brett with weary suspicion. "Why would you want to do that?" she asked slowly.

So the laughter will come back in your pretty green eyes, Brett thought, as he closed the distance between them affably. Besides, he wanted her to save Camellia Lane. She belonged here. "Because I'm a great guy," he said.

"Uh-huh."

"And because I like to see you smile." He touched the tip of her nose. "And because you need the help." *You need me.* "Don't you?"

Choosing not to answer that, Charlotte considered Brett a long moment. "You promise to behave?"

And not try to kiss her? Brett thought. "That's a tall order."

"Promise me you'll try, anyway." Charlotte rested both her hands on his biceps and looked deep into his eyes.

When Miss Charlotte looked at him that way, her green eyes quietly beseeching, Brett knew he could not deny her anything. "Okay, no kisses. Just work," he said softly. The kisses, he promised himself, would come later. As soon as the time was right.

"Race you to the middle," he said, picking up the vacuum.

Charlotte wielded the push broom with a grin. "You're on."

Ten minutes later, they met in the center of the ballroom. "I won!" Charlotte announced triumphantly.

"Only because the cord to my vacuum didn't reach," Brett objected.

"I admit you lost time when you went to plug it in again," Charlotte allowed.

Brett pushed both broom and vacuum out into the hall. He strode back to her side, all leashed male power. "We'll call it a tie so far," he announced.

Charlotte handed Brett a rag mop and a bucket of sudsy water. She picked up the sponge-style mop for herself. Not knowing which type of mop would work best, she'd brought both.

"Now for the tiebreaker," Charlotte challenged.

Brett nodded. "You're on!" They took up positions, exchanged hell-bent-for-leather glances. "Ready, set, go!" Brett said. And they were off....

To Charlotte's dismay, he finished first without even breaking a sweat.

"No fair!" she cried breathlessly, scrambling to cover the last three feet of floor with wild swishes of her mop. "Your mop is bigger than mine."

"Ah, but your mop rinsed quicker than mine," Brett chided, mopping his way to her side with large, dashing strokes.

Their mops met. And so did they. Greatly relieved to have her chores finally over in less than half the time she had expected, Charlotte faced Brett with a playful smile. "What do you say we call this another tie?" she offered.

"As long as I get my victory hug," he said, enfolding her playfully in his strong arms. "And—" he reared back to look at her "—a glass of lemonade."

"IT'S AMAZING WHAT a difference a simple cleaning makes," Charlotte said, handing Brett his glass of celebratory lemonade.

"What's amazing is the way you look in those jeans and a man's shirt," Brett said. He'd have liked to see her in one of his shirts, and very little else.

Charlotte grinned at him and shook her head in silent rebuke at his bad-boy antics. She clinked glasses with him in silent toast, then glanced around her at the gleaming wood floors with satisfaction. "You know what?" she said softly, lifting her glass to her lips. "We make a pretty good team when we're working together."

Brett had noticed, too. "That could be all the time," he remarked, testing the waters. At least, it could be once they got the Sterling business behind them.

"I don't want to think about the future right now," Charlotte tossed over her shoulder. In a theatrical display of exhaustion, she stretched out on the velvet window seat that rimmed the entire ballroom. "I don't even want to think about tomorrow. I just want to enjoy the scent of camellias and honeysuckle floating in through the open windows on the warm spring breeze." *And you, Brett,* Charlotte added silently. *I want to enjoy you.*

Brett sat down next to Charlotte so they were facing each other. "You're really looking forward to this shindig you and your sisters are throwing, aren't you?" he said, searching her eyes. He had thought this party was a money-making idea, period; obviously it meant a lot more to her.

Charlotte's face glowed with anticipation. Still smiling, she lifted the glass to her lips and took a sip of lemonade. "My parents gave parties here all the time when I was growing up. Big, magnificent affairs. Everyone who was anyone in the county was invited. There was always dancing and often a live orchestra, as well.'' Her soft lips curved into a reminiscing smile.

"And you attended these parties?''

"Oh, yes. Both my sisters and I did. It would have been unthinkable of us not to go.'' Finished with her lemonade, Charlotte set the glass on the floor and turned slightly away from Brett so she could lie down all the way. One leg was crooked at the knee. Her mahogany hair spread out over the seat, touching his tensed thigh.

Brett traced the silky ends of her hair with his fingertips. "When did the parties stop?''

"The year my mother died.'' Charlotte's expression grew pensive. "It didn't seem right to throw one, while we were all in mourning. Then later, my father got sick and, well—'' Charlotte shrugged ''—you know the rest.''

Brett sympathized with her for all she had been through. He even admired her tenacity. "If this party is the success you hope, and you're able to raise the money you need, then there'll be no reason for you to go after Sterling, will there?'' Then he'd be free to pursue her, no holds barred.

Her slender shoulders stiffened. "I always start what I finish.''

Brett braced an arm along the back of the window seat and leaned over her. "Even if what you start is wrong?'' he asked mildly.

"I don't want to talk about that.'' Charlotte's pretty chin took on a stubborn tilt.

Brett rubbed his thumb across the sudden crease in her temple. "Could it be your conscience is bothering you?''

Charlotte folded her arms in front of her. "Could it be you're meddling in affairs you have no right to meddle in?'' she retorted hotly. "Namely, mine.''

Brett continued rubbing her temple tenderly. "I care about you, Charlotte. I don't want to see you make a mistake that you'll have to live with the rest of your life.''

"Aren't we being a little overly melodramatic, Brett?'' She struggled to sit up.

Brett faced her equably. "I don't think so.''

"Well, I do, and I refuse to talk about my work anymore." She stalked to the end of the ballroom and studied the grand room. "All I want to think about is what's on my third of the To Do list." Charlotte shook her head and pressed a hand to her brow dramatically, looking as if she felt the weight of the entire world on her shoulders once again. "I can't believe we're actually going to have a party here in just two days."

"Let's just hope it's a success," Brett murmured. He still hadn't given up hope of eventually talking Charlotte out of her misguided quest for Sterling, even though he knew it would take some doing.

"It will be. Camellia Lane is the kind of place that inspires dreams. People will want to come here and live the fantasy of life in another time."

"Is that what *you* do while you're here?" Brett asked, unable to help but marvel at how beautiful she looked, even in cleaning clothes. "Fantasize?" Somehow, he could see Charlotte doing just that. Maybe because he had been doing his fair share of fantasizing, too. He had wondered what it would've been like had they come together here, in the days of the Civil War, when Camellia Lane had first been built. Of course, if they had come together then, he mused, he would've been a Yankee soldier, Charlotte a Southern belle. So there would have been trouble even then, yet somehow he sensed they would've found a way to overcome their differences, just as they were doing now. And that was darned surprising, too.

"Fantasize?" Charlotte put a hand to her breast. "Me?"

"Yes, you," Brett said, knowing from the way she was blushing that she was guilty as hell of fantasizing, too.

Charlotte shook her head. Silken hair went in every direction. She moved away from him elegantly, offering a splendid view of her backside. "I don't know what you mean."

The hell you don't, Brett thought, amused by her unwitting coquettishness as he rolled lazily to his feet and followed her across the room. He laid his hands on her shoulders and pressed a fleeting kiss on the nape of her neck. "I think you do," he whispered in her ear, then turned her to him. "I think when you were dancing around that ballroom you were pretending you were dancing with a lover. And I think that lover was me."

Charlotte laughed nervously as she backed away from him. "You have some imagination, Brett Forrest."

Determined to make her admit to some of her feelings for him, Brett studied the feminine line of her jaw as he drank in the light floral fragrance of her perfume. "You're telling me you've never fantasized about making love with me in this grand old place?" he asked as he studied her upturned face.

"Yes, I am."

It irritated to have her evade him, when they had been so close just moments before. "Now, Miss Charlotte, tell the truth!" he goaded, flashing her a grin.

"I am!"

Oh, no, you're not, Brett thought. And then he did what he had wanted to since he had first entered the ballroom— he took her into his arms. "Tell me that again after I've kissed you, and I'll believe you."

She tried to push him away, but he outmaneuvered her, sidestepping her and clamping both arms about her waist. His lips touched hers, deliberately robbing her of breath. She froze, and he knew he had scared her. He knew, too, that he couldn't leave it like that. He would have to take another gentler, more romantic approach . . . so he softened his lips over hers. Charlotte moaned, confusion sweeping through her.

Again, he brushed his lips softly, insistently, against hers.

A tremor of unwanted desire spiraled through Charlotte with treacherous speed, melting her insides, weakening her knees.

Her lips softened, becoming sexier, but not quite pliant. She wreathed her arms about his neck and leaned against him, as if she were savoring his warmth and his strength. It was all the encouragement he needed. He tunneled his hands through her hair and deepened the kiss provocatively, drinking from her again, wondering all the while what it would take to make her feel as dizzy with longing and mad with desire as he felt this instant, wondering what it would take to make her surrender.

And it was at that instant that she came to her senses. Trembling, she pushed away from him.

Reluctantly, he let her go. He might not have thwarted her efforts to unmask Sterling yet, but he had succeeded in diverting her attention—and his—at least, for a little while. But that wasn't the only reason he was kissing her.

Charlotte studied Brett from beneath her lashes as she composed herself. She didn't know what it was about him that drew her so. She only knew that whenever she was with him, her problems seemed less troubling, her life more romantic. He made her want to laugh and dance and play every day away. But Charlotte wasn't a carefree girl anymore. She might be feeling lovestruck, but it didn't make her problems any less real, or a liaison with the charming, reckless, irresponsible Brett Forrest any less dangerous.

She could not afford to let him divert her.

Not until Camellia Lane was saved.

Tilting her chin defiantly, she gave him a quelling look and warned, "Kiss me like that one more time and you're fired!"

Brett stroked the ends of his dark mustache thoughtfully. Charlotte had her knickers in a knot again, chiefly because he had taken the lead, and she had nearly surrendered despite herself. He grinned, pretending to misunderstand. "But if I kiss you even more passionately I'm not?"

A fiery blush heated her cheeks. "You'll be fired if you kiss me any way at all!" she said, ignoring his attempts to tease her into a more congenial mood. She folded her arms in front of her. "Furthermore, I want you to stop following me around."

Brett paused. His expression sobered. "Does that mean you want me to stop giving you your messages, too?" he asked, deadpan.

Charlotte's glance narrowed. Darn it all if he wasn't getting under her skin again with his deliberate and mischievous inefficiency. "What messages?" she demanded, agitated.

Brett scrambled around in his pocket with an ineptitude he knew would irritate Charlotte to no end. Finally, he produced a crumpled piece of paper and peered down at the illegible handwriting on it. "This guy's secretary called.... Umm, what was her name? Oh yeah, here it is—Marcie. She said she works for Franklin Dunn, Jr., and that she wants you to call her back right away, that it's very urgent."

Charlotte propped both hands on her hips. Her look grew even stormier. "When was this?" she demanded incredulously.

"Well, probably an hour or so before you made me start cleaning up in here. It took me that long to figure out where you were."

She pushed her fingers through her hair and looked at him in complete exasperation. "I don't believe this."

"Wait a minute...where are you going?" he asked innocently.

"You just mind your own business, Brett!"

His mustache twitched as he curbed the urge to smile. "Don't I even get a thank-you?"

"Thank you. In fact, you can even take that day off you started to take earlier, before your car malfunctioned." That quickly, she was gone.

Brett had no time for second thoughts.

"MARCIE?" CHARLOTTE began without preamble. "Charlotte Langston. I had a message you called."

"Yes, I did," Marcie replied with a sweetness that immediately had Charlotte on edge. Why was Marcie suddenly being so nice to her? "You know that information you wanted, that I was unable to get for you at the time you were in Mr. Dunn's office? Well, I have it for you now."

Charlotte paused. This was almost too good to be true. And that made her wonder if it was a trick.

On the other hand, who was she to look a gift horse in the mouth? She could at least investigate the situation—with her guard up, of course. "Okay. I'm ready."

"Sometimes we send packages of material that needs to be proofread by Mr. Sterling prior to publication to this address in Memphis." Charlotte scribbled madly as the secretary quickly, quietly recited the information. "And we have also, upon occasion, used this address in Santa Fe."

Charlotte scribbled the address as it was read to her. "What name is the material sent under?"

"Mr. Franklin Dunn, Jr. It's kind of a code between Mr. Dunn and Mr. Sterling," Marcie explained.

"So you don't know Sterling's real name, either?" Charlotte asked. She was disappointed if this was indeed the case.

"No, I don't. But if you could find out who owns the residences at the above addresses," Marcie suggested, "you'd probably have the real name of Stephen Sterling."

Charlotte put down her pen slowly. It might not be wise, but she had to ask. "Why are you so eager to help me locate Stephen Sterling now? You know how Mr. Dunn feels about me. And when I telephoned you earlier in the week, you hung up on me."

"Let's just say I thought it over and decided I owe Mr. Dunn a favor," Marcie replied dryly, "and this is it. Uh-oh, someone's coming. I've got to go." There was a click as the line was severed.

Charlotte stared at the two addresses. Part of her protested at how easily this information had come into her possession. The other part wanted to just take the information and run with it. She picked up the phone and, after pausing to look up the number for Confidential Investigations, began dialing again. She quickly reached the detective assigned to her case via his cellular phone. "Hi, this is Charlotte Langston. How's it going?"

"There's been no activity at all at the Arlington, Virginia, post-office box."

"There may not be, either. I have a feeling the clerk at Sterling's publisher's warehouse may have tipped off the author that I was trying to track him down that way. Fortunately, I have another lead." Charlotte read off the two addresses. "I want you to check these out as soon as possible and get back to me. It's possible Sterling may be at one of these addresses or own them under his real name."

At least, Charlotte hoped that was the case. Time was running out. The balloon payment was due in six days and she had not yet raised all the money they needed to keep the bank from foreclosing on Camellia Lane, although she was getting closer every day.

No sooner had Charlotte hung up the phone and locked away all her notes in her desk, than there was a knock at the library door. She got up to unlock it, and found Brett on the other side.

He inclined his head in the direction of the parlor behind him and said in a low tone, "Hiram Henderson, from the bank, is here to see you. He's waiting in the parlor. I knew you were busy, so I went ahead and put on some tea for you."

Charlotte was amazed. She had never known Brett to be so efficient. Maybe he really was trying to make it up to her for being so nosy and judgmental this morning. "Thank you, Brett," she said quietly. She looked past his broad shoulder and saw Hiram cooling his heels in the parlor beyond.

In the background the whistle on the teakettle sounded. "I'll get it," Brett said. "Just see to your guest."

"Hello, Hiram." Charlotte walked in. She wished her sisters were here to help her deal with the Poplar Springs banker, but both were at work, so it would just be her, Charlotte thought.

Hiram stood. By the time they'd finished exchanging pleasantries, Brett had returned with the tea tray. To Charlotte's pique, he did not simply put the tray down, as she wished, but began serving them.

"Brett, I can do that, thank you," Charlotte said.

"Oh, no problem," Brett replied, eager to help.

"I don't have a lot of time, Charlotte," Hiram cut in as he accepted a cup of tea from Brett, "so I'll get straight to the point. As not just your banker, but also a Poplar Springs city councilman, I have no choice but to inform you that your 'gift-suggested' costume ball is in violation of local zoning laws."

"What are you talking about?" Charlotte asked, forgetting for a moment that Brett was still in the room, fussing over a bowl of sugar cubes.

"Camellia Lane is in a residential area. It is not zoned for commercial business."

Charlotte put down her tea with a thud; it sloshed over the rim onto the saucer. She leaned forward earnestly. "My sisters and I are not trying to run a business here, Hiram."

"You will be if you and your sisters charge people to attend a party here, and keep the money for yourselves, for your own financial gain."

Charlotte tried to think how her mother would have handled a difficult situation like this. She imagined her sitting back in her chair and drawing a deep breath, so she did the same, and before she spoke again, she put a sweet steel-magnolia smile on her face. "This is a one-time-only occurrence, Hiram. And we're not charging people to attend, exactly. We're only suggesting they make a donation to help save Camellia Lane. And furthermore, I would think that you'd be happy we're trying to pay back the bank, Hiram."

Hiram put his teacup aside and steepled his bony fingers together. "How do we know that? For all we know, Charlotte, you and your sisters could be planning to turn this into a party barn."

Brett cleared his throat, his action reminding Charlotte he was still in the room. Charlotte and Brett traded glances, and she noted he was on her side. She turned back to Hiram. It was odd, but she felt somewhat stronger, just knowing Brett was there. "I give you our solemn word we are not trying to do that, Hiram."

"Good. Nevertheless, if you continue with your plans to collect money at the ball, then you will leave the council no choice but to get an injunction to stop you."

Charlotte frowned as Brett moved to stand by her side. "You're telling me I can't have a party?"

"No. I am telling you that you can have a party here," Hiram corrected. He sat back in his chair, crossed his legs at the knee and sipped his tea. "You can even allow your guests to donate their two-hundred-and-fifty-dollar-a-plate fee to his or her favorite charity. You just cannot keep any of the money raised here for your own profit, not as long as Camellia Lane is located in a residential zone."

Charlotte's heart was beating double time. She felt like she was in the middle of a nightmare and couldn't wake up. "What if I get the zoning changed?" she asked desperately.

Hiram gave her a sympathetic smile that didn't reach his eyes. "Feel free to try, but zoning is regulated by the county, and the board only meets once a month. Even after an appeal is made, it could take weeks to have it acted on, one way or another. More, if they'd like to study the proposal."

"You're trying to force us out, aren't you?"

"Sounds that way to me," Brett drawled.

Hiram shot an annoyed look at Brett, then turned back to Charlotte. "I think it's time you and your sisters sold Camellia Lane. It's a beautiful home, but it's outlived its usefulness."

"If that's all, I think you should leave," Brett interjected mildly. Brett moved close to Charlotte and assumed a protective stance. "You're upsetting my employer."

Hiram shot an amazed look at Charlotte. "You permit your hired help to talk to guests this way?"

Charlotte sighed. Much as she wished for a different outcome, she saw no point in continuing this conversation. "In this instance, Brett is right, Hiram. It is time for you to leave," she replied bluntly.

Hiram stood obediently. He traded sharp looks with Brett, then turned back to Charlotte. "When you calm down, you'll see I'm right, Charlotte."

"Don't bet on it." Charlotte escorted him out and slammed the front door after him.

"I can't believe I never saw how self-serving Hiram was before this," Charlotte muttered to Brett. All along, Hiram had probably hoped to repossess and sell Camellia Lane for a tidy profit.

Brett closed the distance between them and consoled Charlotte with a glance. "Maybe Hiram was just better at hiding his own agenda in years past," he said softly.

Charlotte looked up at Brett. How she wished she could be a true Southern belle and let a man solve all her problems for her. But even as she wished it so, Charlotte knew she couldn't back away from family business. This was her dilemma and she had to solve it.

Brett touched her shoulder gently.

"I think I'll call Jared." Charlotte turned abruptly toward the phone, her heart racing at the dark, possessive look she saw in Brett's eyes. The look that said she already belonged to him.

"Why call Jared?" Brett shoved his hands in his pockets and sauntered closer, in a drift of Old Spice. "It's obvious he isn't on your side in this battle with the bank—and now the city—any more than Hiram is."

"Jared can still change his mind," Charlotte said firmly.

Brett gave her a pitying look. "You don't really think he will?"

"The two of us go back a long way," Charlotte said stubbornly, refusing to even consider that things might not work out for her, after she had come this far, in arranging the costume ball. "Besides, Jared has a lot of clout in this part of the state. If anyone can pull strings and get me a permit at the last minute, he can."

Charlotte looked at Brett. Again, their eyes clashed. Held.

Finally, Brett shrugged. "Do what you want," he advised, "but just for the record, I think you're wasting your time."

Her feelings wounded by Brett's lack of faith in her, Charlotte marched back into the library. Aware of Brett's eyes on her, she picked up the phone and punched in a number. "Jared, we've got another emergency here."

A few moments later, Charlotte hung up the phone to find Brett watching her from the portal. Again. His posture was relaxed, but there was a censuring light in his vivid blue eyes, a definite downward slant to his dark mustache.

"You know, this is probably none of my business," he drawled, "but, local legal clout aside, should you really be leaning on Jared Fontaine, given the way he feels about you?" Brett asked mildly.

If she didn't know better, she would have thought Brett was jealous. Charlotte's heart soared at the possibility, even as she worried over the problems Brett's feelings would cause. "Jared is an old friend, and that is all."

Brett pushed away from the portal and ambled toward her. "An attorney who happens to want to marry you," he corrected.

"Well, all I want from Jared is legal help," Charlotte murmured. The truth was, she wasn't any happier with Jared's recent amorous advances than Brett was, but she saw no reason to let Brett know that. He would just use it to further his own argument.

Brett shook his head at her. He looked like he wanted to either shake her or kiss her senseless—she couldn't tell which.

"I'm telling you, Charlotte. Ten to one, Jared is going to take your call for help the wrong way," he warned.

Charlotte stiffened. She didn't like grasping at straws, either, but that was what she'd been reduced to. "If I want your advice, Brett, I'll ask for it," she said stubbornly. Charlotte went to a window as a car pulled up outside.

She watched as Jared got out of the car.

"That was fast," Brett said.

Peculiarly fast, Charlotte agreed.

"I was on my way home when you called. You got me on my cellular phone," Jared explained when he saw her stunned look.

"Oh. Well, please come in." Charlotte looked at Brett pointedly. "Don't you have something to do?" *Like get lost, so I can prevail on my old friend in private,* Charlotte thought.

Brett smiled, deliberately misunderstanding. "Oh, right, the butler thing." He looked at Jared. "Care for a drink?" Brett asked sociably.

"Sure. Scotch on the rocks," Jared said.

"I meant nonalcoholic, since you'll be driving again shortly," Brett said helpfully.

Briefly, Jared looked like he wanted to punch Brett out. Charlotte knew exactly how Jared felt. She had much the same impulse herself.

Jared gave Brett a quelling look that, to both Charlotte's and Jared's chagrin, didn't seem to weigh on Brett in the least. "A glass of mineral water with lime would be fine then, thanks," Jared said.

"Coming right up." Brett winked at Jared. Charlotte was sure he was just trying to be doubly annoying. Picking up the tray, Brett exited the parlor.

"When did that man become your butler?" Jared demanded as soon as Brett turned the corner.

"It's a long story," Charlotte said with a sigh. Right now, Brett's compunction for nosing into her business was the last thing she wanted to think about. Quickly, she told Jared about Hiram's visit.

"I'm afraid Hiram's got you where it hurts," Jared said when she'd finished.

Charlotte's heart sank. "There's nothing we can do?"

He shook his head. "Not in time to be able to charge money to get into your costume ball. Unless, of course, you take the money you collect and give it to another charity."

"But we're not charging money," Charlotte said. "We're just suggesting the attendees make a donation or gift of two hundred and fifty dollars to help us save Camellia Lane."

"Semantics, Charlotte," Jared said. "It's the same thing."

"Well, you're an attorney. You should have warned me about zoning laws."

"I never figured Hiram and the city council would call you on it," he explained. "Now that they have, there's nothing I can do. They're within their rights."

Charlotte frowned as Brett returned with a tray.

"All right. Forget the party as a way of raising money fast, for now. What if we sold part of the property?" Charlotte asked Jared, ignoring Brett as best she could. "After all, we've got plenty of land here—two hundred acres. I hate the idea of parting with a single inch of Camellia Lane, but if we have to do that to save the house and the gardens, then so be it," she said grimly.

"You can't do that, either, Charlotte," Jared said with lawyerly calm.

Behind Jared, Brett made a face. His disruptive antics served their purpose.

Charlotte struggled to keep her mind on the conversation. "Why not?" she asked.

"Because that area of the county has been zoned primarily for farms. There's an ordinance that states the land can't be sold in parcels under two hundred acres, remember? If you want to sell, you're going to have to sell all of Camellia Lane. Either that or make an appeal and try and get the county zoning board to change the requirements they've set for that part of the county, and that could take weeks."

Charlotte shifted in her chair, wishing she weren't still wearing the clothes she had worn to clean the ballroom. Not that Jared seemed to mind. As usual, he looked completely smitten with her. "If this is the case, then why is the Heritage Homes company so hot on buying my property?" she asked.

"Because they've already taken options on the three two-hundred-acre farms adjacent to your property. If they can purchase your land, they'll own roughly eight hundred acres of prime land. That's room for at least 2,400 homes and 2,400 new taxpayers. They figure, with that kind of clout, they can get the board to change the zoning in time for them to get the subdivision up and running before the new auto plant opens next year."

Charlotte stood and roamed the spacious parlor restlessly, her sneakers thudding softly on the parquet floor. "And if we don't sell?" Reaching the windows, she turned back around to face Jared.

Jared drained his glass of mineral water with lime, then glared at Brett, letting him know his continued presence was not appreciated. "Then they'll probably let their options lapse and look elsewhere. But they're not thinking that that is going to be the case, Charlotte."

How well she knew that! "So what are my options here, Jared?" she asked wearily.

Jared sighed. "Damn few."

"Well, thanks for stopping by," Charlotte said.

"I only wish I could've been more help," he said.

So do I, Charlotte thought.

Aware of Brett's gaze upon her, Charlotte walked Jared to the door and said goodbye.

"Well, what next, Miss Charlotte?" Brett asked as soon as Jared had driven off and the two of them were alone again.

"Nothing—for you," Charlotte said. The depth of her worry gave her tone a sharp edge she couldn't prevent. "This is my problem. Not yours." And it was high time she started concentrating solely on her problem, instead of allowing herself to be distracted by her budding romance with Brett. Because time was running out.

Brett was silent. Charlotte wasn't sure, but she thought she saw hurt flash briefly in his dark blue eyes. "You're telling me you don't want my help?" he asked, his tone edgy, too.

Charlotte sighed. She didn't want to blame Brett for her problems, but the simple fact of the matter was that her current situation probably would not have been nearly so precarious if her sexy caretaker hadn't been working night and day to distract her. If not for Brett's teasing antics and passionate passes, Charlotte thought, she would have been on top of the situation here. She would have been her normal aggressive self and found Stephen Sterling by now. But that hadn't happened...because when Brett was around, all she could concentrate on was him. She had to get rid of him. And get back down to business before she lost everything. Charlotte turned to Brett with a decisive glare. To get her point across, she would have to be blunt to the point of cruelty. For once, she was up to the task. "I want you out of the way," Charlotte said.

Heat flashed in Brett's dark blue eyes. He put down the tray. "Lady, you'll never get me out of the way." That said, he pivoted sharply on his heel and strode from the room.

Chapter Seven

"I'm Brett Forrest," Brett told the electric-company clerk early Friday morning. "The new caretaker at Camellia Lane."

"I know. Everyone in town has heard about you." The pretty clerk looked him up and down, focusing on his Yale Lacrosse sweatshirt. "Some sort of student, aren't you?"

In a manner of speaking, Brett thought. He certainly was *learning* a lot, and none of it was what he had expected. He had come to Mississippi thinking Charlotte Langston was obsessed with finding Stephen Sterling, only to find out that wasn't it at all.

She was obsessed with saving Camellia Lane. So determined she would do whatever it took to come up with the money to save the beautiful old plantation.

The idea for the antebellum ball had been a blessing at first, because that—plus his persistent passes—had distracted Charlotte and kept her from concentrating on her work.

She'd really been thrown for a loss yesterday on learning that she couldn't keep any of the funds raised for the ball. She'd been furious with Hiram Henderson and rightly so.

But there Brett's sympathy for Charlotte ended. She shouldn't have called Jared Fontaine for help, not when she knew how he felt about her. She should have accepted *his* help, Brett thought. But just because she hadn't, didn't mean he was not going to give it....

Aware the electric-company clerk was waiting to hear more about what he was doing in Mississippi, Brett explained, "I'm studying farming methods in the area."

"Oh, yeah, I heard that, too. You've been talking to all the farmers."

He had also spoken to the county agricultural extension agent, just to make sure the facts and figures he had gathered were accurate.

"Everyone has been very helpful," Brett admitted. He turned serious. "But right now I'm doing some kind of confidential stuff to help out Miss Langston. And I need a copy of the utility bills and payments at Camellia Lane for the last two years," he finished matter-of-factly.

The clerk raised a brow.

Brett shrugged. It was no hardship to look as if he'd been through the mill out there. "I don't know why Miss Langston wants this stuff. A big part of my job is just doing what I'm told, if you know what I mean."

"I surely do." The clerk smiled back at him. "Wait right here. I'll get you a copy of what you want. You'll need to sign for it, of course," she cautioned.

"Fine," Brett said. Ten to one, Charlotte would never find out about it. And by the time she did, he would have everything worked out on his end, anyway.

The clerk returned, paper in hand. "Here you go."

"Thanks a lot." Brett accepted the papers.

He headed on over to the courthouse. "I'd like to see the property card on Camellia Lane," he told the public records clerk there.

She made a copy for him, and he added that to the growing stack of financial papers he had hidden in his car. Now all he needed was the estimate on the homeowner's insurance, and he would be all set.

"So THERE'S NO WAY around this injunction the city council has asked the judge for," Brett remarked to the sheriff an hour later, in the back room of Rosie's Red Garter Saloon.

The sheriff dealt the last card. "Nope. Everyone in town knows how much of a mess the Langston gals are in. They're afraid they'll see how easy it is to raise money that way, and turn Camellia Lane into a party barn. Which wouldn't necessarily be a bad thing if the plantation were up to current fire codes and had the appropriate number of emergency exits, a sprinkler system, alarm and so on. But right now it doesn't. So they can have a private party there, but they can't turn it into a business. Not until they take the appropriate safety measures—"

"Brett darling, you've got a visitor," Rosie interrupted.

Brett looked up from the cards he'd just been dealt. The daily lunch-hour poker game in the back room of the Red Garter was serious business, even if the stakes were penny ante. No one received visitors during a game. He was especially irritated to be interrupted when he was talking to the sheriff and the judge about Charlotte's options. He frowned. "You're joking, right?"

Rosie smiled and flounced forward, her breasts spilling out of the low-cut red leather dress she wore. "No, Brett darling, I'm not. Charlotte Langston is waiting in the saloon."

Brett quirked a brow. He and Charlotte hadn't talked since she had thrown him out of the main house the day before. And truth be told, even though he was busy trying to help her at the moment, he was still extremely ticked off about the ungracious way she had refused his help in saving her precious Camellia Lane. "Charlotte said she wanted to see me?" Brett ignored the sudden pounding of his pulse.

"That's what I said, isn't it?" Rosie said, with a wink at the others gathered around the table. "She's all gussied up, too."

Warning bells went off in Brett's head. It sounded like Charlotte was up to her usual Scarlett O'Hara tricks. "Gussied up how?" Brett bit out, more irritated than ever.

"In one of those frilly, Southern-belle sundresses."

Brett shook his head in silent admonition. Charlotte needed to learn that trying to manipulate men into doing what she wanted would only lead her into trouble. Luckily, he was just the man to teach her a lesson. He traded hell-raising glances with the other men at the poker table and gave Rosie his most wicked grin. "Do me a favor?" he drawled.

"Sure thing," Rosie promised with a wink.

Brett picked up a cigar from the table, unwrapped it slowly and bit off the end. "Take Charlotte to one of your back rooms and have her wait for me there. I want to finish this hand."

Rosie watched as Brett lit the end of his cigar and took a deep drag. "Charlotte will be furious."

"I'm counting on it," Brett retorted. The men at the table guffawed and traded ribald winks.

Rosie laughed and patted Brett's shoulder. "You are a devil," she said.

Brett continued to study his cards, the cigar clamped between his teeth. "Yep. I know." And soon Miss Charlotte would know it, too.

"HE WANTS ME TO do what?" Charlotte asked indignantly.

"Wait for him up here," Rosie said as she led the way up the back stairs.

Charlotte put aside her shock long enough to follow the saloon's proprietress. "But—but these rooms are—"

"Reserved for my customers."

Charlotte swallowed as Rosie opened the door to a small bedroom with a double bed, dresser and private bath.

"Sometimes they're in no condition to drive," Rosie continued her explanation. "In which case I rent them a room."

That wasn't all that allegedly went on in Rosie's upstairs rooms, Charlotte thought, setting the wicker picnic basket she had brought with her on the foot of the bed. The rumor was Rosie did some business in the romance department, too. Whether that was really true or not didn't matter. People *thought* hanky-panky went on in the upstairs rooms. So Charlotte knew that if she met Brett Forrest in one of these rooms...people would think the two of them had actually...

Damn Brett, Charlotte fumed. He probably knew exactly what people would think if she met him in one of the back rooms. Which was why he had suggested it—to punish her for unceremoniously throwing him out of the house.

Charlotte smiled at Rosie. Rosie was a smart businesswoman who would have had a much better reputation among the local females if her tastes in clothes hadn't run to tight-fitting leather garments and décolletage. "Isn't there somewhere else I could meet with Mr. Forrest?" Charlotte asked politely.

The glimmer in Rosie's eyes said she could cooperate if she was of a mind. But, to Charlotte's disappointment, Rosie was not going to. "Brett wants you here," the woman said matter-of-factly. "He said he'll be up directly." She shut the door.

Oh, no, Charlotte thought, examining the tiny room that was barely big enough to fit a double bed, and the adjoining bath. What was she going to do now?

To her displeasure, Brett strolled in a good twenty minutes later, a cigar clamped between his teeth.

"Well, don't you look pretty, Miss Charlotte," he drawled, looking her up and down in a comic parody of a Southern gentleman. His glance swept her frilly white off-the-shoulder dress with its tight-fitting bodice and full skirt. "What do they call that?"

Charlotte knew he was giving her a hard time on purpose. She also knew she had a lot to make up to him, and that the surest way to do that was through his admitted susceptibility to her.

Playing the coquette to the hilt, Charlotte plastered a breezy smile on her face. "It's a sundress."

"No." Brett's glance swept her figure again. He waved his cigar until Charlotte nearly choked on the odious smoke. "I mean the holes in the fabric," he said.

Don't let him know he is annoying you. "It's eyelet lace."

"Nice. Very nice." Brett's blue eyes glimmered with pent-up mischief.

The room was quickly filling with the odious smell of his cigar smoke. Unable to help herself, Charlotte waved it out of her face. "Must you?" she asked coquettishly.

"Must I *what?*"

Charlotte stifled a cough. "Never mind."

"Oh, you want me to put this out? Well, I suppose that could be arranged." Brett stubbed the tip of the cigar in the ashtray. Since there were no chairs in the room, he sank down on the bed, propping his spine against the headboard, and stretched his long legs in front of him. "So, what brings you all the way into town to see me? Especially since the last time we saw each other you told me you wanted me out of the way. Or should I say just out of *your* way?"

He was obviously going to make this as difficult as possible for her. Charlotte leaned against the window, next to the wall. She worked to maintain her dignity. "Perhaps I was a little hasty," she said.

"Oh, really." He favored her with a curious, off-kilter smile. "In what way?"

"Telling you that you weren't welcome at Camellia Lane. And to make it up to you, I brought you some lunch." Charlotte pointed to the wicker picnic basket.

Brett flipped open the lid and looked inside. "You've gone all out here." His dark blue eyes glimmered suspiciously.

"I hope you like it."

"Uh-huh." Brett folded his arm behind his head and simply looked at her.

"Aren't you going to eat?" Charlotte pretended to be hurt, though in truth she was more annoyed that she had sprung for a lunch that he didn't seem to have any intention of eating.

"I'm more interested in why you're really here," Brett continued.

Charlotte saw suppressed fury in every line of his body. She plucked at her skirt, fluffing it out around her. "Well, now that you mention it, there is another reason." She gave him her best smile.

"Don't give me one of those Southern-belle smiles," he said. His brows lowered over his stormy blue eyes. "I'm not Jared. And I'm not one of your local admirers. Your charm won't work on me."

Charlotte paused. This was the dangerous Brett, the man that defied manipulation. Her false smile faded. Deciding to try the unvarnished truth, she looked at him earnestly. "I need your help, Brett."

"Why?" he asked, his tall body thrumming with pent-up emotion. "Another shutter come loose? The ballroom floor need polishing and you plan to do it with my backside?"

"Don't be silly, Brett. I didn't mean at Camellia Lane. Here in town, I need your help."

Unfortunately, that revelation seemed to only put him more on edge. "Doing what?" he ground out.

Charlotte looked down at the toe of her basic white pump. "Well, you're good friends with the sheriff, aren't you?" They had to be, if they played poker together every week.

"Yeah, so?"

"So I might be needing you to put in a good word for me."

"How's that?" Brett asked with a casualness that suddenly seemed very deceptive.

Charlotte swallowed around the knot of tension in her throat as unobtrusively as she could. "Well, you recall that Hiram Henderson says it's against current zoning regulations for us to have a money-making party at Camellia Lane, unless all the capital raised is given to a charity of some sort?"

"I recall," Brett said, and his nostrils flared slightly as he spoke.

"And that if I try it, anyway, he's going to get an injunction to prevent us from having the party at all?"

Brett dropped his hands and settled his spine a little more comfortably on the bed. "Then you better change your plans."

Charlotte's heart began to beat a little faster. "That's one alternative," she agreed with a careful smile.

Brett's tall, strong body tensed even more. "And the other?"

With effort, Charlotte trained her eyes on Brett's and kept them there. "The other is to find someone who has a lot of influence with the sheriff and the judge...someone who knows just how much Camellia Lane means to me. Someone, like you, who is not afraid of local chastisement and who might persuade the sheriff into accidentally mislaying the injunction. Or the judge into delaying ruling on the issue, until after the party is held tomorrow night."

Brett cocked a brow. "Why not ask them yourself?" he offered with an insufferable grin.

Charlotte squared her shoulders and retained her calm. "They're elected officials, too. They count on the support of the local business people to win reelection."

"Ah." The corners of Brett's mustache twitched. "So you don't think they'll help you because Hiram runs the bank and is more influential in this town."

"Right." Charlotte beamed, glad he at last seemed to be getting it. Now all she had to do was convince him that he needed to be on her side, not the bank's. "On the other hand, if one of their very good friends—one of their poker-playing buddies—were to help me convince the sheriff or judge that my sisters and I are doing the right thing, then all our problems will be solved," Charlotte said. "Because as of last night, we have two hundred and sixty-two acceptances for the party tomorrow evening. That translates to enough donations to pay the balloon note, if we're allowed to collect them!"

"I see your dilemma." Brett frowned. "I only have one question."

"And what might that be?" Charlotte asked.

"What would you be offering this very good friend of the elected officials—namely me—in the way of compensation if I were to put in a good word on your behalf?"

"Why, my eternal gratitude, of course," Charlotte said, aware she was swiftly veering into dangerous territory again.

Brett frowned and shook his head disparagingly. "I don't think that would cut it."

Charlotte took a bolstering breath. She had feared all along he would be difficult and uncooperative. She had been counting on his obvious desire for her, and his inherent gallantry and protectiveness where she was concerned, to compel him to help her.

Obviously, that wasn't working. He would much prefer to make her grovel.

Charlotte did not want to beg.

She did, however, want to save Camellia Lane, and that called for desperate measures. What was the sacrifice of a little pride if her groveling ultimately got her what she wanted?

Steeling herself to take every bit of orneriness Brett could dish out—and he looked prepared to dish out plenty—Charlotte suggested sweetly, "What if I gave you money to help me out, then?"

"Ah, but money is something you don't have," he pointed out sagely.

"*Now* I don't," Charlotte corrected, color flowing into her cheeks. She had a very good idea where this conversation was going to lead, judging by the amorous light in his dark blue eyes. "But I'll have some in the future," she promised.

"Still not interested," Brett said flatly. He leered at her in a way that Charlotte was sure he knew would make her hot with indignation. "What else have you got to offer?" he asked lazily, crossing his arms in front of him.

Charlotte's gaze sharpened impatiently. Still aware she had a goal to meet and very little time in which to do so, she kept her voice sweetly civil. "How about a lessening of your duties at Camellia Lane?" she proposed.

Brett clucked his tongue thoughtfully. "I don't know, Charlotte. What you're asking me to do, well, it could jeopardize my friendship with the sheriff and the judge, and hence cut me out of those noon-hour poker games. I've been winning quite a *lot* at these games."

Charlotte politely ignored his needling. "Well, I don't have anything else to offer," she lamented, batting her eyelashes at him.

Brett gave her a wolfish grin that radiated sensuality. "Don't you?"

Charlotte stiffened resentfully. There was an arrogance in his amusement that made her distinctly wary. "What are you suggesting?" she asked calmly. *Besides our making love?*

Brett shrugged his broad shoulders laconically. "I'm not suggesting anything. I'm just curious to see how determined you really are to save Camellia Lane."

Charlotte could tell from Brett's cynical expression that she hadn't yet won him over. But, like a poker player, she had another ace up her sleeve. It was time to make a last appeal. One that went straight to his heart. One that he knew was true. "Camellia Lane means everything to me," Charlotte said softly.

"I see. Enough to do this to save it?" Brett asked. Before Charlotte even knew what was happening, he caught her wrist and pulled her across the bed, onto his lap. She landed hard on top of him. She was still off balance as his mouth covered hers in a searing kiss. There was no time to think, no time to resist. She could only feel. And what she felt was a mixture of hot temper and passion. She might not trust Brett Forrest—she might not even like him—but he sure knew how to kiss. And as his lips and tongue continued to work their magic, Charlotte felt herself doing the unthinkable, succumbing to the moment, to the dazzling seduction of his embrace. She leaned her head against his shoulder, and her muscles went lax.

And that was when he stopped, Charlotte realized abruptly as she was jerked out of her dreamworld. When he knew he had won her. The cad, she thought, as he slowly lifted his mouth from hers.

Brett grinned down at her, tracing the exasperated color flowing into her cheeks with his fingertip. "That was for you, Charlotte," Brett said. "This kiss is for me."

Ignoring her gasp of indignation, he shifted her in his arms, so she was settled more firmly across his lap, her bottom nestled securely in the cradle of his thighs. Tunneling one hand through her hair, he tilted her head back and pressed her lips to his.

He grinned as she made a muffled protest, and then all was lost in the swirling, tempestuous meeting of their hearts and minds. She might not want to desire him, but she did. She might not want to love him, but she was getting there, too.

One day, Brett thought, as his tongue coaxed tremors of sensual delight from her softly parted lips, Miss Charlotte Langston was going to be all his. But she wasn't going to be his as part of a barter. And she wasn't going to get away with any more innocent manipulations of the male sex. Not if he had anything to say about it.

And right now he did, Brett thought triumphantly as he languorously continued their kiss. Even though Miss Charlotte wouldn't like that, either.

Ever so gently, ever so reluctantly, he ended their kiss once again...before he forgot what he was about. "Let that be a lesson to you," he said in mock sternness, watching with delight as a new wave of color flooded her pretty face.

"A lesson about what?" Charlotte sputtered, struggling to sit upright.

"About trying to wrap me around your little finger," Brett said, meaning it with all his heart. "I'm not some lovesick calf who can be led around by the nose, Miss Charlotte."

The next thing Charlotte knew, she was off his lap. Standing again. And so was he. She had never seen him looking angrier or more indomitable.

Hands on his waist, Brett paused, looking down at her with narrowed eyes. "If you want to see me, fine—I'll be happy to be with you, Charlotte. If you want me to do something for you, forget it. I'm not interested in being used in any of your schemes.''

"But...Brett..." Charlotte said softly, her lips still tingling from his ardent kiss. She didn't want him to be angry with her! She wanted him to be her comrade-in-arms, possibly even her lover! "I only meant—"

Brett held up an admonishing hand, silencing her with a look. He wasn't about to hear any more excuses. "Find someone else to do your dirty work, Charlotte," he advised in sharp disgust. He picked up the untouched picnic basket and shoved it into her hands. His mouth thinning, so that his lips were barely visible beneath the dark mustache, he finished flatly, "Jared Fontaine might let you get away with playing these silly little games of boy-chase-girl, but I'm not interested."

"WHAT HAPPENED? I can tell by your faces it's more bad news," Isabella said upon arriving home that evening.

"Hiram did what he threatened," Charlotte said wearily. "He got the injunction."

The three sisters stared dispiritedly at the legal paperwork that effectively robbed them of their dream of saving Camellia Lane.

"Now what are we going to do?" Paige sighed, looking more depressed than ever.

"We'll find another way, of course," Charlotte muttered. She wasn't about to lose Camellia Lane. After all, they still had five days left!

"Have you talked to the sheriff?" Isabella asked.

"He's the one who served me with the injunction papers right before I left the Red Garter Saloon!" Charlotte scowled. "They specifically state any money raised at the party must be donated to charity."

"Camellia Lane is a charity," Paige interrupted. "Well, sort of...in the sense that we need the money, anyway."

"No joke, Sherlock," Charlotte muttered. "But when the judge says charity, he means one that has already been established legally. Camellia Lane does not qualify."

"Perhaps if we tried to get the judge to see reason," Isabella offered hopefully.

"Too late." Charlotte scowled as she paced angrily back and forth. "We had a chance, of course, before the injunction was actually served. If Brett Forrest had been willing to use his powers of persuasion during their noon-hour poker game, then we might not be in hot water tonight. But no! Mr. Integrity-Only-When-It-Suits-Him decided that in this case the law should be upheld."

"Oh, Charlotte," Isabella said, her lower lip quivering with emotion. "I am so sorry. This is terrible."

"I'll say! I wanted to have that party!" Paige said. "Now what's the point?"

"The point is we've already invited people, so we're still having the party," Charlotte told Paige. "We have no choice. Our reputation is on the line. We can't disappoint the guests who have already accepted and bring dishonor to the family name. We'll have to go ahead with the party, and make it spectacular to boot."

"But the money—" Paige sputtered.

"Is our loss," Charlotte said glumly. "The best we can do is turn a bad situation to our advantage and figure out to whom we want to donate the proceeds of the party."

"How are we going to save Camellia Lane now?" Isabella asked, her expression worried.

"We'll never raise the fifty thousand dollars needed for the balloon payment now," Paige projected glumly. "Not with only five days left."

"Oh, yes we will," Charlotte said.

Someway, somehow, she would see to it. And furthermore, she would do it without Brett's help!

As it turned out, Charlotte had little time to worry over her fight with Brett. She spent the rest of Friday and all day Saturday working with her sisters and making sure everything was set up properly for their guests. Finally, about five o'clock, the three of them went upstairs, retired to their rooms and began to get ready for the ball.

As Charlotte sank into a hot bubble bath, her thoughts turned to Brett. Lathering herself with lilac-scented soap, she wondered if he was still angry with her. And she wondered if he was going to be coming to the ball tonight. The few times she had seen him that day, he had offered no clue. He'd been busy running errands for Isabella and Paige. They'd had virtually no time to talk, which was the way Charlotte had wanted it then. She'd had enough to do trying to organize the caterers and sort out the garlands of flowers and fresh greenery that had been delivered. Not to mention making sure the formal gardens were ready for visitors.

Now that they were, she wondered if she'd have a chance to stroll the beautiful gardens in the moonlight or share a romantic kiss there with Brett.

Not that it had been easy for her to forgive him for the last kiss they'd shared, Charlotte thought with a sigh, as she leaned her head on the back of the tub and closed her eyes.

In retrospect, of course, she knew he'd had a right to be angry with her. She shouldn't have tried to manipulate him into helping her fight the injunction. She should have asked him straight out to help her. If she had, maybe he would have reacted differently. And even if he hadn't agreed to help her, at least he wouldn't have kissed her just to prove a point.

But all that was over now, Charlotte thought, as she toweled herself dry with a thick, fluffy towel and smoothed lotion onto her skin with generous strokes. Brett had made his point. She had learned her lesson. They had both had time to cool off and, more importantly, anticipate the costume ball tonight.

Feminine intuition told her he would come to the ball. And once he was here, Charlotte thought as she scented herself with her signature lilac perfume and slipped on her lace-trimmed chemise and petticoats, Brett would be as caught up in the highly romantic atmosphere as everyone else. There would be chances for walks in the moonlight... and slow romantic waltzes. They would see each other in a new and different light. And at last they might find out where this stormy but oh so intriguing relationship of theirs was going to lead.

BRETT WAS STANDING just inside the front hall as Charlotte descended the staircase. Their gazes locked, and he knew even as it happened that this was a moment he would remember the rest of his life.

She was beautiful, Brett thought.

So stunningly, heart-stoppingly gorgeous, in fact, that he could only stand and stare at her, his heart pounding in his chest. The off-the-shoulder blue damask dress bared her lustrous shoulders as well as the enticing curves of her breasts and the shadowy valley between them. Two inches of ruffles edged the bodice and the short capped sleeves. From there, the gown clung to the fullness of her breasts and ribs with enticing accuracy. A wide blue velvet ribbon that Brett wanted very much to undo was tied into a pretty bow at her waist. The swirling skirt of the ball gown covered every inch of her beautiful legs and had four separate tiers of blue damask. Her dainty feet were encased in blue satin slippers that peeked beneath the hem of the gown.

Her glossy mahogany hair had been wound into tight curls and swept away from her face, in the style of the antebellum era. She wore a cameo choker of dark blue velvet around her throat and elbow-length gloves in the same dark blue. But mostly it was the look in her emerald green eyes that gripped him and made him feel like molten lava inside. He couldn't say exactly what it was, but something had changed. Something within her.

A wall had come down. And her heart had opened up.

Picking up her skirt with one hand, Charlotte glided toward him, her eyes on his. Knowing she was waiting for his reaction, Brett grinned as he swept off his Union blue captain's hat and bowed low to acknowledge her presence.

Charlotte laughed softly, excitement bringing rich color to her cheeks. "Leave it to you to come to a Confederate ball and dress as a Yankee," she said.

Brett straightened and shrugged. Tonight was going to be something, all right. "Gotta honor my roots somehow, Miss Charlotte," he teased, enjoying the vivacity of her manner, "and I am a Yankee, born and bred."

"So I've noticed." Again, Charlotte held his eyes. Her glance traced the white collar of his shirt, and the high neck of his uniform and the strong column of his throat, before returning to his face. Gently, she took his hat and put it aside for him, then curled her hand around his elbow possessively. "Have my sisters come down yet?"

Brett folded his arm in close to her side, enclosing her soft hand in the warm cove between his chest and his arm. He liked having her hang on to him this way. It was a new sensation, one he could see himself getting used to. "Isabella came down a few minutes ago," Brett said. He walked with Charlotte to the foot of the staircase. "Paige is still getting ready, I guess."

Charlotte looked over her shoulder. At the other end of the great hall, Isabella was in yellow silk, directing the caterers. Charlotte turned back to Brett. Again, she looked at him with heart-stopping intensity. "What about our guests?"

"They should be arriving any minute," he said. "While we've still got a minute, let's go look at the formal gardens."

"Is everything all right out there?" Charlotte asked, her petticoats swishing beguilingly as she kept pace with him.

Brett grinned down at her as they threaded their way through numerous formally attired caterers, waved hello at Isabella and headed on out. Brett wondered if Charlotte had noticed he wasn't wearing Old Spice tonight, but had hunted up some bay rum, in an effort to be authentic. "That's what we're going to find out."

Brett kept a firm, possessive hold on her as they slipped out through the kitchen, across the veranda, down the back steps and into the moonlit formal gardens. Expertly trimmed shrubs formed an elegant maze. Multicolored flowers lent a fragrant aura to the warm spring breeze as the fountain splashed water into the stone basin below.

Charlotte looked around in delight, like a child on Christmas morning inspecting the tree. "It's perfect, isn't it?" she whispered to Brett in awe.

Brett wrapped his arms around her waist and pressed a kiss into her hair as he drew her against him. It did his soul good to see Charlotte looking so happy.

"*You're* perfect," Brett whispered, taking off first one white glove, then the other. He stuffed both in his belt, then brushed his knuckles down the side of her face. "And I'll tell you something else, Miss Charlotte." Brett cupped the softness of her chin and lifted her face to his. Feeling as if he wanted to drown in her eyes, he traced the outline of her lips with his fingertip. "I have never seen anyone look as beautiful as you do tonight. In fact—" he bent and pressed a tender kiss on her lips "—you're so gorgeous it ought to be outlawed. You're going to put all the other ladies here to shame."

Happy tears sparkled in Charlotte's eyes. "Oh, Brett, you do go on so," she drawled softly. And again, her eyes met his.

I love you, Charlotte, Brett thought. *I don't know why or how it's happened, but it has.* "Promise me something?" Brett said. He wanted so badly to make love to her right where they stood.

"What?" Charlotte looked into his eyes.

Brett clasped her gloved hand and put it over his heart. "That you'll save the last dance for me."

Brett didn't know if she could feel the heavy thudding of his heart beneath the wool of his Union Army uniform, but her eyes darkened luminously. She stared up at him, seemingly drawn in by the magic of the night and the magic that was them. "I will, Brett," she whispered back as she laced her gloved hands around his neck. She guided his mouth down to hers and fused their lips briefly, sweetly. "And I'll save the first dance, too."

BRETT PUT AN ARM around Charlotte's waist and led her back into the house just as the first guests arrived. During the next hour, they were both busy, welcoming everyone who came through the door. Isabella oversaw the dinner buffet that had been set up in the formal dining room. Paige directed the guests to the third-floor ballroom.

"You know, you're the only Yankee officer I've seen here tonight," Charlotte told Brett as they headed for the ballroom. Locking her green eyes with his, she repaid his mischief with a teasing comment of her own. "Everyone else seems to belong to the Confederacy."

Brett grinned over at her in a way that made her heart skip a beat. Slowing his pace, he paused on the landing between the second and third floors. Taking a quick glance around and finding them alone, he trapped Charlotte against the wall. Bracing his arms on either side of her, he leaned down to study her. "Different is good, Charlotte. Different is nice." And to prove it, she thought, he stole a kiss that started out erotic and turned into a tender expression of their growing feelings for each other.

She was trembling when he let her go. "You are still wicked, Brett Forrest," she said on a ragged breath.

A trace of a smile touched his lips. "And proud of it." Hearing voices coming their way, Brett tucked Charlotte's hand around his arm and headed back up the stairs. "You still owe me a dance, you know," he reminded, his voice low and husky.

"I owe you two dances," Charlotte corrected as the music from the eleven-piece orchestra seduced them closer, "and I haven't forgotten." *Believe me, Brett, I haven't forgotten.*

And in fact, she was looking forward to fulfilling her promise. Maybe it was the beautiful music. The drama of the night. The costumes. Maybe it was just the passion flowing between them, the tenderness. But whatever it was, she wanted to be in his arms again. And soon.

And Brett seemed to want that, too.

Nothing, however, could have prepared her for the vision of her dream come true. Charlotte paused in the doorway of the ballroom. Camellia Lane had not seen such life in longer than she could recall.

The chandeliers sparkled overhead, providing a gentle glow of light that had everyone looking their elegant, romantic best. Flowers and greenery formed garlands that were strung about the room. Women of all ages, in a rainbow of beautiful antebellum dresses, danced in the arms of Confederate soldiers and other gentlemen in period evening dress.

As the orchestra struck up the "Blue Danube waltz," Brett whispered in Charlotte's ear. "I think they're playing our song."

She looked up at him over her shoulder and his arms slipped naturally around her waist. "We don't have a song."

"One day we will," he promised.

Feeling incredibly proud and honored to be with him, Charlotte swept into the ballroom on Brett's arm and then went gracefully into his embrace. Where their joined palms met, warmth radiated out in waves. As she rested her left hand on his shoulder, Charlotte couldn't seem to stop looking at Brett. He was so handsome in Union blue! The cut of the soft navy blue wool emphasized the width of his shoulders and the muscled hardness of his chest. Thick strips of gold braid adorned each shoulder. Twin rows of gold buttons closed his long blue jacket. A black belt with gold buckle cinched his waist. His matching wool trousers were tucked into glossy black boots. He smelled of bay rum, instead of the usual Old Spice, and he had never looked so confident or so very male in his intent.

His blue eyes danced as Charlotte's own smile broadened. "I know just how you feel," Brett teased as she took in his slicked-back coffee brown hair and closely shaven jaw. With the hand on her spine, he guided her close enough to press a kiss into her hair. "I can't stop looking at you, either."

Charlotte blushed as one song segued into yet another and Brett continued to whirl her round and round to the beat of another beautiful waltz. "Sometimes I wish I had lived in another time," she confessed.

"I think we all fantasize," Brett murmured, holding her closer yet. He grinned down at her in a way that let her know he'd spent plenty of time dreaming about her. "Some of us are just better at it than others."

As their eyes met again, Charlotte drew in a tremulous breath. There was no mistaking the sensual intent in his blue eyes, or the deliciously vulnerable way that look of his made her feel. Charlotte had the feeling that Brett was very, very good at fantasizing indeed.

HOURS LATER, CHARLOTTE couldn't believe the time had passed so quickly. The clock had struck midnight, the orchestra had played its last tune. The carriages and cars that had brought all their guests were gone. The musicians had packed up and left, and so had the caterers. Paige and Isabella, both exhausted, had gone to bed.

And Brett, Charlotte thought with a frown, had disappeared sometime just before the evening ended. Charlotte had looked for him as the orchestra struck up the last waltz, but he was nowhere in sight, and someone else had claimed Charlotte. So she had not gotten the last dance with him, after all. Nor had she even gotten to say good-night to him. She looked around her in confusion.

All that was left of the evening were the garlands of flowers lining the third-floor ballroom. Still swishing around in her blue damask ball gown, not nearly ready for bed herself, Charlotte began taking the flowers down. One strand, then another, and another. And that was when Brett walked in again. He was alone, but he wasn't empty-handed.

"I come bearing gifts, milady." He bowed as much as he was able, considering he had a bucket of champagne on ice in one hand and two long-stemmed crystal glasses in the other.

He set both down, then went back out into the hall.

He returned again, carrying a portable stereo and two candelabras.

Ah, so this was where he'd gone!

Smiling and intrigued, Charlotte sat down on the velvet window seat, the garland of flowers all around her, and simply watched as Brett lit all the candles and placed one candelabra at each end of the room. He plugged in the stereo—soft, lyrical Chopin waltzes filled the empty ballroom. With a sensual smile at her, he switched off the chandeliers.

Moonlight and candlelight charged the room with a gentle romantic glow. Charlotte's heart beat in double time as he strode to her side. This, she thought, was the stuff of fantasies...beautiful, romantic fantasies.

He knelt before her, a knight in Union blue serving his rebel queen. "You are still saving that last dance for me, aren't you?" he said quietly. Taking her hands in his, he drew off one elbow-length glove and then the other, and set them aside.

Charlotte nodded as he traced the backs of her hands with his fingertips, thinking how happy she was to be with him tonight. "I thought you had forgotten," she confessed as he pressed tender kisses on her knuckles, wrists and fingertips.

Brett grinned at her as he slowly unfolded and got to his feet. "Not a chance, my darling Miss Charlotte." He leaned closer, admitting mischievously, "I just didn't want anyone else around when we had it."

Charlotte conceded to herself his idea had been a good one, and she smiled as he poured them both a glass of champagne. When they each had a glass in hand, Brett covered her free hand with his. Charlotte felt the warmth and tenderness of his possession all the way to her soul.

"To your father and the reading room being established in his name at his alma mater—Ole Miss—thanks to the proceeds of the ball," Brett toasted.

Charlotte touched glasses with Brett. "I think my parents would have been proud of us tonight," she said.

Brett nodded. Their eyes met, and the music playing on the stereo seemed to fade ever so slightly. "I have to hand it to you, Miss Charlotte. You and your sisters really pulled it off," he complimented her softly.

"With your help," Charlotte added, as she laid her splayed fingers on his chest and felt his heart thump against her palm.

Wordlessly, Brett set their glasses aside. He swept her into his arms and onto his lap, kissed her long and hard. She kissed him back, clinging to him, drowning in the pleasurable sensations sweeping through her. No one had ever asked her to give so much, and a few more kisses robbed her of the ability to think at all. When his hand slipped into the low-cut bodice of her dress and cupped her breast, she arched her back and trembled at the helpless pleasure.

Brett felt Charlotte's breath shudder, heard the low moan as her mouth softened against his and her nipple beaded hotly in his palm. His body trembling with the effort his restraint was costing him, he pulled her fractionally closer, wanting her to the point of madness, yet knowing, for her sake, they had to wait until he had sorted things out and decided just how to break the truth to her.

It was a hell of a choice he was being asked to make here, deciding between honor or love. But he was going to have to make it, Brett told himself sternly. And very soon. Because they couldn't go on like this much longer. He loved Miss Charlotte too much to betray her.

Ever so reluctantly, Brett ended the caress, and then ever so slowly, the kiss. He held Charlotte close for a long time, then took her soft hands in his and inched back. His glance roved her flushed face and diamond-bright eyes. "I want it to be right," he said softly, meaning every word. And it wouldn't be right, until he had figured a way out, for both of them.

"I know," Charlotte said, her green eyes going all misty and vulnerable, even as her low voice remained strong and determined. "So do I."

To Brett's immense relief, Charlotte seemed to understand it was important they hold on to this tenuous truce and build on it. Because he knew—even if she didn't—that there would come a time someday very soon when they would need a strong bond between them if their love was to survive what he had done, and what he knew.

Suppressing the need surging through him, Brett lifted her off his lap, stood and drew Charlotte gently to her feet. The need to hold her again becoming unbearable, he gathered her to him. When she was pressed against him, he bent down and kissed her lips with all the warmth and tenderness he could muster, promising himself all the while that when the time came he would take Charlotte and make her his. And when that happened, it would be a night they would never, ever forget.

Chopin was still playing softly in the background. The ballroom was filled with moonlight and flowers. They had half a bottle of champagne to drink and the night was still young. There was lots to celebrate. He had the most beautiful woman in the world in his arms, and one day soon she was going to be all his.

Hand splayed on her waist, he lifted one of her hands to his shoulders and clasped her other hand firmly in his. "Ever danced till dawn, Miss Charlotte?"

She shook her head, her cheeks flushing with anticipation, her eyes signaling that most of her commitment to him had already been made. "Can't say as I have," she murmured.

Brett grinned down at her. "Then it's past time you did."

Chapter Eight

Charlotte awakened to see the late afternoon sunlight streaming into her room. For a second, she couldn't imagine why she'd slept so late, then her eyes fell on the blue damask ball gown, and she smiled, remembering.

Who would have thought a dress made out of her bedroom curtains would have been such a success? But it had been, and so was the evening.

Stretching lazily, she lay back on her pillow and closed her eyes. The Confederate ball had been so much more romantic than she could ever have imagined. She would never go into the ballroom again without remembering what it was like to be held in Brett's arms, or to dance with him all night long, until the first pink streaks of dawn lit the sky.

He had walked her as far as her bedroom door, where he'd delivered the last of many slow, sensuous kisses. Charlotte had clung to him, not wanting the fantasy-filled night to end.

But it had. And the last thing she recalled was tumbling into bed. She must've been more exhausted than she'd realized, Charlotte thought sleepily, for she'd fallen instantly asleep.

But now that she was awake again, she had to get a move on. Time was running out for her. She still had to save Camellia Lane. And more important than that, she had to find a way for her and Brett to stay together.

"How is the search for Stephen Sterling coming?" Charlotte's editor asked an hour later.

Not so good, Charlotte thought, as she shifted the telephone a little closer to her ear.

"I've got a private investigator tracking down a lead," she admitted, reluctantly giving the weekly progress report she had promised her editor. "But at the rate things are going, it could be weeks before I've got anything more concrete on him."

Her editor sighed. "That's a problem, Charlotte. We've saved space for the article on Sterling in the July issue of the magazine, and that's going to press in three weeks."

Charlotte waved goodbye to Paige and Isabella, who were leaving to return some borrowed crystal punch glasses to friends in town. After that, they were going to spend some time at the library researching bankruptcy and foreclosure law and procedure. They had already warned her they didn't expect to be back until very late Sunday evening.

"How long can I wait to turn my article in?" Charlotte asked.

"Ten days, but I'd rather have it in seven."

It was Charlotte's turn to sigh. "What happens if I still can't locate Sterling by then?" she asked.

"Well, for starters, there's no bonus for you," her editor said.

"That I know." Her spirits sank even lower. "What else?"

"Then I'll assume Sterling can't be found, and we'll go with Plan B."

"You think that will satisfy *Personalities* readers?" Charlotte asked, rubbing at the tense muscles in the back of her neck. Anything less than unmasking Stephen Sterling to the world would be a failure to her.

"It'll have to satisfy them, at least for the moment," the editor replied. "That doesn't mean you have to stop looking for Sterling entirely."

No, but it did mean she would lose Camellia Lane, Charlotte thought.

"We could always do another article later, after you find him," the editor added. "In the meantime, maybe you should go ahead and start compiling what you do know on Sterling, Charlotte."

That wasn't much, Charlotte thought dispiritedly. "And what do I do with the gaps in my knowledge?" she asked.

"Fill them in, however you want—perhaps with some select passages from Sterling's books. Just make sure whatever you write adequately conveys the excitement and romance of his books. We want this profile to be highly entertaining to our readers, whether or not we're actually able to find out who Stephen Sterling really is."

Charlotte and her editor said goodbye, and she hung up the phone. How hard could it be to write a speculative article, anyway? she wondered wearily. Especially since she had been fantasizing and daydreaming about what Stephen Sterling the person must be like since first reading his books. And that curiosity had doubled in intensity since she had started her search for him.

Deciding a change of pace might stimulate her creativity, Charlotte retreated to her bedroom with her material and lapboard.

Breezing past her bedroom window, she stopped and looked out into the night. Darkness had fallen since she had gotten off the phone with her editor. Brett had turned on the interior lights and left the cottage windows open. Charlotte could see him sitting at the table, typing away on his laptop computer.

So he was working tonight, too.

She wished she could forget all about the article and just go down to the cottage and be with him. But the practical side of her knew she had better get started on her work. She was at such a loss as to how to even begin the article, that there was no telling how long it would take her to finish. Brett was probably making up for lost time, too. After all, he had devoted much of the last week to helping her and her sisters prepare for it.

Charlotte would just have to see him tomorrow. Maybe, she thought, if she made good progress on her work tonight, she could take some time off in the morning and go down to the cottage and see him.

In the meantime, there was still her article to do.

Perhaps the best way to start, she told herself as she undressed and climbed into a long white nightgown, was to get really comfortable. If she thought about how much she loved Sterling's novels, instead of Brett, then her angle for the speculative article would surely emerge.

Charlotte sat down at the antique writing table in the corner of her bedroom and picked up her pen. And for the first time she could recall, she stared at the blank page in front of her with absolutely no idea where she should start or what she would write when she did.

A more relaxing mood, Charlotte told herself firmly, was what was needed. Getting up, she went downstairs and picked up twin candelabras from the dining room and matches from the kitchen. She carried all upstairs, lit both sets of candles and put them on either side of her desk. She turned out the light. Her room glowed with an old-fashioned, highly romantic light.

There, that was better, Charlotte thought.

She opened the window, letting in the warm spring breeze and went back to her desk. She sat down, opened one of Sterling's novels and began to read....

"I thought I'd find you here," Matt Justice said.

The frightened heiress whirled around with a soft, startled gasp. The dark-haired intruder stepped from the balcony outside, and into her bedroom. Matt Justice was dressed as he had been earlier that evening, in a black tuxedo and crisp white shirt, but the heiress had already gotten ready for bed. She drew her thin negligee around her. "What are you doing here?" she demanded in a voice that trembled.

"I had to see you." He stepped closer. "I had to know if you were going to betray me."

The heiress had not made up her mind. She was torn between her love for her homeland and her love for him. "You shouldn't be here," she insisted fiercely. "My fiancé would have you arrested if he knew...."

Matt Justice touched a finger to her lips. "But your fiancé won't know, will he, for I'm not going to tell him and neither are you."

Furious about the way Matt Justice had deceived her from the first moment they met, the heiress glared at him and said, "You think you've won, but you haven't. You're an enemy agent, an enemy to my country, and I'm not making any promises." Stepping away from him, she backed into the table with a crash.

Matt Justice glanced at the papers on her writing table. She tried to cover them. Too late, he had already seen. A smile curved his lips. "You're writing about us, aren't you?" Matt whispered. "About what you feel for me, what you know to be true."

"That isn't so," she cried. "I know nothing about you!"

"Perhaps," he said, his voice lowering to a sexy whisper, "you know everything you need to know." Giving her no chance to argue, he tangled his hands through her hair and lowered his mouth to hers....

BRETT SAVED THE DATA on the computer, then turned it off. He unplugged it and put it back in the linen closet beneath a folded blanket and an extra set of clean sheets. He covered it carefully and shut the door. He didn't want Charlotte or any of her sisters finding that.

Not that they'd suspect he had two computers on the premises—the one with his real work on it that he kept hidden in the linen closet, the other a decoy he left out on the table.

No, his cover was secure. As was Stephen Sterling's identity, at least thus far, despite the efforts of Miss Charlotte Langston.

And speaking of...

Brett wondered what Charlotte was doing. He had stopped by earlier this afternoon, only to discover her still sleeping. Later, he had tried to call and found the phone busy. Flagging down Isabella and Paige on their way into town, he had asked about Charlotte. They had said she was on the phone with her editor and was planning to work tonight.

So Brett had worked, too. And he'd gotten a lot accomplished, although Charlotte had never been very far from his mind.

Still thinking about her, Brett stepped outside into the darkness of midnight and glanced longingly at the main house. Camellia Lane was completely dark, except for Charlotte's bedroom on the second floor. Beyond her windows was a pale, wavering light.

Brett frowned. That wasn't an electric light—at least, not one that was functioning properly. Nor did it seem to be a flashlight, he thought, alarmed. Was it possible there was a fire starting up at the main house? His heart pounding, Brett set off to find out.

Using the keys Isabella had given him, he entered the house through the front door. "Charlotte?" he yelled up the stairs. "Charlotte? Are you there?"

No answer.

Brett took the steps two and three at a time, and raced down the corridor to her bedroom. He stopped short at what he saw. Charlotte in a long white nightgown, slumped over her desk. Twin candelabras, with three candles each, burned on either side of her. Whether she was unconscious or asleep, he couldn't tell.

Brett reached out to touch her shoulder gently. "Charlotte?" Brett said.

She jerked awake so quickly she nearly upset one of the candelabras. Brett jumped to get it before it fell. He righted it carefully while Charlotte stumbled sleepily to her feet, colliding with the hardness of his chest in the process. Still leaning against him sleepily, she shoved her hands through her dark, tousled curls. "What is it?" she asked, her low voice husky with confusion.

Brett breathed a sigh of relief. Now that he was here, he felt a little foolish for panicking the way he had. That wasn't like him, either, but then, he had never cared about a woman the way he cared about Miss Charlotte.

"From the cottage, it looked like your room might be on fire," he explained softly, thinking how much she looked like the heroine in Stephen Sterling's latest book. Particularly in that negligee, which was sexy as hell on her. "I came up to check," Brett went on as Charlotte continued to cuddle against his chest drowsily. "Didn't you hear me calling you?"

She shook her head.

Deciding she was too sleepy to stand up, he hooked a shoe around the chair and pulled it farther away from the writing table. He sank down into it and snaked a hand around her waist and guided her onto his lap. Stroking his hands through the softness of her hair, he asked, "Is something wrong with the electricity in the house?"

"No."

Basking in the delight of having her close again, Brett cupped a hand beneath her chin and lifted her face to his. "Then why were you writing by candlelight?" Brett persisted, taking in the soft golden glow of her skin and the softness of her bare lips. He could feel the curve of her breast resting against his chest, the slender warmth of her thighs on his.

Charlotte hooked one hand around his neck and slid the other around his waist. "Because I felt like it," she said, more awake now. Her glance slid over his face slowly, sensually.

"Hmm." Aware she was wearing next to nothing beneath the thin nightgown, it was all Brett could do to sit still.

Needing to take his mind off making love to her, he glanced at the paper she had been working on. Frowning, he read aloud. "'Sterling gets to the heart of every woman, evoking romantic thoughts and forbidden fantasies.'"

Charlotte blushed and tried to squirm out of his lap, but he clamped both arms around her and held her still as he continued grimly reading the notes she had jotted down. "'Sterling's many devoted fans can only speculate about the mysterious author, and the "personal expertise" he brings to his love scenes. . . .'"

Brett regarded Charlotte, absolutely dumbfounded. He was filled with so many conflicting feelings he could hardly think straight. But one thing he knew for sure—this felt like a cunning betrayal of every principal he believed in. "*What* are you writing here?" he demanded, both shocked and incensed. As far as he knew, Charlotte hadn't found Sterling, hadn't even come close! So if she was writing an article about the author, she had to be conjecturing the information out of thin air.

Her chin set stubbornly, Charlotte wrested free of his grip, slid off his lap and whipped the papers up before he could read more. Her cheeks flaming, she said in a highly aggrieved tone, "If you must know, I'm working on a speculative article on who Stephen Sterling is."

"What do you mean *speculative?*" Brett interrupted, rising slowly to his feet, his own heart pounding. He clasped both her shoulders and held her in front of him when she would've run. "I thought you wanted the truth and were prepared to stop at nothing to get it."

Charlotte stiffened defiantly. "I haven't given up," she explained reluctantly. Her jaw set as she turned her glance away. "This is just an insurance policy in case I don't find him in time to meet my deadline."

"You really think you can speculate enough of the truth about Sterling to do an accurate portrait?" Brett was both amazed and a little disheartened. The Charlotte he had come to know never gave up on anything, period.

"No, of course not. I know this—" Charlotte tapped her notes impatiently "—is all conjecture on my part, Brett, but *Personalities* magazine has slated an article about Sterling and worked a teaser for it into the cover for that month's issue, so something must be written. This is what will run if I can't track him down.''

Brett hoped Charlotte was finally starting to realize she wasn't going to be able to find Sterling, no matter how hard she looked. If she gave up her search, that would let *him* off the hook. His secret mission would no longer stand between them. There would be nothing to stop them from becoming lovers, or even more.

Brett glanced at her notes again. He frowned at the romantic nature of her writing. Why now? he thought irritably, shoving both hands through his hair. This was the last thing he needed. Another twist on this incredibly complicated situation.

"Now what's wrong?" Charlotte demanded hotly, slapping her notes down on her desk and folding her arms in front of her, in a way that drew the thin white nightgown against the plump curves of her breasts.

Trying not to notice the way her nipples protruded against the delicate cotton, Brett looked back at her.

She didn't look the least bit nonplussed to have him in her bedroom at this time of night. Maybe because she thought— erroneously, of course—that she could handle him. And destroy Sterling with unwanted, untrue publicity, all at the same time.

"I'll tell you what's wrong," Brett said. He leaned a little closer, drinking in the lilac scent of her perfume. "You're making Sterling sound like an aphrodisiac in print!"

"So?" Charlotte shrugged. Arms folded in front of her, she began to pace back and forth, the skirt of her gown tangling about her slender legs.

Brett drew his eyes from the slenderness of her waist and the delectable curviness of her derriere. "So, I'm sure that isn't what any novelist would want," Brett countered emphatically, shifting his stance.

Charlotte whirled to face him. Her eyes on his, she asked contemptuously, "How in the world do you presume to know that, Brett Forrest? Aren't you taking on a lot, presuming to speak for all writers this way?"

Brett swore silently. In letting himself get sucked into an argument with Charlotte, he had revealed too much.

It was time to distract her again, perhaps with more kisses, before she got wise and figured things out on her own.

He stepped toward her, arms outstretched. "Because I know, that's all," he said softly, taking her gently into his arms.

Charlotte tilted her head back and narrowed her eyes at Brett. As always, she looked incredibly beautiful in the soft candlelight.

"It's a guy thing," he continued, picking up steam as he decided on a tack. His glance roamed the elegant contours of her face. Letting his voice drop a persuasive notch, he admonished, "You're going to offend Sterling if you print any of that garbage." *I ought to know.*

Charlotte rolled her eyes and shook off his tender grasp. Stepping away from him, she tossed her head. "Look, Brett. These are just very rough notes for a draft of an article. Some of my private thoughts." She reached over and turned the pages face down on her writing desk. "And I would appreciate it very much if you didn't read them!"

Brett raised both hands in surrender. Maybe he was over-reacting here. Charlotte hadn't done anything wrong—yet. There was still time to dissuade her.

"I'm sorry, Charlotte," he said softly, meaning it. "I understand how you feel. I don't like anyone reading my rough drafts, either."

Charlotte folded her arms in front of her. Brett could tell she was trying to decide whether or not to stay mad at him. He could also tell he had hurt her feelings in criticizing her writing, which he hadn't meant to do.

"And by the way, what I read just now—even if I totally disagree with the content—was damned good. Tantalizing, even." Brett paused. He decided there was no harm in revealing his opinion of her writing. "But then, so are all the articles you write," he continued softly.

Surprise registered in her eyes, followed swiftly by wariness. "How—?"

"Isabella gave me some copies to read the other day at the library. I don't mind saying I was impressed." And it was the truth. Charlotte was an extremely gifted writer.

She blushed with pleasure. But, as usual, she wasn't about to take a compliment from him without first asking questions. "What do you know about the kind of writing I do?"

Brett shrugged as his glance skimmed her nightgown. It was chaste to the point of being ridiculous, with its high neck, long sleeves and floor length. Beneath the thin opaque fabric, he could see the rounded fullness of her breasts and pouting nipples. Lower still, the flatness of her abdomen, the slenderness of her waist, the long, lissome thighs.

Just looking at her made his heart race, and he stepped forward slightly, trying to adjust his weight to accommodate the arousal straining against the front of his jeans.

"For that matter," Charlotte continued emotionally, new color flooding her pretty cheeks, "why would you even presume to give me your opinion on such a thing?"

"You're right, of course," Brett said in a low, steady voice. He had the feeling that she just wanted to cut short their conversation, which had grown disturbingly intimate in a very short period of time. Charlotte didn't like revealing herself to him, because it made her vulnerable.

"It's like me presuming to give an opinion of a doctoral dissertation when I know nothing about the subject," she continued.

"Again, you're right," Brett said with a shrug. He wished she would put on a robe. *Anything* to stop these decidedly erotic fantasies that were swiftly crowding his mind.

Aware she was still studying him carefully, he said, "I guess I don't know as much as you when it comes to how women think, Charlotte."

She tossed her head again as she paced back and forth, the tension in her seeming to come from a new, different source. "You're damn straight about that!" she said, and her lips trembled.

"But I'd like to learn." He stepped closer, inhaling the rich fragrance of her perfume.

"Then try reading a Sterling novel. I highly recommend them. Now, there is a man who not only understands women—he savors them."

Brett frowned. Back to her being a fan again. He really wished that weren't the case. Because then there was no hope for the two of them. "Your devotion to Sterling's novels amazes me, Charlotte," he said. "A practical, hard-hearted woman like you should be reading only nonfiction."

"Hard-boiled mysteries," Charlotte corrected, settling down again without warning. "And you're right—generally I'm not a fan of adventure novels filled with interpersonal complications and steamy romance."

"Ah, I see." Brett worked to suppress a grin. "You prefer to engage your intellect rather than your emotions?" Vintage Charlotte. Very much afraid of falling in love, especially with a hot-blooded devil like him.

Charlotte aimed a censuring finger at his chest. "Listen, Brett Forrest, you write about dirt farming. You're in no position to criticize my tastes in fiction."

Brett captured her hand and tugged her close. "I guess I'm not," he agreed as he studied her hair, which glowed luminous in the soft candlelight. His hands itched to sink into the softness of the long, dark curls, just as his mouth ached to fuse with hers once again. "But just the same, you ought to lay off fantasizing about an author you know nothing about," Brett continued advising her solemnly.

"You know what?" Charlotte frowned, clearly puzzled. "You sound jealous of Stephen Sterling!"

Sterling at least had Charlotte's respect, he thought. Brett was still working on earning it. "Maybe I am," Brett said, his hands stilling on her spine, "I just want to see you concentrate on what's really important—saving Camellia Lane."

"Careful, Brett." Charlotte turned so she was facing away from him, her head resting on his shoulder, her back against his chest. "You're talking as if saving Camellia Lane is suddenly a noble goal."

Brett cupped the length of her folded arms with his. "Noble or not, it's your goal," he countered.

Deciding his lazy-scoundrel act could use a little boost if it was going to continue to be credible, Brett gave in to the temptation that had been plaguing him since he entered her bedroom.

"Fortunately for both of us, I'm not," he said huskily.

He bent her backward from the waist, leaning the weight of her on one braced leg, and his mouth hovered just above hers. He watched the shock in her eyes, a little surprised by how much he enjoyed playing the rogue to her high-spirited damsel in distress.

"Noble, that is," Brett finished softly.

He expected her to fight the coming kiss because they were in the middle of a disagreement. And she did, by going rigid in his arms. That pleased him; he had always enjoyed a conquest. And conquering Miss Charlotte was going to be a pleasure, one he would recall for a long time. Just as making love to her was also something he knew he wanted never to forget. The fact that this went contrary to his mission here—stopping her from finding Sterling—was not lost on him.

Part of him—the romantic part—even wanted to tell her the truth.

But he couldn't—wouldn't—think about that now, as he watched the increasingly stormy expression in her thickly lashed eyes. Now, all he would think about was the desperate hunger inside him—the passion he had felt all last night—and the kiss he was going to steal if she wouldn't give it to him....

His mouth touched hers, lightly at first, like a brush of warm, soft flannel, then with growing ardor.

Charlotte struggled to keep her feelings in check, but it was an impossible task when his arms were wrapped around her like a lover's caress.

His tongue teased her lips apart and then plunged into her mouth over and over again, stroking and arousing. The sexual electricity between them was intense and exciting, as was the wonder that they had come together like this again when they both knew it was so unwise.

They weren't suited for each other, but that didn't temper the intimacy of his kiss, Charlotte thought. The truth of the matter was, he made her feel like a woman. He made her aware of her own needs, feelings that until now had been unsatisfied.

His arousal nudged her, through his jeans and the thinness of her nightgown, and she reveled in the tantalizing sensations their closeness evoked. Magical fantasy touched her heart, and Charlotte was completely caught up in the slow, liquifying pleasure.

Brett unbuttoned the front placket of her gown, then pushed open the edges, baring her breasts to view. Charlotte was as beautiful as he knew she would be and his whole body tightened as he caressed the rounded upper curves and the shadowy valley in between.

Melting against him as if she wished the loving would never stop, Charlotte moaned as the flat of his hand brushed her nipples, caressing them into velvet morsels. Still holding her against him, he slid ever downward, his mouth shaping her nipple for the gentle conquest of his lips and tongue. Trembling fiercely, she caught his head with her hands, threading her fingers through his hair as she held him against her.

To know that she wanted him was exciting. To know she'd surrendered, sent him over the edge. Wanting to show her just how good the loving between them could be, Brett backed her toward the bed, until the backs of her knees were touching the mattress.

Her whole body straining against him, she gave a little cry as he pushed the gown past her waist, and then lower still, over her hips. On his knees in front of her, Brett slid his palms across her thighs and gently parted her legs. Charlotte blossomed beneath his sweet, tender caresses. When the excitement inside her had subsided to a gentle tremor, Brett found his way slowly back up her body, loving and discovering every sweet, fragrant inch of her.

Smiling down at her, he lifted her body onto the big four-poster bed. He laid her down in the middle of the sheets, and then, eyes still locked passionately with hers, began to undress.

Dazed with passion, Charlotte reached up to help him, unzipping the fly of his jeans, pushing them aside. She drew in her breath sharply at the first contact of his hot male flesh with her hands. And then he was on the bed with her, looming over her, touching her everywhere, even as she caressed him wantonly and without restraint. Loving Brett was a dream come true, Charlotte thought, kissing him back hotly.

Her own pinnacle caught her by surprise, and even as she was squirming beneath the skillful ministrations of his hands, he was moving to possess her as she knew he meant to from the first.

Murmuring her name over and over, he braced his hands on either side of her and made love to her passionately.

Tears of happiness fell from her eyes as he lifted her against him until he had made her undeniably his own. And Charlotte knew, as he surrendered himself to her, that he was hers, too. *Not* just for now, but for all time.

Chapter Nine

"Thank you for agreeing to meet me before you went to the office," Charlotte said, as Jared Fontaine joined her on the bandstand in the park Monday morning. Sunlight streamed down through the trees. The scent of azalea blossoms clung to the warm spring breeze. It was a beautiful day, and as Charlotte thought about the way she and Brett had made love the night before, happiness sifted through her. But her relationship with Brett aside, Charlotte had plenty of trouble on her hands.

She had never been this close to absolute failure and she didn't like it. She had been counting on herself to save Camellia Lane. And now she needed that to happen more than ever, so that she and Brett could be together.

Jared closed the distance between them promptly. He took her hand in his. "What was so urgent that you needed to see me this morning, Charlotte?"

Charlotte withdrew her hand from his and paced the small, octagonal pavilion restlessly. "The same thing that *has* been urgent, Jared," she said, albeit a little waspishly. "Saving my family home."

Jared studied the way Charlotte had clipped her hair at the nape of her neck. "I'm sorry your plan to raise money didn't work out."

Charlotte made a small, dismissive motion with her hand. "It wasn't all for naught since there is now a reading room at Ole Miss established in my father's name."

Charlotte walked back over to Jared. "But I still need to raise money to make that balloon payment to the bank, Jared." Charlotte drew a ragged breath, adding, "And time is running out." She had four days left. That was all.

Jared adjusted the Windsor knot on his pale yellow tie. He looked down at her sternly. "What exactly are you asking me, Charlotte?"

"I'm asking you to float me a loan, just until I raise the money myself, so I can repay the bank."

Jared frowned, the shrewd lawyer in him taking over. "Realistically, how long do you think that will take?"

Charlotte shrugged and thrust her hands in the deep trouser pockets of her sage pantsuit. "I'm researching a magazine article now. If everything works out the way I hope—" *and I find Stephen Sterling* "—I could probably have most, if not all of the money, back to you within the next one to two months." She was being overly optimistic, she knew, but what choice did she have but to hope for the very best?

Jared stepped forward and wrapped his arms around her shoulders. Ignoring the stiffness of her body, he tugged her close. "Charlotte, I hate to see you looking so worried, darling."

She stood stiff and inflexible, the weight of his arms around her feeling more like a noose around her neck than the comforting gesture he meant it to be. "Then you'll help me?" she asked softly, wishing all the while that she had never landed herself in such a fix.

Jared stroked the nape of her neck with the pad of his thumb. Frissons of displeasure soared through Charlotte; it was all she could do to suppress a shudder of distaste while she waited for Jared to decide if he would loan her the money.

"If I thought you'd say yes, I'd ask you to marry me...this minute...today."

Unable to bear being close to him a moment longer, Charlotte extricated herself from his arms and turned away.

Jared followed her to the edge of the bandstand. "Think of it, Charlotte. No more chasing after stories. You could live at Camellia Lane again."

She drew a calming breath. Her fingertips tightened on the waist-high latticework trim. "I can't marry you, Jared."

Briefly, hurt flickered in his eyes. His face hardened. "Then what exactly are you offering me, Charlotte?" he asked quietly.

Aware she had never felt more miserable and worried in her entire life, Charlotte looked at him uncertainly. "I'm not sure."

"How about hope?" Jared presumed gently. He put his hands on her shoulders and held her gently to him. "That in time your feelings for me will change?"

Charlotte's heart was pounding. She struggled to hide her revulsion. Whatever fondness she had felt for Jared faded the instant he had tried to turn her personal difficulties to his advantage. "I don't know that I could marry anyone, Jared," she said honestly. "I don't know that I could love anyone that deeply and irrevocably, to make a lifetime commitment." *Except maybe Brett.* "It's a big responsibility."

"Then perhaps I should set my sights a little lower," Jared suggested with a wolfish grin.

Charlotte swallowed. She wasn't afraid of him. She was afraid of the rift that would come between them if he continued with this line. "Jared, don't—"

"Why not?" he prodded just as firmly. "As long as we're laying all our cards on the table, why not be blunt? You know what I want, Charlotte. I know what you want. You need me for a loan to save Camellia Lane, fine. But I'm not a high school kid anymore who's content to worship you from afar. I want something out of this arrangement, too," he said, his jaw hardening.

"Like what?" Charlotte interrupted, her legendary temper heating up.

"Like the chance to prove to you in every way there is that the two of us are a good team."

Jared's proposition was gentle, but matter-of-fact. Charlotte folded her arms in front of her like an invisible shield. "If I said yes, would you give me the money?" she asked, reverting to the proven Southern wile of steel-magnolia sweetness. Desperate situations called for desperate measures.

"If you say yes," Jared said, grinning broadly, "I'll get you the money today."

BRETT RELAXED ON A PARK bench on the other side of the concessions building, watching the unfolding drama to his far left with keen interest.

He had wondered what Charlotte was up to when she had vaulted out of bed at the crack of dawn. Knowing one night of the best lovemaking he'd ever experienced in his life didn't give him the right to question her, Brett had decided to follow Charlotte and find out what she was up to instead. And now he knew.

Barely 8:00 a.m., the area of the park next to the bandstand was devoid of people, except for Jared, Charlotte and himself. Even at a distance of twenty feet he heard their every word.

"You're asking a lot, Jared," Charlotte said hotly.

"I'm prepared to give a lot," he retorted.

Don't do it, Charlotte, Brett thought. He watched with chilly disapproval as Charlotte tamped down her temper with effort and gave Jared the weasel a placating smile.

"What if I just say maybe?" she suggested in a low tone that trembled.

Clearly, Brett thought as he studied Charlotte's profile surreptitiously, she was on the edge of physical and emotional exhaustion. And that was not surprising, considering all she had put herself through in the last week. Nevertheless, she wasn't about to give up or throw out any options. Which showed how very much Camellia Lane meant to her.

Brett watched as, up on the pavillion, Jared wrapped both arms around Charlotte's waist and tugged her close.

"*Maybe* won't cut it here, Charlotte," Jared said in what Brett assumed was an attempt to be masterful.

Brett's hands tightened into fists as Jared bent to kiss Charlotte.

To Brett's immense satisfaction, Charlotte turned her head just in the nick of time and Jared's lips landed on her cheek. To his dissatisfaction, she made no move to completely extricate herself from Jared's embrace. Rather, she continued to look to the side.

Brett could see the wheels in her head turning. And so could Jared Fontaine.

Jared continued forcibly, "I have to know if I come up with the money that you'll be mine...for however long you stay in Poplar Springs."

Brett relaxed slightly as Charlotte wedged her arms between herself and Jared. "I told you," she said pleasantly but firmly, "I don't love you."

"And I told you. I have enough love for the both of us," Jared soothed. He tangled his hands in her hair and tilted Charlotte's head up to his. It was all Brett could do to stay put as Charlotte deftly avoided Jared Fontaine's kiss.

Brett wasn't sure, but he thought Charlotte's face was losing some of its usual glow. *Don't kiss him, Charlotte,* Brett willed her silently. *You'll regret it if you do.*

Finally, Charlotte swept her hands through her hair and said tersely, "I can't think about starting a romance with anyone now, Jared. I'm too upset about losing Camellia Lane."

"Then when?" Jared asked curtly.

Charlotte folded her arms in front of her. "After Camellia Lane is safe."

CHARLOTTE'S HANDS were shaking as she got in the car and started back to Camellia Lane. She couldn't believe she had sunk to such a low level. Listening to Jared lay out his outrageous provisions for a personal loan had been bad enough. But to actually think for one insane, desperate minute about beginning a romantic relationship with him was terrible.

Of course she couldn't do that. She had morals, a sense of right and wrong, and selling herself—for any reason—was wrong.

So it was back to Plan A again. She would have to find Stephen Sterling, and she would have to find him quickly!

As soon as Charlotte arrived home, she went straight to the library and sat down at her desk. Seconds later, she had dialed New York.

"Surely there must be something else you can tell me about Stephen Sterling," Charlotte begged Marcie Shackleford over the telephone. "After all, you're Franklin Dunn, Jr.'s secretary! He handles all of the author's contracts!"

"Don't you understand?" Marcie whispered, sounding very nervous and upset. "I could get fired for just talking to you!"

"Sterling's social security number—anything!" Charlotte begged.

"I gave you those addresses where Sterling's galleys are sometimes sent!" Marcie reminded, incensed.

"And I have a private detective looking into who owns those properties," Charlotte shot back. "In the meantime, I need another lead."

"I don't know," Marcie whispered back. "I'll have to think about it."

Again, she hung up on Charlotte.

Charlotte sat glaring at the phone. She picked it up again and began calling in every favor she had ever been owed.

To her deep disappointment, no one knew anything more than she did about Stephen Sterling.

Everything for the author went through his lawyer, and no one there, save Marcie Shackleford, was even talking to Charlotte! And the secretary, it appeared, wasn't giving Charlotte any more information.

Defeated, Charlotte laid her head on her desk. She had been at this nearly all day, she realized wearily. And all she had to show for it was an exorbitant number of long-distance phone calls and a lot of frustration.

And yet something inside her—the indefatigable reporter—refused to give up. She knew there was a way to find Sterling. A clue. A lead. Something. It was probably staring her in the face. She just had to find it, zero in on it and—

The front door slammed, breaking Charlotte's thoughts. Resenting the interruption of her brainstorming session, she frowned as footsteps thudded firmly on the parquet floor.

Seconds later, Brett stormed into the library. Charlotte hadn't seen him since the previous night, but she knew instantly something was very wrong.

As she continued to study the tense expression on his face, instinct told her she didn't really want to know what was bothering him.

Brett didn't stop until he had reached her desk. Then he leaned over and placed both hands flat on the desk so she was caged in by his arms and their faces were very near. His electric blue eyes glittered with anger. He seemed to be having a lot of trouble controlling himself. "You must be awfully proud of yourself," he said.

Charlotte sat back with studied casualness. She rested the back of her head on the cool leather of the chair and steepled her fingers together in front of her. "Why would you say that?"

"Because I heard something awfully interesting at the hair salon in town just now."

Brett didn't look as if he'd just had a haircut, Charlotte thought. "Really? What?"

"Seems Hiram Henderson is fit to be tied."

Charlotte wasn't about to pretend she had any concern left for the banker trying to force her and her sisters out of their family home. "What does *that* have to do with me?" Charlotte pushed the words through gritted teeth.

"I'm getting to that." Brett straightened, shoving his fingers in the back pockets of his jeans. "Jared Fontaine was at the bank shortly after it opened. It seems he didn't much care who overheard his business. It's all over town that he had a cashier's check drafted for fifty thousand dollars.''

Charlotte's heart pounded. She had hoped Jared would recall how long they had been friends and come through for her. Obviously, he had. And Brett had assumed the worst about Jared's actions, and the reasons for them.

She could let Brett off the hook by telling him that she had promised Jared nothing in return. But why should she reward him for thinking the worst about her...especially after the night they had shared. He should know she would never do something like that! Since he had, there was going to be hell to pay, Charlotte decided furiously. Brett was always teaching her lessons. Here, at last, was her chance for a little payback.

Charlotte tilted her chin up defiantly and waited for the next blow. It wasn't long in coming.

''Furthermore, the check wasn't drafted in Jared's name,'' Brett continued. ''It was drafted in yours.''

Caught off guard by that little tidbit of information, Charlotte could barely contain a flush of embarrassment. Damn Jared! He knew Poplar Springs was a small town, with old-fashioned standards of conduct. Jared had to know the gossip an action like his would cause. Was he trying to force her into marrying him, to save her reputation in the community?

Seeing how much this was bothering Brett, Charlotte pushed all thoughts of his passionate lovemaking from her mind and offered him a civil smile. ''I fail to see why this upsets you, Brett,'' she said.

''Then let me spell it out for you.'' He circled around the chair. Hands braced on his waist, he towered over her. ''The talk at the lunchtime poker game over at Rosie's saloon was that you sold yourself to get that money.''

Charlotte pushed the swivel chair back and away from Brett. Once there was adequate room between them, she shot to her feet. ''I did not sell myself to anyone,'' she said hotly.

Brett quirked a brow. "Does Jared Fontaine know that?" he asked silkily.

"I don't have to answer that!"

"I see." Brett regarded her coldly. Another heartbeat of silence fell. "Don't you have anything to say for yourself?" he demanded.

It was clear, Charlotte thought, as she pretended to study the hundreds of books her father had collected, that she and Brett had a lot to work out if they were ever going to have a lasting relationship. And the first thing he needed to learn was that she was an independent woman who made her own decisions. "I don't have to explain myself to you," she said.

Brett merely continued to look at her. His lips compressed until they all but disappeared beneath his dark mustache.

Charlotte's conscience gave her another nudge. "But just for the record—you figured wrong here, Brett." Her eyes lasered into his with heartfelt accuracy. "I don't want Jared for a beau. He's just helping me out as an old family friend."

Brett was not at all convinced. "Then why is the check in just your name and not Isabella's and Paige's, too?"

Charlotte shrugged. "I don't know."

Brett pinned her to the spot with his sexy gaze, his sensual mouth curling in contempt. "The hell you don't!"

It was all Charlotte could do not to grin. This was sure turning out to be some lesson for Brett. "You know, Brett, you presume an awful lot," she drawled.

"Unfortunately, so does everyone else in town. You and Jared were the hot topic of conversation at the bank, the grocery, the sheriff's office all day today."

Charlotte didn't mind what he thought. It served him right for jumping to conclusions. But she did not want her sisters suffering the town gossip for anything Charlotte had done.

Charlotte rubbed at the tension gathering in her temples. "Does Isabella know?"

Brett gave her a look. "She works at the library. What do you think?" he asked sarcastically.

Charlotte's heart pounded all the harder. Despite herself, she began to blush. "What about Paige?"

Brett shrugged. "Haven't seen her. But if she's anywhere in town today, she knows."

Charlotte swallowed. This was turning into a royal mess, regardless of her noble intentions in going to Jared for a loan. "I've got to call Isabella."

Brett blocked her path to the phone on her desk. "You won't be able to get her at the library."

Charlotte stopped dead in her tracks. "Why not?"

"Heritage Homes is having a Meet and Greet session in the community room there tonight. They're going to talk about their plans to build new homes in the area, providing an appropriate site can be found, of course. Isabella is out getting refreshments for it."

A reprieve! Charlotte thought. "Oh. Well, then... I'll just have to wait until later this evening to speak to her." That way, Charlotte thought, she'd have time to think about what she wanted to say.

"Oh, no you don't," Brett said, reading her mind.

Charlotte blinked. "I beg your pardon?"

"You're not going to leave your sisters to face the gossip in town alone. You're going to that Meet and Greet session tonight along with Isabella and Jared and Paige, if I have to throw you over my shoulder and haul you in myself."

Charlotte smiled tightly, refusing to think about how fast and hard her heart pounded, or how alive she felt, whenever Brett was near her. Or how much she was looking forward to kissing him again when they did make up. "That, sir, would be kidnapping."

Brett's confidence increased. "As you have pointed out on many occasions, this is a small town and the sheriff is a friend of mine, so I am not worried about getting arrested. Isabella and Paige have been beloved residents of this town for the last decade. You've embarrassed both of them pub-

licly with your behavior, Charlotte. You won't leave them to
face this scandal alone.''

"ARE YOU SURE WE'RE doing the right thing?" Franklin
asked Brett. "After all, that woman is still hot on Sterling's
trail and making a tremendous nuisance of herself.''

Brett picked up the stack of money Franklin had wired to
the Jackson, Mississippi, bank that very afternoon. He
curled his hands around it and forced himself to concentrate on the predicament.

Something had to be done here. Like it or not, it was up
to Brett to get involved. He frowned pragmatically. "Look,
Franklin, we want to keep Miss Charlotte Langston from
writing an exposé on Stephen Sterling. From what I can tell,
the only reason she's writing it—other than the fact she has
something of a crush on Sterling's writing—is because she
needs to save Camellia Lane.''

"Camellia Lane is not Sterling's problem," Franklin reminded him.

"Yes, but Miss Langston is. I feel sure that she would stop
behaving in such a desperate manner and concentrate on
other things—'' *like her love life, for instance* "—if her ancestral home were secure.''

"So, in other words, it would be fifty thousand in cash
well spent,'' Franklin theorized.

Sterling would never miss the money, but if his identity
was revealed, his private life would be public knowledge. He
would never be comfortable with that.

"What are you going to tell Miss Langston about where
the money originated?" Franklin asked.

"From a high-stakes poker game in Atlantic City last
year.''

Franklin laughed. "That, my friend, would not be far
from the truth. You have a gift for cards.''

"Among other things.'' *Like spying on unsuspecting
women and making love to Miss Charlotte.*

"You think Miss Langston will accept the money?''

Brett sighed. "I plan to do everything in my power to convince her to do just that tonight." He also planned to make love to her, well and thoroughly, and get Jared Fontaine out of her mind once and for all.

After tonight, the next time Charlotte needed help she would come to him, Brett thought.

"And if Miss Langston refuses your offer of money?" Franklin asked. "Then what?"

"She can't refuse. She has no other real options," he said. "Not if she wants to save her beloved Camellia Lane."

But even as he spoke, Brett began to have some doubts. What if Charlotte preferred to go to someone else for help? What then?

Brett scowled. Whether Charlotte admitted it or not, accepting a check from Jared was like accepting a loan from the devil. Jared could make Charlotte's life hell. And Brett didn't want to see her hurt.

On the other hand, it was high time someone taught Charlotte that the end never justified the means. Brett'd made a start, forcing her to go to that meeting in town tonight. The rest would come when she returned home.

"Listen, my friend, do you think maybe you're getting too involved with Miss Langston?" Franklin asked after a moment. "I could always send someone else down to handle the situation."

"No," Brett said shortly. The *problem* was he wasn't nearly involved enough with her for his own comfort. Furthermore, he had come here to do a job. He would finish it, and then do what he really wanted to...make Miss Charlotte his for all eternity.

"How about I send in some help, then?" Franklin persisted.

"No," Brett said roughly. "Charlotte Langston is all mine." Realizing how abruptly possessive he sounded, Brett adapted a lighter tone. "Besides, you know what they say. In for a penny, in for a pound."

Brett was in this for the long haul. So was Miss Charlotte, he thought, grinning. She just didn't know it yet.

Chapter Ten

"So how was the meeting?" Brett asked the moment Charlotte stepped through the front door of Camellia Lane.

She stopped dead in her tracks and pivoted slowly around to face Brett. He was standing in the open doorway of the library. Arms folded in front of him, feet planted solidly on the floor, he looked like a warrior ready to do battle.

Charlotte lifted her chin, aware her heart was beating too fast, and it was all his fault, damn him. He was tying her into knots, making her doubt everything she knew to be true—in this case, saving Camellia no matter what it took.

"What are you doing here?" she demanded autocratically.

"Why, I'm waiting up for you, of course."

Charlotte surveyed him coolly as she struggled to make sense of her own soaring emotions. "Well, you needn't have bothered," she informed him curtly. She was still angry with him for insisting she go to the meeting at the library.

Brett merely quirked a brow and made a low, dissenting sound that swiftly got under her skin. His glance raked her slender form, taking in her slim skirt, long-sleeved silk blouse and blazer. Charlotte couldn't tell if he approved of her businesslike apparel or not. She assured herself she didn't care, either way. "The development company win any converts?" he drawled.

"Lots, as you might well imagine, since new housing starts, or the need for them, have been down for some time in this area of the state,'' she said stiffly. ''They still aren't getting our land.''

''Thanks to Jared Fontaine,'' he said bluntly.

Charlotte was silent as she met his probing glance. Damn him if he wasn't making her feel guilty for accepting Jared's help when Brett knew that she and her sisters had no other place to turn.

''Do you have his check with you?'' Brett asked.

She shrugged, refusing to let Brett get to her. Her parents would've understood what she was doing, even if he didn't, she assured herself firmly. ''Jared said he'd give it to me tomorrow.''

Brett's fist hit the newel post on the stairs like an auctioneer's gavel. ''Sold, to the highest bidder.''

Charlotte gave him a seething look and said nothing. She refused to dignify his crude comment with a response.

''This is a business arrangement, Brett, and I will be signing papers to that effect.''

''Papers or no, you know what Jared expects from you?'' Brett continued.

Unfortunately, Charlotte knew Brett was right. Jared was likely to continue to pressure her. And she was still grappling with that. Had she somewhere else to turn, she would've declined Jared's aid. But she didn't. So she'd told him where they stood tonight after the meeting, and he had still offered his help.

''All I'm doing is accepting Jared's help temporarily,'' she explained, threading a hand through her hair wearily. ''As soon as I find Stephen Sterling, write the article and get the bonus the magazine has promised me, I should have enough cash to pay Jared back.''

Brett's expression turned unaccountably grim. For a moment he was silent. Finally, he recovered enough to say, ''If I were you, I'd read the fine print first, before you sign anything. And I still say any contract with Jared Fontaine is a contract with the devil.''

Charlotte narrowed her glance at Brett. She did not appreciate his interference in her private family affairs. ''This conversation is getting far too personal." And so were the two of them. They had only had one night together. If he was going to be this jealous and difficult all the time, she wasn't sure she wanted another!

Her feelings more confused than ever, Charlotte started to breeze on by.

"What's the matter?" Brett taunted, blocking her way to the stairs. "You certainly look upset. Could it be your conscience is finally bothering you?"

Charlotte propped her hands on her hips. Brett seemed determined to get a rise out of her. Well then, so be it, she thought. "For hired help, you certainly have an attitude," she drawled.

Brett's mouth curved upward in a dangerous smile. "Lady, you ain't seen nothing yet. And you haven't answered my question," he said softly. He surveyed her ruthlessly. "Does Jared know you aren't planning to become his mistress?"

Charlotte stiffened at the contemptuous note in Brett's low voice. "Of course he does!"

Brett merely smiled at her assertion. His eyes took on a challenging glint. He rubbed his jaw in a parody of thoughtfulness. "Uh-huh. What if he changes his mind and demands you express your gratitude before you have enough cash to repay him?"

Charlotte had enough problems without worrying about future disasters that might never occur. She decided Brett was being entirely too ridiculous, in his fierce desire to protect her. "I can't think about that today," she said with a dismissive wave of her hands. "I'll think about it tomorrow."

Brett shook his head at her in an emotional display of remonstration. "In true Scarlett O'Hara fashion. You're so naive sometimes you really *ought* to have lived in another time."

Charlotte set her chin and glared at him. She was all too aware that it was just the two of them in the house. And that

Paige and Isabella were dining with friends and not expected back for hours.

"And you, sir, are judgmental and narrow-minded enough to be Rhett Butler," she shot back.

Brett lifted a brow. He was intrigued, rather than put off, by her insult. "Maybe what you *need* in your life is a Rhett Butler. You know, someone who is not afraid to stand up to you or let you know when you are wrong."

Her pulse racing, Charlotte stared at him in mute consternation. He seemed different tonight. He seemed like he wanted to do battle with her to the bitter end. Determined not to let him intimidate her into meekness, she glared at him and tossed her head imperiously. "I've heard enough. I'm going to bed!"

Brett put out an arm to block her way. He leaned against the newel post. "Not before I've had a chance to place my bid."

Her heart pounding, Charlotte tightened her fingers on the other side of the post and stared up at Brett. She could see the jealousy in his eyes.

He was furious with her for accepting Jared's help. But that didn't mean he had a right to pass judgment on her.

"What are you talking about?" Charlotte demanded, tossing her head as if she hadn't a care in the world.

Brett smiled down at her. His eyes were filled with a dangerous light. "You like a man with money." He looked her up and down with sizzling intensity. "I've got money," Brett announced casually.

Sensing danger, Charlotte took a step back. "I don't want your money."

"Too bad." He closed the distance between them in a heartbeat. Charlotte gasped as he swung her up into his arms and carried her up the stairs.

"Stop this, this instant!" she demanded.

Brett paused on the landing. He looked down at her. His grip tightened possessively. "As the lady wishes," he said with a mock gallantry that kindled her senses.

The next thing Charlotte knew he was shifting her in his arms. His mouth dipped to hers. Panic rushed over her. One hand clung to his neck, the other pushed at his shoulder— to no avail. Her lips were already parting under the firm, warm pressure of his.

She didn't want to give in to him, but his will was stronger than hers.

With a low moan of surrender, Charlotte tilted her head to give him deeper access, which he immediately took. His tongue curled against hers, and he delivered a searing kiss that scored her soul and left her limp with longing, faint with acquiescence and wondering at the magical power he held over her heart. She didn't want to desire him, but she did. And she was afraid that desire was going to lead them down a dangerous, heady path from which there was no return. She was afraid if she spent much more time with Brett, she was going to fall head over heels in love with him. If she hadn't already....

Brett had the power to break her heart, she realized suddenly, stunned. She had to stop this now. She pushed at his shoulders and tore her mouth from his.

Brett broke the kiss off, but he didn't put her down. Still holding her in his arms, he studied her flushed, upturned face for a long moment. Charlotte was mad as hell—he was enjoying her obvious distress and the ardent way she had responded to his kiss.

"Speechless, hmm?" he teased. "Well, this is a first."

"Don't bet on it," Charlotte returned, refusing to let him get to her.

Brett chuckled and, to Charlotte's dismay, looked all the more pleased. She could feel his erratic heartbeat as he resumed his trek up the stairs, strode determinedly into her bedroom and then set her down with unexpected gentleness on the floor beside her bed.

She stared at the coverlet. Her mind was still swimming from his kiss. Her bed was littered with one-thousand-dollar bills. Now what? she wondered. And then thought, Damn him. "Very funny," she muttered sarcastically beneath her breath as she picked up a bill and examined it. "They even look real. Too bad they're not, Brett!" Determined to get the best of him yet, she ripped the bill in half.

Brett swore and made a grab for the damaged currency. "What are you doing?" he gasped.

"What do you think I'm doing? I'm getting rid of your joke!" she shot back.

"It's not a joke!" He snatched her hand and tugged her close. "That money is real," he continued as she stumbled against his chest.

Refusing to indulge in something as undignified as a struggle, when they were already standing chest to chest, Charlotte braced a palm on his shoulder and tilted her head up at him. "Sure it is. And next you have some swampland to sell me."

Brett shook his head in mute admonition. Releasing her as abruptly as he had taken her into his arms, he leaned across the bed. Quickly, he picked up the money, bundled it all together, forcibly opened her hand and pushed it into her palm.

Charlotte looked down at the crisp green bills. The currency certainly looked real, but since she was no expert she couldn't be certain.

Which was, Charlotte supposed as her next idea hit, what Brett was planning on. "Oh, I get it," she said slowly. "If I take this to the bank tomorrow morning, they'll likely have me arrested for trying to pass counterfeit money."

Brett shook his head in obvious exasperation. "You think I'd do that to you?" he asked, incensed.

Charlotte studied him. Her pulse was racing. She felt on edge. In a way that had everything to do with the fact they were together in her bedroom again. "I think the depths to which you would go to teach me a lesson know no bounds."

"Suppose I tell you the money is real." He regarded her reasonably. "And that I intend to give it to you outright."

Charlotte's pulse pounded even faster. Her sense of danger intensified. "Why?"

Brett shrugged, his shoulders looking impossibly broad beneath the fabric of his soft sweatshirt. "So you won't have to hunt Sterling down like a criminal, destroy his privacy and regret it later—when it's too late to do anything about it, of course."

Charlotte had been struggling with mixed feelings about unmasking Sterling for days now. He was an excessively private person, true; but there was no evidence he was a fraud like others she had written stories on.

Consequently, Charlotte knew that her heart hadn't really been in the search for Sterling. As desperate as she was to save Camellia Lane, she wasn't anxious to destroy an innocent person's life. She had Brett to thank for that realization. And because Brett was continually sticking his nose in her business, Charlotte didn't trust him. She had more doubts about him than ever.

"No one gets something for nothing, Brett Forrest," Charlotte reminded him reasonably.

Which brought her to the next point. What exactly did he hope to gain from this little monetary display of his?

A lot, she supposed, judging from the expectant look on his handsome face. Charlotte frowned as she began to pace back and forth. "Assuming, just for one minute, that this money is real, what do you want really from me, in return for it?" Charlotte tested him aloud. "A night of lovemaking?"

Brett quirked a dark brow. The corners of his mustache twitched with mirth. "*Is* a night in your bed being offered?" He looked delighted at the thought.

"In your dreams." Her adrenaline flowing, Charlotte paced the floor, thinking. "Either you're nuts—"

"I must be to be this involved with you."

"—or you are simply working for Heritage Homes and First Unity Bank." Her newest theory voiced, Charlotte crossed her arms in front of her and regarded Brett bluntly. "So which is it?" she demanded.

"I don't know what you're talking about," he denied flatly. And for a second all traces of his characteristic arrogance was gone. But he looked a little uneasy about something just the same.

Charlotte's reporter's instincts went on full alert. She tapped her chin in a parody of thoughtfulness. "The gentleman—and I must say, in your case, Brett, I use that term very loosely—does protest too much, methinks."

Brett hooked his thumbs through the belt loops of his jeans. His eyes lasered into hers. "I agree," he drawled. "I'm no gentleman."

Charlotte ignored the come-on in his low voice. She tapped her foot contemplatively. "You know what else I think? Despite the college sweatshirts and jeans, you never did look like a scholar to me. There's a bit too much of an edge to you. And isn't it funny how you always keep showing up in my face at the most inopportune times, spying on my private conversations."

She was getting close to the truth here, even though she hadn't yet figured it out precisely; she could feel it in the way he looked away from her uncomfortably. Exasperation exuded from his every pore.

"Has it occurred to you that maybe you're the one who is the problem?" Brett countered, an irascible gleam in his eyes. "That if you weren't always doing something underhanded yourself that it wouldn't matter how, when or even why I showed up, because there'd be nothing to see?"

Charlotte crossed her arms in front of her defiantly. She didn't know why she had let this encounter with Brett go this far. She, better than anyone, knew that to give him an inch was to give him a mile. "You've overstepped your bounds here," she warned.

Brett shook his head at her in mutual disapproval and offered up a censuring frown. "Lady, from what I know of what you've been up to, I haven't even begun."

Silence fell between them. As they glared at each other, Charlotte became aware that he was breathing as quickly and erratically as she was.

Feeling like she was in the midst of a Mexican standoff, Charlotte turned her attention back to the bills. "Where did you get all this?" she asked.

Brett closed the distance between them with sensual grace. "Does it matter?" He moved closer yet, in a drift of Old Spice.

Charlotte drew a tranquilizing breath. "That's a funny question for you to be asking me," she said as her heart pounded harder. "Hell, yes, it matters! Is this money really yours?" She studied him intently while waiting for his reply.

Again, Brett shrugged his broad shoulders contemplatively and sidestepped the real issue. "I don't see anyone else here."

Charlotte had suspected from the very beginning there was something not quite on the level about Brett Forrest. Now that feeling intensified. Surely, she prayed, he wasn't a criminal! She drew another deep breath and worked to keep her hands from shaking. "Did you get it from a loan shark?"

"No," Brett said matter-of-factly. "I won it. Playing high-stakes poker in Atlantic City."

"And it's real," Charlotte supposed, deadpan. How much of a fool did he take her for?

He nodded, affirming her premise. "The money came straight from a bank."

Yeah, right, she thought. "And you're giving it to me?"

Half his mustache took on an upward tilt. His vivid blue eyes danced with mischief. "I figure you need it more than me at the moment. Besides," he offered candidly, "you can pay me back."

Charlotte continued to look at him. His offer seemed sincere. And that was crazy. "Assuming this is real—and for the record, Brett Forrest, I am still not nearly gullible enough to believe that—I can't take your money." She pushed it resolutely back into his hand.

He promptly set the stack of bills on the bedside table. "Why not?" he asked with deceptive affability. "You could take Jared Fontaine's money."

Charlotte drew in a ragged breath. "That's different!" And she hadn't yet accepted Jared's check, mainly because he had said he wanted to come out and see her in the morning.

"How is it different?" Brett ground out.

Charlotte flushed self-consciously. "I knew why he was doing it! He was very straightforward about what strings were attached."

"Ah, I see." A new, dangerous light entered Brett's eyes. He closed the distance between them and sifted his hands through her hair. "Would it make you feel better if I attached some strings of my own?" he countered silkily.

"What kind of strings?" Charlotte asked nervously.

Brett shrugged noncommittally. "A few passionate kisses."

"And that's all? Fifty thousand dollars for a few kisses?"

"Want to give it a trial run?" Brett asked facetiously as he drew Charlotte into his arms.

She had never been one to look a gift horse in the mouth, but neither had she made a practice of working the high wire without a net. And right now, just his nearness overwhelmed her. She hated to think what his kiss would do to her.

Charlotte adapted a contentious stance. "I would but... frankly, my dear Brett... I think you would have a hell of a time stopping at just a few kisses if I were to indulge in them." He certainly had before and so had she!

His arms still circling her waist lightly, Brett studied the soft curves of her mouth. Charlotte felt his tender scrutiny like a lover's caress. Her insides melted a little more.

Finally he returned his attention to her eyes. "You really think I couldn't handle it?" he taunted softly.

By an act of sheer willpower, Charlotte reined in the desire flowing through her in undulating waves. "If I gave it my all? Yes, I do," she insisted stubbornly. She didn't want him to think he had the upper hand, just because they'd made love.

Brett tilted his head to the side. "Maybe that'd be the case. Then again, maybe you're the one who is afraid. Maybe you're the one who would have trouble stopping at a few kisses," he suggested, dropping his hands from her waist and stepping back.

Charlotte turned her back to him. "Don't be ridiculous," she scowled. She didn't know why she was suddenly feeling so upset. She ought to be relieved he was no longer touching her.

Brett tapped her lightly on the shoulder, interrupting her censuring thoughts. Charlotte turned halfway around to face him, wondering what he wanted now.

He grinned as she regarded him with sharp suspicion. "Care to put that claim of yours to the test?" he taunted.

It was all Charlotte could do to stifle a low moan of dismay. Her life was changing too fast. In retrospect, of course, she could see the crisis had been coming for some time now. She just hadn't wanted to acknowledge it, just as she didn't want to face that she was falling in love with Brett Forrest.

If it were just passion between them, maybe she could have handled that. But she knew there was more than that between them. Brett saw into her heart and her mind. And she found that almost as unsettling as his kisses. But she wasn't about to let him know that, not when he had already deftly located her every weakness and somehow managed to turn them all to his advantage.

But not this time, she vowed silently. Propping her hands on her hips, she pivoted back around to face him, angled her chin up at him and retorted with a mildness of manner she couldn't begin to feel inside, "What kind of test?"

"Indulge in a few kisses with me...and see if you can stop."

It sounded so innocent. Furthermore, beneath the recklessness he exuded whenever he was around her, she sensed at heart Brett was, like her, as solid and dependable as they came. The kind of person you could count on to be there in

a crisis. "What will that prove?" Charlotte asked, unim
pressed.

"That you're as in control of your environment as you
would like to be."

The truth was, she would settle for just being in contro
of him, and the soaring emotions she felt whenever she wa
near him. Maybe there was some value to this madness, af
ter all. "If I do this, and succeed in resisting your irresist
ible charm," she bargained plainly, "I want something from
you in return."

He perked up. "What?"

"I want you to stop following me around and spying or
me."

Brett inclined his head slightly to the side. "I prefer to
think of it as trying to keep you out of trouble."

Charlotte sighed in exasperation. "Call it whatever the
heck you like, your shadowing me is beginning to get on my
nerves!"

"Fair enough. But if I win—" Brett pointed to his ches
"—and you can't resist my kisses, then *I* want something in
return."

No surprise there, she thought. Like her, he would at leas
try to turn any situation to his own advantage. "Name you
prize," Charlotte ordered shortly.

Brett grinned. "Another night in your bed."

"You are wicked, Brett Forrest."

"Never claimed not to be," he drawled. "So are we on?"

"Oh, we're on." Now that he'd made the stakes so high
Charlotte had no intention of letting him win. "All right
Let's go back downstairs," she said.

He grabbed the back of her suit jacket and plucked he
back into easy reach. "Let's not."

"Now wait just a darn minute," Charlotte sputtered.

"What's wrong with right here?" Brett asked, his ex
pression all innocence.

She studied him in exasperation. In the dim light of he
bedroom, his eyes were the deep clear blue of a mountair
lake. His dark hair was rumpled, his mustache neatly

trimmed and quivering with the barely suppressed mirth of a man who never took himself—or her, it seemed—too seriously. "Well, for one thing," Charlotte said, "the proximity to my bed."

His dark brows lifted speculatively. "Don't think you can stay out of it?"

Ha! "I think I could get on it or in it with you and not have a damn bit of trouble saying no when the time came," Charlotte vowed impassionedly.

"Let's see about that," he suggested.

Did she want to put her declaration to the test? Her cautious side said no. The other part of her—the more hedonistic part—simply wanted to see if he could make her feel the way he had when he'd kissed her on the stairs.

But she couldn't say that. "Brett, no," Charlotte said.

"Charlotte, yes," he whispered back.

Anchoring both hands around her middle, he turned her around and danced her backward to the bed. He lowered her gently, covered her body with his own. His weight was like a warm blanket on a cold winter's night. Charlotte's heart pounded harder as she studied his face. There was no force here. All she had to do was say the word and he would release her. But then it would look as if she was afraid of kissing him again. And she was not afraid of his kiss, only of her own powerful reactions to him. "You're going to be disappointed," she vowed.

"I'll be the judge of that," Brett said. Then his mouth was on hers and she was swept up into a kiss that was shattering in its possessive sensuality. He kissed her like he was in love with her. He kissed her like he meant to have her. And then all conscious thought fled as he held her close and fused his mouth to hers. Longing surged through her, overwhelming her heart and her mind. Charlotte felt his intent in the fierceness of his kiss. She felt the challenge in his embrace, the desperation. Coupled with his wanting, it was enough to drive her toward abandon. She made a soft, helpless sound of protest in the back of her throat.

"Well?" he said at last, uttering a soft, thoroughly satisfied sigh of contentment when he finally lifted his head. "How was that?"

Like heaven on earth, Charlotte thought, successfully suppressing a contented sigh of her own. "No problem," she fibbed.

Brett's eyes darkened smugly at the breathlessness in her voice. "Really?"

"Really." Charlotte drew a bolstering breath. "So now I've said no and—" She shoved at his chest and started to get up; he rolled onto his back and folded his hands behind his head.

"Don't you want to see if I can say no?" he asked.

Charlotte paused at the edge of the mattress. "Oh, right," she said dryly. *Like I am really going to fall for this!* Aware he was waiting for her retort, expecting her to turn and flee, she regarded him with a newfound patience of her own. Maybe it was time to put him in the hot seat, she thought slyly. She pretended to think about it. "How do I know I can trust you?" she asked finally.

"That's the risk." Brett stretched out lazily on the center of Charlotte's four-poster bed and gave her a bad-boy grin. "You can't."

"You really are a rascal, Brett."

He threw his arms out on either side of him, as if offering himself up for sweetest sacrifice. "Okay, sweetheart, your turn," he drawled, deadpan. "Do your worst." He winked at her salaciously. "Not that it will move me."

Well, we'll just see about that, handyman, Charlotte thought, determined to make him feel as light-headed as he had made her feel.

Mindful of the satin comforter on her bed, she kicked off her heels and let them drop to the floor. Brett looked askance as the second heel dropped to the floor. "This is interesting," he murmured.

Not, Charlotte thought, as interesting as it was going to get. Before she was done with him, Brett Forrest was going to be totally in her power and begging for mercy. Then, and only then, would she have the pleasure of turning him down.

Charlotte noted the way the pulse was throbbing in his neck as she hiked her slim skirt to midthigh and swung one stocking-covered leg over his legs. His expression remained smugly watchful, but a bead of perspiration broke out on his forehead. Good, Charlotte thought. That meant she was getting to him.

Planting a palm on either side of his broad shoulders, she bent over him and lightly touched her lips to his.

No response. She tilted her head so that their lips met in perfect alignment and deepened the kiss. Again, no reaction. She might as well have been kissing a stone.

Damn him.

Charlotte straightened and, still straddling him, began to push up the hem of his sweatshirt.

Brett's glance narrowed. At last, Charlotte thought smugly, she had his attention. "What are you doing?" he asked mildly.

Charlotte pushed until the sweatshirt was bunched beneath his arms. Then she tugged the T-shirt beneath it free of his jeans, and pushed it up, too, until it barely cleared his ribs. "You look a little warm. Too warm, in fact, to be able to accurately test my kiss. Not to worry," she finished as she smoothed a hand over his ribs, to his waist, and then back up again, until her hand nestled in the mat of silky hair in the center of his chest. "This ought to help center your awareness."

"It's doing something," Brett said. His glance said he was clearly interested, but also in control.

Not for long, Charlotte decided. Calmly, she began to take off her suit jacket, revealing the thin, long-sleeved silk blouse beneath. "You know," she said as she undid the first button, then the second, and began to play with the third, "I think it's a little warm in here, too."

Brett's thighs were rigid inside the cradle of hers. "Now, wait a minute. We said a kiss here—"

"A few kisses, and there was no stipulation of how we had to be dressed or undressed," Charlotte corrected. On impulse, she undid the third button on her blouse. "Unless . . . you're afraid you can't take it?" she taunted.

"I can take it," Brett declared. But the words sounded more like a groan of dismay.

Sensing victory, Charlotte leaned over him, her breasts spilling out of the cups of her lacy, translucent demi-bra.

Brett shut his eyes.

She could feel the rigidness of his arousal as she settled her weight more fully over him. "Ready for those kisses now?" she whispered.

He nodded tersely.

She bent to kiss him. Looking like a man in pain, he kept his lips closed. She touched her lips to his. The taste of him, so hot and dark and male, set off a fire storm of sensation within her. Their bodies melded in an instant of boneless pleasure. She stretched out over top of him. He rolled, taking her with him. As he positioned her squarely beneath him, his fingers dug into her hips. Then need took over once again, making them both reckless and relentless.

There was no denying his kiss, no denying the feelings swirling around inside her heart. This might have started out as a battle of wills, but it had swiftly evolved into so much more. She wanted him. Needed him. Needed this. The knowledge lent a reckless edge to an already dangerous evening. Bit by bit, Charlotte felt the last of her inhibitions melt away.

Her lips parted and she drew his tongue more intimately into her mouth. He moaned and his hands drifted lower, to the soft silk blouse. Tugging the hem from the waistband of her skirt, he slipped his hand between the silk and her skin. She whimpered as he moved past her ribs, beneath the lacy bra, and cupped her breast. Warm ribbons of pleasure flooded her as he caressed the taut, aching tip and covered her mouth in another searing kiss. She arched against him. She wanted to love him. And she wanted out of these clothes.

"Brett—"

"I know. They're in the way." He unbuttoned her blouse and slipped it free. His eyes were dark with desire as he dispensed with the lacy bra, and then his mouth was on her, moving from her throat to her breast, kissing, caressing, sending her into a frenzy of wanting. She arched against him, burying her hands in his hair.

She was trembling when he returned to her mouth.

She trembled even more as she helped him tug off his sweatshirt and T-shirt. His jeans followed in rapid succession, and so did her skirt. He settled between her thighs, his hips nudging them apart. She drew in a shaky breath. She was in over her head and sinking fast. Her muscles trembled, then tensed. She wanted . . . She didn't know what she wanted. She only knew as he began to kiss her again that her world was him, and only him.

Brett hadn't meant for this to happen, not any of it. He had only brought her up here to give her the money. But when she'd started challenging him, everything had taken a different turn.

He wanted Charlotte as he had never wanted any woman. He wanted to court her relentlessly. He wanted to sweep her off her feet until she was as crazy about him as he was beginning to be—hell, who was he kidding here?—as crazy as he was about her.

Charlotte moaned as Brett's lips found her breasts. She had known from the moment she laid eyes on him that this was inevitable.

He kissed her again and again, until desire streamed through her like fire, until she felt warm and safe.

He touched her languidly, knowingly, until sensation layered over sensation, until that tenderness was almost her undoing. She gripped his shoulders, hard; he caught her soft cry with his mouth. She arched up to meet him. He entered. She embraced. He took her to heights and depths. Taught her every subtlety, every nuance of desire. Taught her that she didn't need to think her way through this, didn't need to do anything but feel.

She gave back everything tenfold and demanded more. She wanted everything, and then nothing. She conjured up passion and pleasure, tenderness and surrender, until she wasn't the only one who was lost in the moment.

Brett didn't care about the future or the past. He only wanted this moment, this woman, the discovery that—at least, for now—she was his. And his, he vowed, she would remain....

Brett woke sometime later. How had it come to this? he wondered. He shouldn't be in bed with the enemy, but he was. He should have given her the money in a straightforward business deal and then used all his powers of persuasion to encourage her to give up the search for Sterling.

CHARLOTTE WOKE TO FIND herself alone. For a moment, she thought she had dreamed the wild lovemaking with Brett the night before, and the crazy dare that had preceded it, but all she had to do was look at the rumpled covers, at the clothing she'd left discarded at odd points all around the bed, at her own nakedness, to realize it was true. She had made love with Brett last night, wild passionate love.

She knew she ought to be ashamed of herself for falling into bed with Brett during a quarrel simply because the two of them had earth-shattering chemistry, but she wasn't. What she wanted, when they weren't fighting and even when they were, was more of him.

"You're awake." Brett walked in. He was dressed in a T-shirt, sweatshirt and jeans. His hair was neatly combed. He had shaved and showered.

"When did you get up?" Charlotte asked as he stretched out on the bed beside her and delivered a minty-fresh kiss to her lips.

"A while ago, after I heard your sisters leave. Don't worry. Neither of them realize I spent the night in here."

Charlotte breathed a sigh of relief. She wasn't ashamed of the fact she'd made love to Brett; she just didn't want to explain it to anyone—not yet, when it was all so new and wonderful.

"I could have slipped out before they'd even awakened, but I hung around because I wanted to talk to you about something."

He looked serious. Charlotte sat up and brought the sheets up, tucking them beneath her arms.

"It's about the money," Brett said softly, pointing to the cash on her nightstand. "It is real, Charlotte, and I meant what I said last night. I want you to have it."

Charlotte took a deep breath, aware she was trembling from the inside out. "I don't know, Brett. I don't think it's such a good idea."

Hurt flickered in his vivid blue eyes, but it was gone almost as soon as it appeared. He reached behind her to fluff up a pillow. "Why not?" he asked casually.

"Because it's not a good idea to borrow money from friends. And if I accepted money from you, it would just complicate things between us unnecessarily."

His glance was troubled as he pointed out, "You're accepting it from Jared."

Charlotte shrugged her shoulders helplessly. "And look what it's done to my relationship with Jared, even before I take the cash and sign on the dotted line. Suddenly, after years of knowing each other, our friendship is really feeling the strain." Charlotte swallowed as she took Brett's hands in hers and held tight. "I don't want that to happen to us," she said softly, her eyes searching his. "I don't want the money to come between us, particularly since we're still in the process of becoming close." Charlotte knew she was wearing her heart on her sleeve here. She didn't care.

Brett sat back against the headboard and pulled her into his arms. He smelled of her soap and shampoo. "I wouldn't be putting any strings to the money, Charlotte. Except—" Brett paused.

Tingles crept up Charlotte's spine; it was all she could do to suppress a shudder of dismay. "Except what?" she asked in trepidation, almost afraid to look him in the eye for fear of what she'd see. This was precisely what she'd meant about even the discussion of money ruining things!

Brett seemed loath to look at her, too. Instead, he was staring at the stack of novels on her bedside table. "Except I'd want you to stop looking for Stephen Sterling," he confessed after a moment.

Here we go again, Charlotte thought, biting down on her lower lip. "Why?"

Brett looked at her in concern as he tenderly pushed the hair from her eyes. "Because I think it's wrong, what you're trying to do."

Charlotte refused to let the prickles of her conscience dissuade her. "But don't you see that's my decision to make?" Charlotte said passionately, twisting around to face him. "Even if we are lovers?" This was important. It was a precedent-setting situation that would dictate the tone for all future conflicts with Brett.

Brett paused, his expression conflicted as he stared down at her. "I know it's your decision, Charlotte," he said finally. Sighing, he looked away from her again. "I'm just being selfish, I guess." He rubbed her arm with long, tender strokes. "I don't want anything to stand between us, either."

Charlotte shook her head and settled back into the warm curve of his arm, knowing by the conciliatory nature of his low tone that the battle was over—for now, anyway. "The only way you can help, Brett, is to give me my freedom and let me do things my own way. As long as you do that, I promise you, everything will work out all right."

Chapter Eleven

"You look lovely this morning, Charlotte."

"Thank you, Jared." Charlotte smiled, trying not to show how anxious she was to simply get this over with. She escorted him into the parlor. "You brought the check?"

"Yes." Jared wrapped his arms around Charlotte. "But I want to do a little celebrating of our own first," he murmured as his wet mouth grazed her ear.

Charlotte felt sick inside as she pushed Jared away. The gossip in town was right. Obviously, he still expected a lot more from this arrangement than she was prepared to give.

"You surprise me, Jared," Charlotte chastised, extricating herself from his embrace.

Jared followed her across the parlor. He looked frustrated but no less determined. "Why?"

This was an awkward situation, but she would just have to make the best of it. Charlotte looked at Jared evenly. "I've never known you to be so forward."

There was a desperate edge to his placating smile.

"You've been gone a long time, Charlotte. I've missed you," he said softly. His eyes hardened. "And I'm tired of not getting what I want."

And what he still wanted was her. Something in Charlotte went very cold at the thought. She moved around the back of a wing chair, keeping it between the two of them, and returned his smile tensely. "From what I can see, you've already got everything you want," she pointed out reasonably. "A thriving law practice, a nice car and home."

Jared smiled and stepped behind her, trapping Charlotte between him and the chair. He lifted the hair from the back of her neck and rubbed it with the back of his thumb.

"But I don't have you."

Her temper flaring, Charlotte jerked away. She didn't want a moment's madness to end a friendship that went back more than twenty years. But unless Jared came to his senses, that was exactly what was going to happen. "Please don't equate me with your happiness." She pushed by him and started to walk away. "It's not fair to either of us."

Silence fell between them, as thick as molasses. Jared stared at her unhappily. He shoved a hand through his straight blond hair. "You're the one who is not being fair, Charlotte," he said, his voice rising. "You're the one who's never given us a chance."

There was no *us*, Charlotte thought on a fresh wave of exasperation. Resting her hands on her hips, she met his eyes, and suddenly, she knew a door had closed. It didn't matter that they had known each other for years, or that in the past she had always been able to turn to Jared for help. She shook her head at him sadly. "I thought our friendship was strong enough to withstand the strain of you loaning me money, but obviously that's not the case."

"I was afraid this was going to happen." Jared's voice was harder now. "It's that Brett Forrest, isn't it? You're in love with him, aren't you?" he demanded hotly.

"How do you—?" Charlotte began. She hadn't thought her feelings for Brett were so obvious.

Jared's mouth thinned. "Everyone saw you dancing with him at the Confederate ball. They saw the way you two looked at each other."

Charlotte swallowed. She had never seen Jared look so unhappy, so bitter. "What I do or don't feel for Brett has nothing to do with this, Jared. I asked you to help me out of the goodness of your heart, with no strings attached, like a true friend would. I *never* agreed to anything else. In fact, I explained to you that just the opposite was true.''

"That's precisely the point, Charlotte," Jared interrupted stonily. "You told me what you want. You never once asked me what I wanted here. Well, I've had time to think, too. And I've also reconsidered." Jared paused, his lips thinning. "If we do this, then we'll do it my way or not at all."

Charlotte had expected she would be disappointed if it came to this. Instead, she was only relieved. "Then it's going to be not at all," she said firmly.

Jared pulled an envelope from the inside pocket of his suit jacket. Charlotte saw the amount typed on the check. She knew she was this close to saving Camellia Lane. She realized she only had three days left to find another way to come up with the money.

Jared looked at the check, then at her. "You realize I'm not going to offer this check to you again?"

Charlotte's heart pounded, but she felt free. "Yes," she replied flatly. "I still won't change my mind."

"MORE BAD NEWS for Stephen Sterling," Franklin told Brett later the same morning. "We've got three more reporters tracking him down. Two of them are getting close. One of them even tried the same route as Miss Langston and infiltrated the law firm."

"Great," Brett said sarcastically.

"Fortunately, we were onto him before any damage was done, but I don't think it's going to stop anytime soon."

Brett didn't, either. Phone in hand, he walked to the cottage window. His heart in his throat, he stood, looking out at Camellia Lane.

"With Sterling on the bestseller list, interest in him is only going to grow," Franklin said.

"So what are you suggesting?" Brett asked wearily, rubbing the back of his neck.

"That you come back to New York and sit in on a strategy session."

Brett searched the back veranda and gardens for any sign of Charlotte. "I can't leave yet."

Franklin paused, his confusion evident. "I thought everything with Miss Langston was all settled," he said slowly.

It should have been, Brett thought, if only he had handled things right. "She didn't take the money."

"What do you mean?" Franklin asked, stunned. "I thought she needed it badly!"

That was what made Charlotte's actions all the more telling, Brett thought, the fact that she would value her relationship with him above her fierce desire to save Camellia Lane. But how was he going to tell this to Franklin, without revealing how much Charlotte had come to mean to him? Finally, he said, "Miss Langston has come to trust me."

"So? All the more reason for her to take the money," Franklin said.

Normally, yes, Brett thought, that would have been the case if he and Charlotte had just been friends. But they were lovers, and soon, if he had his way, they would be more than that.

Brett swallowed. "Charlotte thinks accepting a loan from me would put a strain on our friendship," he said quietly.

"Do you agree with her on that?" Franklin asked.

"I don't know. I see her point." Brett didn't want anything to come between him and Charlotte, either. Which made this mess he had gotten himself into all the more untenable.

Brett scowled in silent misery. Things would be so much simpler if he could just tell Charlotte the truth about why he was here. Then the two of them would be free to pursue the love they had found, with no limits or restrictions.

The only problem was, if he told her now, after having made love to her first, he feared she would never forgive him for the duplicity. And, thinking about it, he couldn't really say he would blame her if she did feel that way. He had known all along he should tell her the truth first, before getting in over his head with her. He wanted Charlotte, heart and soul, for now and forever. The question was, Brett ruminated, how was he going to make it happen?

"Brett, you still there?" Franklin tapped the phone at the other end of the line.

"Yeah. I was just thinking, that's all," Brett said.

"Hmm," Franklin murmured on the other end of the line. "So you say our dear Miss Langston trusts you?"

"More every day," Brett confirmed reluctantly. And that in turn added to his guilt.

There was no telling what Charlotte might do if she discovered the real link between Sterling and himself, Brett thought. He didn't want to risk her doing something they'd both regret. Because once Sterling was unmasked, there was no going back.

But he still had time to put everything to rights.

"So what next?" Franklin prodded.

Brett shrugged and concentrated on what he could tell Franklin. "I guess I keep an eye on Charlotte. With only three days left until the bank forecloses, she must be getting pretty desperate."

"What makes you think that?"

"Rosie, the owner of a saloon in town, phoned a few minutes ago to tell me Charlotte turned down a loan for Camellia Lane from another source."

"A legitimate source?" Franklin asked.

"A weasel of an old friend," Brett explained. It warmed his heart knowing that she had thrown Jared out on his ear. Not that Jared had admitted Charlotte had passed on the opportunity to be his lady friend. Rather, he had stormed back to the bank and redeposited the cashier's check in his own account. He had termed Charlotte's refusal of the money as a matter of family pride. "Speaking of Charlotte,'' Brett told Franklin, ''I better go up to the main house and check on her.''

There was another telltale pause on the other end of the line, reminding Brett how well Franklin knew him. ''Even though Miss Langston has turned down those loans, you still don't trust her completely, do you?'' Franklin guessed.

When it came to saving Camellia Lane? Not an inch, Brett thought. ''She has this saying. 'Desperate times call for desperate measures,''' he told Franklin. ''And she really loves this old place.''

''Meaning, I suppose, there's no telling what she could do in the next few days?'' Franklin said.

''You got it,'' Brett added grimly.

Tamping down his worry, Brett looked out at Camellia Lane once again. Whether Charlotte wanted to admit it or not, she needed his help—now more than ever.

''SO WHERE ARE WE?'' Charlotte asked the private investigator. She had been putting pressure on him for days now, even knowing he had a limited budget to work with.

''I was able to convince a postal worker in the Arlington, Virginia, post office to check on Sterling's mail.''

''And?'' Charlotte waited anxiously.

''According to my source, all the mail is now being forwarded from Arlington to a post-office box in Atlanta, under the heading of S. E. Sterling.''

''And?''

''From there, it's being sent to Miami, Florida, and then mailed out to a box in nearby Jackson, Mississippi. I don't know if it's being forwarded from Jackson to anywhere else, but I figure you might want to check that out yourself, since you'll be able to do it faster than I can.''

''Good idea.''

Charlotte paused to take down the number of the post-office box in Jackson. ''What about the addresses Dunn's secretary gave me last week? Any luck tracing down ownership of those?''

"No. It took me almost a week to find out those properties are both leased by a complicated series of holding companies within holding companies, but of course that's just a smoke screen for the real owner. I'm going to Memphis to see if I can uncover anything on my own about who really lives there. I'll call you as soon as I know anything."

Charlotte had the feeling they were getting close. "What's my bill so far?" she asked. The investigator told her, and she groaned at the tally. "Just do your best."

She hung up the phone to find Brett watching her from the portal. The sweatshirt he had on molded softly to the muscled contours of his chest and shoulders. His faded jeans clung to his legs and lower torso like a lover's caress. His handsome face bore the golden glow of the spring sun, and a hint of sunburned pink across his cheeks and nose. Just looking at him, Charlotte felt her heartbeat pick up a pace.

Brett straightened laconically and moved away from the doorframe. His eyes held hers as he moved lazily toward her. "I just came in to bring you the reports on the soil samples I took last week." He set a sheaf of papers on her desk.

Charlotte trusted him enough not to read the reports herself. She just wanted to cut to the chase. "How did they turn out?" she asked anxiously.

"Actually, a little better than I had hoped." Brett cleared a corner and rested a hip on the edge of her desk. "I think with proper management and the implementation of crop rotation, you could grow cotton here again and make enough to pay the day-to-day expenses and taxes on Camellia Lane."

Charlotte leaned back in her father's old leather swivel chair. It was so intimate in here, talking with him. "What kind of cash outlay are we talking about?" she asked softly.

Brett frowned, the dark edges of his mustache curling down. "That's what I wanted to talk to you about. I know you said you didn't want to accept a loan from me, but we didn't say anything about our being *business associates,*" he emphasized slowly.

Charlotte's heart took up a steady, mesmerizing beat. It sounded like Brett was making long-range plans that involved her, too. She admitted to herself there was nothing she'd like better than to spend her immediate future with him.

Unable to completely contain her happiness, she asked with reluctant gratitude, "What do you mean?"

Brett picked up a paperweight on her desk and shifted it from hand to hand. "I've learned a lot about growing cotton in the course of my studies. But I've had little chance to actually apply what I've learned. This would be the perfect opportunity for me. And for you, too. So what do you say?"

Charlotte studied his face. He seemed awfully anxious for her to take him up on his offer. And that made her cautious. Leery of being taken in again, the way she and her father had been by J. H. McMillan, she narrowed her glance slightly. "You're proposing you become the overseer for Camellia Lane?"

Brett shook his head. "More like a sharecropper," he explained. "I'd want to lease the fields from you for a period of five years, bear the expense and responsibility for growing the crop and then keep a percentage of the profit and give the rest to you. We'd both gain, and best of all, you'd be off the hook financially because you could give the leasing fees I give you up-front to the bank to pay off your balloon payment. We'd put all this under strict legal contract, of course."

Brett had impressed her from the first that he was very good at protecting his own interests, yet in this case he seemed to be putting her concerns first. This was sounding a little too good to be true, and that made Charlotte nervous.

She turned her pencil end over end, her mind spinning with the thought of Brett being at Camellia Lane for the next half decade, minimum.

"Why would you do all this for me?" she asked cautiously. There was only one reason in her mind... because he loved her as much as she loved him.

"I told you." The curve of Brett's mouth hardened slightly. He looked as if he resented her persistent questioning of his motive. "I want a chance to test my knowledge."

Charlotte pushed aside her disappointment, telling herself that she didn't really need to *hear* him say he loved her, not when she *felt* it all the way to her soul every time he kissed her. Still there was something amiss here, and until Charlotte could pinpoint what it was, she wouldn't rest.

"Besides that," Charlotte prodded, "why here? Why not some other place? For goodness' sake, Brett, you could put a down payment on a small farm for what you're proposing to pay to lease the property."

"I'm doing it because you need me," Brett said softly. He slid off the desk, circled her wrist with his hand and tugged her unceremoniously to her feet. Sitting back, he drew her between his legs and wrapped an arm about her waist.

Charlotte basked in his warmth, wanting so much to believe that Brett's intentions were noble to the core, yet not sure she should. From the very first, there had been something that didn't quite fit about him. Now, after a brief respite, it was surfacing again. She angled her head up to study his face. "Is that the only reason you're proposing this?" she asked, tracing the strong line of his jaw with her fingertips.

Brett shrugged. Although he kept his eyes on hers, Charlotte had the sense he was shutting her out again. "I know how much the plantation means to you," he said, looking down at their clasped hands. "And this way you could keep Camellia Lane, without sacrificing your pride or having to do anything ignoble."

"Like tracking down Sterling," Charlotte said, guessing at what was coming next.

Brett sighed, exasperated. "You already know that's iffy," he pointed out, his sensual mouth thinning once again. When Charlotte said nothing, he slid a hand beneath her chin and guided her face up to his. "Isn't it?" he asked.

"You know it is." She scowled back at him.

Both of them tensed. Charlotte hated it when they disagreed, and even more when he made her examine her own motives, yet she could not make herself move out of his arms.

"So what do you say?" Brett continued persuasively, stroking his fingers through her hair. "Do we have a deal?"

Charlotte studied him from beneath her lashes. He seemed to be waiting for her answer with bated breath. This proposal was very important to Brett. More important than it should have been, she thought. The reporter and the woman in her both wanted to know why. And until she did, she wasn't agreeing to anything.

"Thanks, but I'd still prefer to do this on my own," she said firmly. Hand to his chest, she stepped away from him. There was no use complicating her relationship with Brett unnecessarily, she thought. It would be enough if they could make something of the love they were feeling, rather than muck it up by adding a business element, too.

Brett looked aggravated by her decision. He shoved both hands through the windswept layers of his coffee-colored hair. "At least think about it for a few days, Charlotte," he urged impatiently.

"Why?" Charlotte knew when she was being pressured, and she didn't like it. Her chin tilted up defiantly as she tested him once again. "I won't change my mind."

Again, Brett frowned. Charlotte had the sensation there was so much more he wanted to say to her. But the moment passed and he stubbornly kept his silence.

Disturbed by the turn their conversation—and their whole relationship—had just taken, Charlotte hunted around for her car keys, finally finding them beneath the dictionary.

"Why are you being so hardheaded about this?" he asked.

Hearing the thread of hurt in his voice gave Charlotte pause. Drawing a deep breath, she forced herself to meet his eyes. "Because I don't want what happened to Jared and I to happen to you and me," she said softly.

Brett's blue eyes held a tinge of male satisfaction. "I heard you turned down his loan."

Charlotte nodded. Just recalling her last meeting with Jared made her miserable. She looked down at the toe of her shoe. "What's really sad is that this loan business probably ruined our friendship. I don't think I'll ever look at him in the same way again, and I imagine the same is true for him."

Wordlessly, Brett gathered her in his arms, intuitively giving her the comfort she needed. "If that's the case, then your friendship wasn't all that great to begin with, Charlotte," he said, stroking her hair.

Although it hurt her pride to admit it, Charlotte knew Brett was right. She laid her head against his shoulder and leaned against him, loving his warmth and his strength. "Somewhere along the way Jared changed," she said.

"Happens to all of us," Brett pointed out agreeably.

Hooking his thumbs beneath her chin, he tilted her face up to his. He kissed her gently, his tongue mating with hers. Needing the closeness as much as she needed air to breathe, Charlotte turned all the way into his arms and wreathed hers about his neck.

Brett released a ragged breath as his fingertips flattened on her spine, bringing her as near as their clothes would allow. His fingers threaded through her hair. Lower still, she could feel the sizzling need in him and the answering need in her.

His lips traced the shell of her ear, the soft slope of her neck, leaving her feeling deliciously distraught. His blue eyes dark with passion, he brought her mouth back to his and kissed her with tantalizing slowness. "Come back to the cottage with me," he whispered urgently as his hands moved restlessly over her, starting fires everywhere they touched.

Charlotte would've liked nothing better than to spend the rest of the afternoon and the entire evening in Brett's arms. But she knew from experience that once she got into bed with him, she would not want to get out again.

She shook her head reluctantly, the problems she was facing making her feel as if she had the weight of the world on her shoulders. "I can't," she whispered, feeling as if her heart were going to break if she didn't find time to be with Brett again. "At least, not right now."

Brett tensed, as he always did when her actions went contrary to his wishes. Hands cupping her shoulders, he drew back so he could see her face. "Why not?"

Charlotte forced her eyes to his, not sure how he was going to take the news. "I've got to follow up a new lead on the Sterling story."

For once, Brett offered no lectures on what she was attempting. Instead, he thought a minute about what she'd said, then shrugged in mute acceptance of her activities. "Let me go with you, then," he said.

Again, Charlotte had the nagging sensation something here was not quite right. Maybe because Brett had gone so suddenly from outright disapproval to supportiveness.

Aware he was still cataloging her every move, Charlotte locked her desk and picked up her purse. "I usually work alone."

Brett folded his arms in front of him. His muscular legs formed a flexed arrow to the floor. "I won't get in your way."

Charlotte met his compelling gaze and knew she wanted to be with him, too. But first she was setting the ground rules. "Okay, but no more chastising me about what I'm doing regarding Sterling," she said.

"Believe me," Brett said on a surprisingly heartfelt sigh, as he slid a possessive arm around her waist and escorted her out of the library, "I don't want Sterling's name to come up, either."

BRETT AT HER SIDE, Charlotte walked into the Jackson, Mississippi, post office where Sterling's box was. Walking up to the service counter, she explained her business. "I understand you have a post-office box here registered under S. E. Sterling. It's very important I locate Mr. Sterling as soon as possible, so I'd like an address or phone number for him, please, if you have it."

The clerk, a freckle-faced girl in her early twenties, frowned. "I'm sorry, ma'am. That information is confidential."

Already dismissing Charlotte, the pretty clerk looked at Brett and smiled. "Was there a problem with your post-office box today, sir? Is your key not working?"

Charlotte turned and gave Brett a sharp look. He shrugged at her as if to say he didn't know what was going on, either. Brett looked at the clerk. "There's no problem," he said.

"You're sure now?" the clerk insisted helpfully, looking as if she recognized Brett, and more, had a faint crush on him. "Because I'd be glad to help you with anything you need—just say the word."

Charlotte looked at Brett. "*Do* you have a post-office box here?" she asked.

"No," Brett said emphatically.

"Then where do you get your mail?" Charlotte persisted, determined to get to the bottom of this. "There's none being sent to the house."

Brett gave Charlotte an irritated glance, letting her know he resented her third degree. "My brother is collecting my mail and sending it to me," Brett answered. "Okay?"

Charlotte turned back to the pretty young clerk. "But just now...you thought you recognized my friend here, right?"

Brett looked at the clerk, his eyes locked on hers. "Maybe you saw me walking around town," he suggested to the postal clerk, almost too casually. "I stayed at a hotel not far from here a few weeks ago, while I was doing some research on cotton-growing techniques."

The young clerk held Brett's look for a breathless moment. Finally, she frowned and shook her head. "I'm sorry," she murmured to him apologetically. "I thought I recognized you from being in here before. Obviously, I was mistaken."

Or was she? Charlotte wondered. Brett's effect on women was legendary. Furthermore, he was too handsome to be overlooked, even in a crowd. Charlotte knew she would never confuse him with someone else. So if this freckle-faced young clerk thought she recognized him, she probably *had* seen him before.

Charlotte had initially suspected Brett might be a rival reporter. She had put those thoughts aside as she concentrated on saving Camellia Lane, but now they had surfaced again, and she wasn't sure she could be so quick to dismiss them this time.

What if he was a journalist and also one step ahead of her? Was he trying to stop her from investigating Sterling so that he could get the true story first?

"Anything else?" the clerk asked sweetly, looking more at Brett than Charlotte.

Charlotte snapped to attention. She had driven an hour to get here, and she wasn't about to leave until she had uncovered something of note. "Can you at least tell me if Sterling has been in here recently to collect the mail from his box?" Charlotte asked impatiently.

"I don't know. Giving out that information seems like a violation of the rules, too." The girl frowned uncertainly at Charlotte.

"Ah, what can it hurt?" Brett interjected casually as he leaned on the counter companionably and continued to smile at the clerk. To Charlotte's irritation the girl capitulated within seconds under the megawatt charm of Brett's infectious smile.

"All right," she whispered. "I'll see what I can discover and be right back."

"Thanks," Charlotte said to Brett as soon as the clerk had headed off to the back.

"Don't mention it. Besides, I'm anxious to see what she is going to uncover, too," he murmured softly.

The girl came back quickly. "There's a lot here waiting to be picked up, so it looks like Sterling hasn't been in in a while." She shot an apologetic glance at Brett before either Charlotte or he could form another question. "And that really is absolutely all I can tell you," she said.

Chapter Twelve

Charlotte's answering machine was blinking when she and Brett walked in the door to Camellia Lane. Although she had been doing her best to hide it, he seemed to know what suspicions had been on her mind the last hour. "That's probably a business call," she murmured.

Brett looked at her pointedly. "Do you want me to leave?"

His question seemed a test. Charlotte could see that he wanted her to trust him enough to take the call in his presence. Heaven knew she wanted to trust him. She wanted to believe she had not fallen in love with the wrong man. What quicker way to find out, Charlotte mused, as she stared at the blinking light, than to put him to the test, too?

"No, stay," Charlotte said impulsively. Already reaching for the phone, she slipped out of her shoes and sat down behind her desk. "Make yourself comfortable. I'm sure this will just take a few minutes."

While Brett prowled the room, Charlotte listened to the cryptic message from the private investigator. To her surprise, he had left the number of a Memphis hotel. Things must be moving much more quickly for him now, she thought as she began to punch in the appropriate numbers.

Or maybe all the legwork the detective had done the previous week was finally beginning to pay off; she'd had things happen for her that way, too. Her hopes soared as she dialed the number and was connected to his room.

"Good news!" the investigator told Charlotte while Brett continued to watch her surreptitiously from a distance. "I was finally able to get some information on the condo in Memphis. Capt. Iam Hook is subletting the condo there from a Mr. P. R. Pan. Pan allegedly purchased the condo from a Ms. W. Darling, who had bought it from Sterling's attorney, who purchased it about a year ago and then leased it back to a holding company within another holding company."

Charlotte had been writing as the investigator talked. She glanced down at what she had written and sighed. "Damn him," she muttered.

With a frown, Brett crossed to Charlotte's side.

"The names look fishy to you, too?" the investigator said.

"Iam Hook. P. R. Pan. W. Darling." Charlotte scowled as she read. "They're all names from Peter Pan."

"Or, in other words, we only wish we had found Stephen Sterling." The detective sighed on the other end of the line.

Charlotte noted Brett's impassive expression.

"What do you want me to do?" he asked Charlotte, as she continued to watch Brett. "I still have that address in New Mexico to check out," he continued.

"That property is probably owned by Mr. Dunn, too." Charlotte scowled as she jumped to her feet. So far the attorney hadn't proved to be a great deal of help, she thought, pacing the room restlessly in her stocking feet.

"So I should just forget it?" the investigator asked.

Charlotte paused. Her eyes locked with Brett's. He seemed to be waiting for her decision, too.

With effort, she glanced away from the raw yearning in his eyes and turned back to the dilemma at hand. Time was running out. She had less than three days left now to find Sterling. But she was getting close. She could sense it. Excitement began to build inside her. "There really was a condo in Memphis, right?" she ascertained thoughtfully.

"Correct," the investigator said as Brett turned to look out the window.

"So maybe Dunn's secretary was telling the truth. Maybe Sterling has read his galleys there. Maybe he has always stayed in the one in Sante Fe. Maybe he's even there now," Charlotte said excitedly.

"It's possible," the investigator theorized.

"And if he's not," Charlotte continued, "you might be able to get a description from a neighbor or something. I'd go myself, but I've got pressing business here." Namely, checking out Brett.

The detective paused. "You still want me to check the Santa Fe place out, then?"

"Yes," Charlotte said. It was a risk. She faced losing money, yet what other choice did she have?

"All right, I'll get back to you as soon as I can," the investigator said before hanging up. Charlotte replaced the receiver just as Brett turned back around to face her.

He had his hands shoved in the pockets of his jeans. "Why don't you forget all that and just let me help you?" he said.

Charlotte sighed. "We've been over this."

"I know you have your doubts. But I think our relationship could withstand the rigors of a business association. We could handle it any way you wanted, Charlotte. Draw up a contract—"

"Maybe we could handle it," she said. "But only as a last resort."

"Meaning?"

"I can't give up yet."

Brett's frustration was evident. "Why not?" he rasped impatiently.

"Because I've got to try and do it on my own first. And besides—" Charlotte folded her arms in front her "—I don't want to take *all* your money, Brett."

"It wouldn't *be* all my—" He stopped abruptly, cutting off what he'd been about to say.

"More poker earnings?" Charlotte quipped.

Brett looked at her.

And suddenly all the cryptic clues and half-finished sentences made sense and Charlotte knew. "You come from money, don't you?" she said.

Brett regarded her with a maddening innocence. "What makes you think that?"

Charlotte advanced on him determinedly. "Your lack of interest in it. Poor, starving students tend to count every penny. You don't. Furthermore, that Yankee costume you wore the night of the ball cost a pretty penny and was obviously made just for you. I, on the other hand, was so broke after paying for the party that I had to have my own gown made out of my bedroom curtains."

Brett grinned. Wrapping his arm about her waist, he reeled her in to his side. "The curtains looked better on you than any window."

"Don't change the subject." Charlotte wedged her arm between them. "And don't try and distract me with any more kisses, because it's not going to work."

Brett grinned and pulled her all the way into his arms. Locking both arms about her waist, he tugged her close, until they were pressed together from the waist down. "Sure about that?" he asked wickedly.

Not about to be dissuaded from her quest, Charlotte tossed her head. "I mean it, Brett. Who are you—really?"

"I told you." Spreading his hands out, he gently caressed her back. "I'm Brett Forrest, regular guy. Bookworm. Agricultural scholar."

"And what else?" Charlotte taunted softly.

"Now who's being hopelessly nosy?" he teased as he bent to kiss her neck.

"I am. And I want to know, Brett, where are you really from? What haven't you told me? What are you still holding back from me?"

Brett hesitated. "You're right to think I haven't told you everything. And we need to know each other better, Charlotte. And I will tell you everything you want to know, I promise."

"When?" she bit out.

"Well, I'm not sure we can cover everything in one day, but we can start tonight," Brett promised silkily, his low, sexy voice doing marvelous things to her insides. "Down at the cottage."

Charlotte blew out an exasperated breath. "You keep trying to get me down there," she accused.

He gave her a maddening grin. "You know you want to go, too."

Charlotte couldn't deny that, so she held tight to her suspicions and moved on. "Why can't we just talk now?" she protested, wanting more than anything for him to set her mind at ease.

"Because," Brett retorted reasonably, "you still have to finish your speculative article on Sterling for the magazine, and I have some errands to do, too."

Cursing herself for her curiosity and possessiveness, Charlotte allowed herself to ask, anyway. "What kind of errands?"

"Just the usual." Brett shrugged his broad shoulders carelessly. "Go to the bank. Buy groceries." He glanced at his watch, noting it was after four, then gave her a slow, leisurely smile that made her heart rate pick up with a jolt. "What do you say we meet back at the cottage around seven-thirty?"

Charlotte paused. Experience had taught her she would never get her way entirely when it came to any romance-laden battle with Brett. It was enough, she decided finally, that he was finally beginning to open up to her—and more, willing to meet her halfway. It wasn't a victory, exactly, but it was a start. And who knew where they'd go from there?

IT WAS A BEAUTIFUL NIGHT, quiet and warm, with just a hint of spring breeze and a full galaxy of stars overhead as Charlotte walked through the formal gardens, toward the caretaker's cottage.

Happily anticipating the evening ahead of them, Charlotte paused to gather a whimsical collection of flowers for a centerpiece.

Brett hadn't asked her to bring anything when he invited her for a picnic supper, but she didn't want to show up empty-handed. So with a gardener's practiced touch, she began cutting yellow alyssum, golden marigolds and other vibrant flowers. She continued filling her white wicker flower basket, until it was nearly full, then added sprigs of greenery.

Charlotte sighed. Pausing, she broke off a blossom and smelled its delicate fragrance and then slipped it into her hair. She had taken a lot of care in getting ready for this evening. And that puzzled her. Usually, she didn't take such risks. Especially when the levelheaded reporter in her knew Brett could easily have spent the rest of the afternoon trying to steal her story after the clues she'd deliberately let him see and overhear that very morning.

She didn't want to believe that he had betrayed her, of course. Her heart said she could trust him.

The cynical half of Charlotte was less sure. She kept wondering if she was falling into the same trap her father had with J. H. McMillan. Was she trusting the wrong person, just because he promised her everything she had always wanted and needed? Or did she trust Brett because she loved him and he loved her? Charlotte wondered as she started back down the path to Brett's cottage.

If only her life were simpler. If only she could tell Brett what was in her heart, that whenever he kissed her or held her in his arms, everything felt right. Then the evening would be perfect.

A ROMANTIC NIGHT under the stars was what Charlott
needed, Brett thought as he spread thick quilts on the gras
behind the cottage. He brought out the rest of the essentia
gear he had collected just for tonight—a picnic basket fille
with goodies, several outdoor candles, a bottle of chille
white wine and two long-stemmed glasses, and, of course
his portable stereo and a stack of CDs.

He had just switched on Tchaikovsky's Symphony No. 5
when he glanced up and saw Charlotte moving gracefull
through the formal gardens, toward him. Dressed in
floaty, feminine, long-sleeved dress, the moonlight shinin
on her hair, she looked like an angel.

He wondered what she would say if she knew all he ha
secretly done to help her this afternoon. Would she be happ
he had come to her rescue? Or would she be furious at th
way he had intervened, and at the liberties he had taken?

Brett wanted to be her knight in shining armor. He wante
Charlotte to be his queen. But he also wanted her to com
to some very important realizations on her own first. So h
would play the waiting game another day, give events tim
to unfold and Charlotte time to change her course. He wa
sure she would, when she understood her future happines
was not tied to Camellia Lane so much as to the dictates o
her heart, and his.

Charlotte came to the end of the path. Her eyes locke
with his, she crossed the yard to his side. Brett brushed hi
lips across her temple in lieu of hello, then looked down a
the basket in her hands with a smile. "What's all this?"

She gave a playful curtsy. "I brought you flowers, kin
sir." She rose slowly, her soft mouth curving ruefully as sh
confessed, "But I'm afraid I forgot to bring a vase."

"No problem. I'm sure we'll find something that'll do
Come on inside."

Charlotte pointed to the pitcher by the sink. "Is tha
okay?"

"Perfect." Brett filled it halfway with water, then watche
as Charlotte arranged the flowers into a stunning bouque

Admiring the graceful motions of her fingers and the artistry of her arrangement, he said, "You're very good at this."

Finished with her task, Charlotte smiled up at him happily. "I used to do it all the time when I was a kid. My mother loved having fresh flowers all over the house."

Possessive feelings flowing through him, he placed a hand to her spine. Picking up the pitcher of flowers, he guided her toward the door. "Do you miss it?"

Charlotte reached the door first and held it open for them. "To tell you the truth, I'd forgotten what it was like to just step outside your door and pick a bouquet until tonight."

Brett's glance roved the softness of her lips and the vulnerability in her eyes, and he knew they had crossed yet another bridge to where they were going. "Do you like living in New York?" he asked, wondering all the while what he would say if she told him the city was the only place on earth for her.

Charlotte shrugged a slender shoulder and fell into step beside him, walking so close to him that the hem of her skirt swished against his jeans.

"I like writing for *Personalities* magazine." Charlotte kicked off her shoes and sank to the quilt. With a graceful gesture of her hand, she spread her skirt in a ladylike circle around her. "The magazine is located in New York."

Brett heard the hesitation in her voice and grinned. "Why do I get the feeling you're no longer as enthralled with New York as you once were?" he drawled.

Charlotte held the glasses while he opened the wine. "Because I miss my sisters, and I feel guilty about not doing my share to take care of Camellia Lane. Also, it's occurred to me recently that our overall financial situation would be a lot easier if I lived here full-time."

Brett closed his hand around Charlotte's, steadying the glass while he poured. "Could you live here now?" he asked, wishing with all his heart that were so.

Again, Charlotte shrugged. "I couldn't have ten, five o
even two years ago. But now—" she bit her lip though
fully "—I don't know. Maybe I could, if I were willing t
travel a lot, or get a job with another magazine that was lo
cated here in the South. I've even thought about switchin
to newspaper reporting, since so much of what I do is in
vestigative-type work."

She looked like an angel in that silky dress, and Bret
longed to press his lips to the soft exposed skin above th
sweetheart neckline of her dress. Instead, he brought ou
plates of fruit and cheese and fresh-baked bread.

"I can see you writing for a newspaper," he said, paus
ing long enough to dip one of the strawberries in powdere
sugar before putting it to her lips. "What I'm not so sur
about is you living here permanently in such a small town—
at least, as long as you're single." He looked into her eyes
"Or am I wrong?"

"You're right." Charlotte smiled as she nibbled del
cately on a green grape. "I don't want to live here an ol
maid. Part of the reason I left was because I knew there wa
no one here I wanted to marry. I figured in a place as big a
New York I'd be bound to meet the man of my dreams, an
I could nail down a career, too."

"But it hasn't worked that way?" Brett asked gently
Moving around behind her, he formed a cradle with h
thighs so she could sit comfortably back against his chest.

"No," Charlotte admitted reluctantly. Turning her hea
sideways, she looked up cockily, her eyes meshing with h
once again. "It hasn't."

Brett grinned. He wrapped a curl of her hair around h
fingertip and bent to kiss the exposed slope of her nec
"Given up hope?" he teased.

"No. Not at all," she admitted.

Leaning back on him, Charlotte fed him a square o
cheese on a soft piece of bread. Brett returned the favo
enjoying the quiet sensuality of the ritual.

"What about you?" Charlotte asked. "Have you ever been married?"

"No," he admitted on a ragged sigh. "But I would be, if I'd only met the right person prior to now."

Apparently deciding she'd had enough to eat, Charlotte put her own plate aside and stretched out on the blanket. Lying on her side, her head propped on her hand, she surveyed him teasingly. "Oh, I don't know about that, Brett. Somehow, I can't see you settling down into dull, married life," she murmured, contemplatively sipping her wine.

He stretched out the length of the blanket, too. Facing her, only his plate and her wineglass between them, he asked, "Why not?"

"Because you like excitement too much." Charlotte broke off a green grape and popped it into his mouth.

It was all he could do not to groan at the touch of her soft hands on his mouth. But knowing he had promised he would answer her questions, he made a stab at concentrating on the conversation. The loving, he assured himself boldly, would come later. "Marriage could be exciting," Brett said. Damned exciting, if his wife was Charlotte.

Charlotte grinned. Holding her glass carefully to her lips, she took another careful sip of wine. "It probably would be with you," she said.

Finishing her wine, she put her glass aside, and then leaned toward him. Brett took her chin in his hand and indulged in a slow, leisurely kiss. Just as slowly, they drew apart.

Charlotte's mood growing more languorous, she slipped into his arms. They lay quietly, their bodies intertwined. Her head resting against him, she traced a lazy pattern on his chest. "What about you? How did you end up with such an abiding interest in dirt farming? Did you grow up in an agricultural community or something?"

Brett turned his face into her hair, breathing in the soft, fragrant scent. "No. My father is a career diplomat. My family lived all over the world when I was growing up."

Still wrapped in the curve of his arm, Charlotte turned until she could see the stars and the moon overhead. "What was that like?" she asked softly.

Brett shrugged. He could stay here like this forever and never want to move again. "Like anything else, the experience contained both good aspects and bad."

"And the good was?" Charlotte prodded. Lifting the back of his hand to her mouth, she rubbed it against her lips.

His skin tingling, the heat within him building as slowly and surely as her questions, Brett said, "The good part of my childhood was that I saw a lot of the world. It really opened up my mind and my heart, and now that I'm an adult I'm very appreciative of that."

"The bad?"

Brett frowned as he recalled the tough times. "Because I was the son of an ambassador, my whole life was open to public scrutiny. I had to think carefully about everything I said and did, so I wouldn't inadvertently create some international incident just by being a typical mischievous kid."

Extricating herself from Brett's arms, Charlotte sat up. Retrieving their wineglasses, she paused to pour them each some more wine. She slanted him a humorously consoling smile. "Knowing the mischievous streak in you is a mile wide, it must have been really tough on you to live with those kinds of restrictions, especially during your teenage years."

"Yeah, it was." Brett propped himself up on his elbow and accepted the glass of wine she gave him. "I didn't like always being on public display, but I really loved and respected what my father was trying to do in the course of his work. And I didn't want to do anything to him or his career, so I was very serious about living up to the image of the perfect all-American family."

"Is that why you identify so closely with Sterling—because you know firsthand what the pressure of public life is like... how people get locked into roles?"

Brett nodded solemnly, glad she was seeing and understanding so much.

"What about the rest of your family?" Charlotte asked. "Do they feel the same way as you do about public life? And are you still close to them, now that you're older and definitely out of the limelight?"

"One question at a time, Miss Charlotte," Brett rebuked with a teasing grin. "No, my family does not share my aversion to public life," he said solemnly, "but they do understand mine. And yes, I am close to them."

"You have siblings, then?"

Brett nodded. "Five brothers, no sisters."

Charlotte grinned and rolled her eyes. "All those boys in one household. No wonder you don't understand women," she teased.

Brett chucked her under the chin. "Oh, I think I understand *you* well enough, Miss Charlotte."

She fed him another grape. "So where is your family living now?" she asked quietly.

"My brothers are scattered across the states. My father is the U.S. Ambassador to Switzerland at the moment."

"Does your family have a home base here in the States?" she asked.

Brett couldn't shake the feeling her question was some kind of a test. "There's a house in Richmond, Virginia. My brother and his wife live there now. It's not much bigger than this cottage. My parents lived there as newlyweds."

"But for you it has no significance," Charlotte ascertained, her eyes locked on his.

Brett shrugged. "The only times I've been there, it's been for brief vacations. Certainly it's nothing at all like what you and your sisters have here at Camellia Lane."

"What about now?" Charlotte asked quietly, tracing the crease on his khaki slacks with her fingertip. "Do you have a permanent place?"

"I taught at a university for several years, right after I finished my master's, and while I was there I did rent a place. Since I left, I've lived in temporary homes or hotels, wherever I was doing research at the time. A few months here, a few months there.''

Charlotte shook her head. Sighing, she dropped her hand from his knee. ''Just moving to an apartment in New York was traumatic for me. I don't think I could ever live the way you have.''

Brett admitted the last couple years he had felt increasingly like something vital was missing from his life. But it was a partner and soul mate he had been missing.

He caressed the back of Charlotte's hand gently, then placed her hand back on his knee. ''I don't think the place is nearly as important as the person you are spending time with, wherever you are.''

Charlotte twined her fingers intimately with his, even as she continued to rub his knee. ''I see your point. But at the same time—'' she drew a shaky breath, lifting her eyes to his ''—I have lived in a place that's held a lot of meaning for me, and I don't know what I'll do if I lose Camellia Lane.'' Looking like she might burst into tears at any minute, she bit down on her lower lip until it stopped trembling. ''I don't know if I could handle not having a home to return to.''

Brett understood why Charlotte loved Camellia Lane, and on that score his heart went out to her. He had only been here a week and he loved it, too. What worried him was the lengths she seemed willing to go to preserve the status quo. She was still setting a dangerous precedent here. He didn't want to see her do anything she'd later regret.

''I admit I never got particularly attached to any one place we lived,'' Brett said. He paused to kiss her chastely. ''The truth was, we were never there very long, and we were always in official quarters of some sort. Home for me was wherever my family lived at the time, and it could be that way for you, too, Charlotte.''

''I don't know, Brett.'' Charlotte moved so she was sitting in his lap and lay her head on his shoulder. ''What you're saying sounds so reasonable. But at the same time this old place is so much a part of me...it has so many memories..." Charlotte's voice caught. Suddenly she couldn't go on.

Brett couldn't bear to see her hurting. Wordlessly, he brought her even closer. He touched the side of her face with the warmth of his palm, wiping away the traces of her tears, and scored his thumb across her lips, tracing the delicate shape. "I promise you, Charlotte, everything is going to work out for you," he said softly.

She tipped her head up. "How do you know?"

"I just do."

Ever so gently, he laid her back on the blanket and brought his mouth down to hers. She drew a ragged breath as he merged their lips in one long, steamy kiss, and Brett felt his own control slip just a bit. Knowing there was no need to rush, he steadied his kiss and concentrated solely on her pleasure. He waited until she too was treating each kiss as a beginning and ending in itself. He waited until she had melted against him in abject surrender, cradling him with her warmth and her softness, then ever so slowly, ever so reluctantly, he stopped and drew her to her feet.

Wordlessly, he swung her up into his arms, carried her into the house and straight into his bedroom. He lowered her gently, so she was standing upright. Anchoring her against him with an arm around her waist, he kissed her again, arousing her with slow, certain strokes. Until he was certain with every fiber of his being that she was his, and his alone.

Brett had never imagined Charlotte could surrender this way, or kiss him so sweetly. And for a second, he tensed as he remembered the deception still between them. Then he pushed his guilt away as he slowly, lovingly began to unbutton her dress. He would stick to his plan and tell her everything tomorrow evening, he decided. Tonight was for loving her, and for Charlotte...realizing she loved him back.

One arm hooked around her waist, Brett unbuttoned the tiny row of buttons down the front of her dress, then pushed it off her shoulders, letting it fall to her waist. Her breasts were straining against the thin barrier of white silk teddy, and Brett groaned softly.

Charlotte sighed tremulously, clinging to him even as the dress fell way completely and he unsnapped the teddy. Dizzy with desire, she gripped his shoulders as his mouth continued to tease and torment her breasts. Lower still, he claimed her softness with his hands, exploring her gently, until she was dewy and yielding and hungry for his touch.

She unbuckled his belt and lowered his zipper, helped remove his trousers and take off his shirt. Moving her hands along the hot, hard length of him, she leaned forward to touch her lips to his in a kiss that made her insides wild. Charlotte could feel the pulsing of his desire, and she gloried in his unabashed demonstration of need.

Feeling primitive and wholly desperate, Charlotte drew him wordlessly down to the bed. She wanted him, more than she ever would have dreamed.

He moved over her, his body hard and masculine. She caught her breath, welcoming his weight and his warmth. Knowing she was caught up in something too powerful and wonderful to fight, she arched against him wantonly. The time for caution was past. He wanted all of her; all of her was what she would give.

Threading his hands through her hair, Brett tilted her head to his and claimed her in a slow, savage kiss. Lifting her hips, he clasped her possessively to him and sheathed himself inside her, driving unbelievably deeper with each slow, deliberate thrust, continuing until they were as close as they could be.

Afterward, they clung together, tangled in his sheets. Unwilling to move so much as an inch, Charlotte shut her eyes and drank in the scent and feel and texture of him as he continued to hold her close.

This was no simple love affair, she thought on a ragged sigh. They were teetering on the edge of a deeper involvement. Charlotte could feel it, in the way Brett had comforted her and made love to her, and she knew from the look in his eyes that Brett felt it, too.

Charlotte rose to kiss the nape of his neck, the shell of his ear. "I love you," she whispered, risking everything, wanting it all.

Brett clasped her to him and kissed her into silence. He wanted a lifetime with her, but for tonight he would take each moment as it came. His voice husky, he said, "I love you, too."

Chapter Thirteen

The heiress knew immediately, when she saw his face, that Matt Justice had learned of her betrayal. In a panic, she picked up the long skirt of her evening gown and dashed through the doors of the country club. Her only avenue of escape was the moonlit polo field.

Too late—Matt Justice was already gaining.

Heard pounding, she tried to elude him. But he was too quick. He caught her around the waist and swept her into his arms. "You can't run from me," Matt Justice said. "We are meant to be together...."

"Charlotte? How are you coming on your Stephen Sterling article?"

"It's coming along okay," Charlotte told her editor. She sighed her frustration. "I still wish I knew more." She also wished she hadn't been so distracted the whole time she'd been working on this project.

"When can I expect to see something?" the editor asked.

"I'm not sure," Charlotte said. "I'm still working on pulling it all together." *Still trying to feel like I've done a good job here, even though, for the first time, I didn't meet the goal I set for myself.*

"Well, let me know when to expect it, will you?" her editor persisted.

"I will." Charlotte said goodbye and hung up the phone.

No sooner had she replaced the receiver in the cradle than it rang again. "This must be my morning for calls," she grumbled.

"Miss Langston? Confidential Investigations here. I've got some data on the Sante Fe property."

Charlotte reached for her paper and pen, her heart pounding. Maybe all wasn't lost yet. Maybe she could still meet her goal. "Go ahead."

"The property is currently occupied by Mr. S. Bull, who sublet it from a G. Custer, who leased it from Franklin Dunn, Jr."

"Of course," Charlotte said sarcastically, not really surprised. She sighed. She had hocked her mother's jade necklace and earrings to find this out.

"Do you want me to keep looking?" the investigator asked.

Charlotte rubbed her temples. "No. Not at this moment."

"Then I'll be sending you a bill?"

"Please," Charlotte said.

Wearily, she hung up the phone again. She glanced down at her notes, and in a fit of temper, threw her legal pad across the room. A string of unladylike words followed.

The next thing she knew, an arm waving a white hanky was extending past the doorframe. "Is it safe to come in or should I continue to duck for cover?" Brett drawled.

Blushing, Charlotte stood and started for her notebook. As she had feared, Brett got to it first. "'S. Bull. G. Custer,'" he read aloud. He gave her a comically confused look that she did not appreciate at all. "You doing some research on Custer's last stand or something?"

"I only wish," Charlotte grumbled as she snatched her notepad from him.

Brett quirked an interested brow in response. Charlotte noticed he had showered and shaved with extraordinary care before coming up to the main house, although he was dressed in the usual sweatshirt, jeans and sneakers.

He strode close enough that she could smell the aftershave clinging to his jaw and the minty freshness of his breath. Her senses swam at his nearness. "What's going on?" he said.

Charlotte scowled her displeasure at the recent turn of events, the depth of her anger sending color surging into her cheeks. "Stephen Sterling's attorney has had me on yet another wild-goose chase. That's what's wrong!"

Brett shoved a hand through the rumpled softness of his hair. "Well, at least the guy has a sense of humor," he allowed.

"Yeah, right," Charlotte said wearily. "Now I'm more in debt than ever and I have nothing to show for it. Nothing!" she fumed.

"Oh, I don't know about that," Brett drawled. The ardent light in his eyes made Charlotte warm all over.

"I think maybe this whole experience has made you a little wiser," Brett continued. "Certainly a little more considerate."

Charlotte glared at him. She couldn't recall a time when she had been more frustrated. She didn't need a lecture from him this morning on respecting others' privacy. "Who asked you?"

He merely grinned at her display of temper and said nothing for a moment as he checked out her gold hoop earrings. "So what's next," Brett asked. "I take it from the glum look on your face you have no more clues from Dunn's office to check out."

"No, I don't," she answered crisply. Charlotte touched the wide navy bow that held her dark, tousled curls at the nape of her neck, making sure it was in place. "Nor would I accept any at this point."

"Does this mean you're giving up the search for Stephen Sterling?" Brett asked.

"I have to. The article is due as we speak." Notepad in hand, Charlotte circled back around to her desk.

Brett watched as she tossed the pad facedown on her desk. "Are you sorry you didn't find him?" he asked. He sat on the edge of her desk, looking for a moment as if he were savoring their nearness as much as she was.

"Yes and no." Charlotte sat down in her chair. "I'm frustrated I didn't manage to track Sterling down, but I'm also kind of relieved, too. What if I had ruined an innocent person's private life? And don't look so happy." She propped her feet up on the edge of the desk. "You are not entirely responsible for my change of heart."

"But partly responsible?" Brett asked hopefully as he lightly traced the toe of her shoe.

He continued to regard her with an intensity that was both casual and unnerving. "How is the speculative article coming?" he asked softly.

Charlotte wished people would stop asking her that. She made a so-so gesture with her hand and elaborated. "It's frustrating for me to have to rely on conjecture, rather than fact. I'm not used to that and I admit I don't like it."

Brett picked up a paperweight that had once belonged to Charlotte's father and turned it end over end. "Is that the only reason you're upset?"

She shrugged, close enough to Brett now to admit in a troubled tone, "I feel like it's a defeat. Like everyone is going to read this and say Charlotte Langston, snoop extraordinaire, couldn't cut it and had to take the easy way out."

Brett put the paperweight down. He rested his hand on the inside of his thigh, next to his knee. "And that bothers you a lot, doesn't it?"

Charlotte nodded. "Almost as much as the increasing inevitability of losing Camellia Lane." Her jaw set and a burst of temper gave a new intensity to her low voice. "I don't like to fail. I don't like crying uncle."

Brett's eyes fell on the open pages of Sterling's novel. "How come you're highlighting the love scenes?" he teased with a curious look. "Studying up on technique?"

Charlotte pushed away from her desk. "Ha, ha." She cast him a look over her shoulder as she walked away. "Though maybe it wouldn't hurt *you* to give them a read."

He laughed, as she had figured he would. And then he persisted, as she had known he would.

"I'm serious, Charlotte." He pointed to the highlighted section of Sterling's novel. "What are you doing here?"

She paced over to the shelves before answering and looked at the thousands of books her father had collected during his years of scholarly research. The ones at eye level looked old, battered and dreadfully dull.

She whirled back to face Brett. "If you must know, I am looking for a passage that best demonstrates the appeal of Sterling's work."

Brett frowned, looking like he wanted to argue with her again. He put the novel aside. "And you think the love scenes are it?"

Charlotte shrugged. "I think Sterling knows his way around a bedroom," she allowed. *Just like Brett did.*

"Maybe he does." Brett stood and crossed the distance between them at a leisurely pace. "But trust me on this," he teased softly as he drew her into the warm cradle of his arms and lowered his mouth masterfully to hers. "The real thing is so much more exciting." He kissed her with a thoroughness that took her breath away, then lifted his head.

Charlotte knew her mind should be on other things, but there was something so warm and strong about him. So mischievous and interesting, despite the incredibly dull nature of his chosen work. She still couldn't make herself quite believe he actually was as wildly interested in dirt-farming methods of the Western world as he claimed to be.

But maybe that was because she couldn't quite see herself in love with a dirt-farming intellectual. She had always expected that if she gave her heart, it would be to someone with a much more interesting job. Although she had to admit, Brett was certainly exciting. He had a way of keeping her thoroughly distracted and on edge. And that was pre-

isely what she didn't need, considering the severity of the
problems she was facing.

"Brett, it's morning," Charlotte began, still tingling from
his kiss. "I've got a ton of work to do—"

"So do I," Brett said as he stroked her hair and held her
close. "And you know what, Charlotte?" he confessed
huskily. "I really don't give a damn about anything right
now—except you. How's that for being incredibly head over
heels in love with you?"

Pretty damn good, Charlotte thought as their eyes met.
And in that moment, as the two of them locked hearts and
souls once again, she knew what it felt like to be completely
swept away by passion...what the heroine in one of Stephen Sterling's novels must feel....

"Just go with your feelings, Charlotte," Brett whispered
as his fingers fastened firmly on her chin and tilted her face
up to his. He smiled down at her and finished in a lazy
drawl, "Because I sure as hell intend to go with mine."

Charlotte barely had time to gasp before their lips connected again. Sensations sizzled through her. His lips parted
hers, and he began a slow, voluptuous exploration of her
mouth, searching out every nook and cranny.

"Oh, Brett," she moaned as he kissed his way down her
throat and lingered at the delicate U of her collarbone before moving ever so resolutely south, to the soft slopes of her
breasts. What was he doing to her? she thought dizzily as he
began to unbutton her tapestry vest. She had never felt this
way before...never wanted anyone this much.

He drew away from her to look searchingly into her eyes.
Then they kissed languidly, powerfully. And as they did, he
nimbly unfastened the rest of her vest, the buttons on her
blouse. He divested her of both, then her silk trousers. She
kicked free of them and stood before him, clad only in a
triangle of translucent beige lace and matching demi-bra.

She met his eyes. The heat in them shattered her, sending
waves of passion sizzling through her. She knew they were
going to make love again. And this time, despite not know-

ing exactly what the future held for them, she harbored n misgivings. She and Brett might not have forever, but the had now.

Brett locked the door and lay her back on the sofa. Sh thrummed with anticipation, watching as he undressed.

He pulled off his sweatshirt, unbuttoned the fly of h jeans and stepped out of them. Clad only in a pair of sex black briefs, he joined her on the sofa.

"You wear the sexiest underwear," she teased.

"So do you," Brett said. He traced the crowning impri of her nipples through the sheer demi-bra. She raised up o her elbows. He reached around behind her, undid the clas and drew it off.

He draped her body with his. The warmth of his sk burned her. He was all solid male muscle and unyieldi strength and he knew just how to please her. His mouth le its scorching brand on her breasts, tracing her taut nippl until she arched beneath him and pulled him closer. His li moved lower still, across the flatness of her stomach to th suppleness of her thighs. He parted her legs and slid low still, seeking every secret, every silken feminine inch. Cha lotte could feel her control slipping away. The love she fe for Brett pouring through her, she surrendered herself him, heart and soul. He caught her to him, holding h close. When her trembling stopped, he moved swiftly up an over her. Their eyes locked. Charlotte luxuriated in the dee emotion, the longing, in his eyes. "Tell me you want me, he whispered huskily.

"I do."

He caressed the side of her face gently. "Tell me you hav no regrets."

Charlotte had had the whole night to think about it, weigh the pros and cons. "I don't."

He drew a shallow, uneven breath. "Tell me what yo want."

That was easy. Charlotte smiled. She encircled him wit her hand. "This."

His eyes darkened, he braced his arms on either side of er, then they were one. He moved slowly, seductively. The aves of passion inside her returned quickly and with surg-g force. She moaned and wrapped her arms around him.

They moved together, oblivious to everything but the es-alating crescendo of desire between them. Charlotte sur-endered herself as never before. They were meant to be ogether, she thought, as he fulfilled her every need, an-wered her every wish.

Brett reveled in the feel of Charlotte beneath him, all pli-nt giving woman. The lilac-scented softness of her skin, the ot passion in her kiss, the loving feel of her fevered hands aressing his skin, all combined to trap him in a maze of ild sensual pleasure that seemed to have no end.

Charlotte surprised and intrigued him all the time . . . she as the most damnably irritating and perplexing woman e'd ever met. Like the heroine out of the pages of a novel, he was everything he'd ever wanted, everything he'd ever reamed a woman could be. Full of fire and excitement, enderness and love, she drew him to the edge over and over gain. She was the embodiment of every romantic fantasy e'd ever had and he was going to be her hero.

Charlotte surged beneath him, her hands moving over im, working their magic. Brett clasped her to him. His ontrol snapped. Then the world fell away and they cata-ulted together into the cascading pleasure.

Afterward, he held her close and stroked her hair. He uzzled his nose into the soft ivory of her skin, feeling all the hile that he'd never get enough of her. "Sweet," he whis-ered affectionately. "You are so very beautiful."

"So are you," Charlotte murmured languorously. In fact, o one had ever challenged and provoked her the way Brett ad. No one had ever made her search her soul or reach out o another human being the way she had just reached out to im, giving everything she had and expecting and getting verything in return.

Brett grinned, the writer in him objecting to her choice words.

"And wonderful, too," Charlotte concurred as a feeling of contentment and well-being unlike anything she had ever experienced drifted over her. "I mean that, Brett. I've never felt as close to anyone as I feel to you right now."

"Me, too," he said gently.

They were silent for long minutes, enjoying the luxury of simply being in each other's arms as the warm spring breeze wafted in through the open windows and the morning sunlight poured into the room. Was this what it would be like if they were to stay together for more than just a few days, Charlotte wondered. And if that was the case, how would she ever be able to give Brett up? Was there a way to make their relationship work? If she could find a solution, she could have everything!

"Charlotte?" Brett turned her so they were lying face-to-face.

"Hmm?"

He wrapped an arm about her waist, holding her close. "The next few days are going to be hard."

Charlotte's heart contracted at the low note of worry in his voice. "I know."

"But I want you to remember one thing." He brushed a hand through her hair, then kissed her temple. "No matter what happens, I love you with all my heart and soul and always will."

"I know that," Charlotte whispered softly. The breath she hadn't been aware of holding escaped unevenly. "I love you, too."

His eyes darkening, Brett surveyed her, then took her face in hand and kissed her again. She found what she needed in the drawn-out caress, and she melted against him, savoring his warmth and his strength.

When they drew apart, both were smiling. "I have a question for you," he said finally.

Charlotte relaxed at the teasing lilt in his low voice. "When don't you have a question for me?" she teased, stretching out lazily beside him. "You're almost nosier than I am."

Brett grinned at her sassy tone. Then his eyes sobered. "Have you ever been serious about anyone, to the point of getting married, Charlotte?"

"No."

"Why not?"

She shrugged. "Maybe because no one has ever measured up. And because I've never been in love before." She hadn't planned it with Brett, either. It had just happened. But now that it had, she didn't quite know what to do about

"What do you mean, no one ever measured up?" Brett said. "In what sense?"

Charlotte rolled onto her back. She tugged a lacy white afghan down from the back of the sofa and drew it over them both. "I want lots of romance and excitement, a movie version of love, not real life, where the couple is more concerned with who does what chore than each other." She didn't want the dull, mundane existence most of the married people she knew had. She wanted what she and Brett had just shared this morning—only, she wanted it every day the rest of her life.

"I don't think anything is wrong with wanting lots of romance and excitement," Brett said. He rolled so he was on top of her.

"You don't?" Charlotte said.

"No, I don't," Brett murmured as he began to make slow, thorough love to her again. "Because I want it all, too, Charlotte. And," he said, kissing the tip of her nose affectionately as he sought to make all her wishes come true once again, "I want it all with you."

BRETT LEFT JUST BEFORE noon, so Charlotte could finish her article. Before he left, however, he promised to return

late that afternoon to cook dinner for her. The idea of re
turning to New York, of leaving him, was almost unthink
able. There was something so nice about writing in the mai
house, while he wrote in the caretaker's cottage, somethin
great about having him underfoot, alternatingly provokin
her and taking care of her.

She wasn't sure she would find it so easy to slip back int
her old life. But right now she had to get back to finishin
the article.

Charlotte did that in about thirty minutes. She picked u
a mailing envelope and slid the finished pages inside, alon
with a cover letter for her editor. Deciding to see if Bre
wanted to ride into Poplar Springs with her when she wei
to mail the article, Charlotte sauntered down to the car
taker's cottage. The door was open. Brett was nowher
around. Looking for a clue as to where he might have gon
she walked into his bedroom. On the student desk in th
corner was another laptop computer. It was newer and mo
expensive than the one he habitually left out in the livin
room. Why would he have two laptop computers? Cha
lotte wondered uneasily. And why had she never seen th
one before, even when she spent the night in the cottage wit
him? Obviously, he had been keeping this laptop hidde
from her. And that made her wonder what else he was hic
ing.

Deciding she had to check this out—or never know an
other moment's peace—Charlotte sat down at the desk. He
heart pounding, she opened the laptop and switched it on
The main directory had more files on dirt farming. Typic
Brett. The alternate directory held a novel, *The Steel Mag
nolia Conspiracy*.

Only it wasn't just any novel, it was a book penned b
Stephen Sterling, one that had never before been pub
lished.

This time, Matt Justice had ended up on an antebellu
plantation in the old South. It was a brisk change of pace fc
the famous author, who generally preferred European se

tings, and as romantic and fast-paced as all the rest of his novels. The book also appeared to be authentic . . . at least, Charlotte thought, the writing style appeared the same.

What was Brett Forrest doing with an unpublished Matt Justice novel on the hard drive of his computer? Charlotte wondered.

Without warning, a shadow fell over her. She looked up, her heart in her throat, and saw Brett framed in the doorway to his bedroom.

Hands braced on his waist, his expression was exceedingly grim. "Find what you were looking for?" he asked.

Chapter Fourteen

Charlotte stumbled slowly to her feet. "I'm sorry. shouldn't have been snooping. It's just that I had never see this computer before and I wondered what was on it."

Brett folded his arms in front of him and regarded Char lotte with a cold, searching gaze. It was clear her actions ha infuriated him. "I wish you hadn't done that," he sai grimly.

Charlotte did, too. Because what she had just seen ha turned her whole world upside down. And yet she wante to give him the benefit of the doubt, wanted him to prov she was wrong in what she was thinking about him. "Wh is there a brand-new Matt Justice novel on your computer Brett?" she asked cautiously, keeping her eyes locked on his Was he an editor from the publishing house? A friend o Sterling's? An attorney with Dunn's firm?

Brett didn't take his eyes off Charlotte. "I didn't want t have to tell you like this," he said.

"Tell me what?" Charlotte was filled with dread. Sh didn't want to believe Brett had lied to her, but it was ver clear he had, from the very first. And that knowledge dev astated her. Feeling as if her trust and faith in him was o the verge of being completely destroyed, Charlotte deduce slowly, "You know Stephen Sterling, don't you?"

Brett nodded.

"How?" she ground out.

"Because I created him," Brett announced smoothly. "I'm Stephen Sterling. I write the Matt Justice novels."

"Wait a minute," Charlotte said through her teeth. Her temper flared even more as she strode forward and met him, toe to toe. "All this time you knew I was looking for Stephen Sterling and you never once let on who you really were, even after you made love to me!"

"Right," Brett said stonily, looking relieved to finally have it all out in the open. "If you wanted me, I wanted you to want me, Brett Forrest, normal guy, not some big-time author. I keep my anonymity and write under a pen name because I want a private life, Charlotte. And if you can't understand that—"

She could and she couldn't. But there was no escaping the fact he had lied to her. "You totally misrepresented yourself to me," Charlotte said, feeling unbearably hurt and betrayed, "even while knowing all the worst about me." She had confided in him about innumerable things! She had made love with him! Opened her heart and soul to him!

"And I suppose everything you have done, including the way you invaded my privacy, is okay," Brett fumed, a faint tinge of color coming into his cheeks.

Charlotte knew she had crossed the line in her attempts to save Camellia Lane. She probably would have even apologized for it had he not done the same to her. But he had. Therefore, she shelved her own regrets and concentrated on his skulduggery. "I can't believe you showed up here at Camellia Lane in a bizarre twist of fate."

"You're right." Brett shouldered his way past her. He walked over, switched off his computer and shut the lid with a snap. "My being at Camellia Lane is no accident." Straightening, he glared at her again. "I was so annoyed by your sleuthing and the way you kept invading my privacy that I decided to turn the tables on you and investigate you."

"And your getting the caretaker's job here?"

"That was also no accident," Brett confided tightly as he leaned against the sturdy oak bureau. "I wanted to know who the termagant of an investigative reporter was who was making my life so miserable, so I purposefully befriended your sister Isabella and talked my way onto the property.''

Knowing she'd allowed herself to be duped made Charlotte sick inside. Hadn't she promised herself, when she had learned how she and her father had been swindled out of his fortune, that she would never be misled again? "And the Arlington, Virginia, post-office box where your books are sent?'' Charlotte bit out.

"That was real," Brett said. His mouth flattened into a thin line. "My brother used to pick up my books and then he forwarded them to me wherever I was staying at the time. While researching this book, I traveled quite a bit. Hence, the trail of post-office boxes."

"So you really did rent a post-office box in Jackson."

"Yes. And the clerk probably did recognize me, though I was only in there one or two times to pick up my mail."

Charlotte shook her head, marveling at how close she had been. If only she'd stayed on the investigative trail then, instead of letting herself get sidetracked by her efforts to save Camellia Lane, and her romance with him, she might not be in this mess. "And the Nashville and Sante Fe properties owned by Franklin Dunn," Charlotte said tightly. "Did you ever read galleys there?"

"No. Marcie, Franklin and I cooked that up together to throw you off the track."

The heat of her humiliation filled her cheeks. "You know I pawned my mother's jewelry to pay for that private investigator."

Brett shrugged and kept his eyes on hers. "No one told you to take that risk, Charlotte."

An ache rose in Charlotte's throat. She had never felt this hurt. Never. Nor had she ever had such an overwhelming desire to slap a man's face. It was all she could do to restrain herself.

"No one told me to get involved with you, either," she said bitterly. "I suppose I should commend you for that.

You did a great job distracting me, Brett." Hot, angry tears welled in her eyes as she recalled how she had given herself to him, never for a second having dreamed that Brett was the real Stephen Sterling. "Even that legendary lover, Matt Justice, would have been proud."

Brett shook his head, disagreeing with her once again. "Making love to you wasn't part of my plan," he said roughly.

"Wasn't it?" Charlotte said sarcastically.

"No, it wasn't." Brett shoved his hands through his hair and for a moment looked as torn up about everything that had happened as she felt. He swallowed hard. "I admit initially I wanted to drive you crazy with my ineptness as a caretaker, but as for the other—" he released an unsteady breath "—I didn't count on falling head over heels in love with you or going to bed with you. That just happened."

Charlotte shook her head at him. "Like you couldn't have stopped yourself from crawling into bed with the enemy," she muttered hoarsely. "Like you couldn't have just walked away from me at that point, sparing me some indignity."

"First of all, I didn't view making love to you as an indignity."

"Probably not. From your point of view, it must have been a real laugh riot." Charlotte glared at Brett humorlessly, aware he had made a fool of her like no one else ever had or could. "Here I was, searching high and low for you, and you were under my nose all along. What great comedy! The stuff books and movies are made of, right, *Stephen?*"

"It wasn't like that," he informed her grimly.

"No, you're right, it wasn't all fun and games," Charlotte argued bitterly. "There were times when you *were* mad as hell at me for snooping into Sterling's life that way."

"I had a right to be angry with you, Charlotte." Brett advanced on her stoically. "In fact, I have a right to be angry with you right now, for snooping around in my computer!"

"Well, not to worry." Charlotte turned her back on Brett. "It will even out in the long run," she predicted.

"What the hell is that supposed to mean?" he asked before she could so much as take a step away from him. Clamping both hands on her shoulders, he spun her around to face him.

Charlotte looked up at Brett sweetly. "You made a real fool of me. I intend to return the favor."

He dropped his hands from her shoulders abruptly. "How?"

Charlotte shrugged carelessly. She allowed her gaze to convey how little he meant to her. "I still have an article to write, and now that I know the truth, it ought to be a lot more fun this time around."

Brett's jaw clenched. "You can't do this, Charlotte."

"Like hell I can't!" she shot back, just as fiercely. "You may have deliberately deceived me and played me for a fool, but all that is over now, because I am onto you, loverboy! And how!" She whirled away from him and marched out of the bedroom.

"You're misconstruing our romance," Brett warned, following hard on her heels.

Charlotte tossed her head. Silky brown hair flew in every direction as she sent him a quelling sidelong glance. "You forget. I'm one of your fans. I've read every one of your books."

"So?" Brett watched Charlotte pause to pick up her purse and a sealed envelope addressed to *Personalities* magazine.

"So I know Matt Justice always chases and ultimately beds his female nemesis. Thanks to my near-fatal attraction to you, *you've* just lived out your fantasy. And what a sweet, beautiful fantasy it was. Even I have to admit our lovemaking was excessively pleasurable!"

Brett winced at the sarcasm in her low voice. He reached out to touch her gently. "Charlotte, you're overreacting here—"

Again, she pushed his hands away. "Wrong, Brett. I'm not overreacting. I'm finally back on track. And better yet, I still have twenty-four hours left in which to pay the bank and save Camellia Lane." She waved her purse at him for emphasis. "Twenty-four hours in which I can unmask you to the whole world."

"You don't want to do this," he warned, a muscle working convulsively in his cheek.

"Oh, don't I?" Enjoying the new pain on his face, Charlotte gave him a brittle smile.

"No, you don't," Brett said flatly.

"And why would I not want to do this?" Charlotte asked scornfully, her eyes spitting green fire at him.

Brett folded his arms in front of him implacably. "Because if you willfully betray me like this, our relationship will be over."

"I've got news for you, Brett," Charlotte said flatly, aware he had not only just sent her plummeting to the lowest point of her life, but he had broken her heart, too. Blinking back tears, she stormed, "Our relationship is already over. You have lied to me and played me for a fool for the very last time."

BRETT GAVE CHARLOTTE three hours to cool off. Then he went back to the main house to try and talk some sense into her. He found her in the library, lifting pages from her printer. He could only imagine what those pages contained. With her so furious with him, they had to be very damaging to his credibility.

"What's the matter, Brett?" she asked as she slid the newly inked pages into a mailing envelope. "Can't get enough of making me miserable?"

Brett folded his arms in front of him. He had known loving Charlotte was a risk, but he had never imagined he would be in such a mess. "I never meant to do that, and you know that, Charlotte," he said sternly, wondering if her legendary temper would ever subside.

"Right. You just wanted me to sacrifice my reputation as a scandal-hound extraordinaire and give up my search for Sterling. Silly me." Charlotte pressed a hand to her breasts with Southern-belle flair and gave him a simpering smile. "Had I only come to my senses sooner and realized I had already found Sterling, I could have wrapped things up much sooner. Not to worry, though, Brett. All's well that ends well. And thanks to your eleventh-hour attempt at honesty, I intend to see this fiasco ends great."

Although she tried to hide it, Brett could see the tears of outrage sparkling in her green eyes. He knew he had hurt her deeply, and for that he was very sorry. "You act as if this whole affair has been easy for me," he said gently. "It hasn't."

Charlotte stopped what she was doing and rested her hands on her hips. "You want me to work up sympathy for you now, is that it, when you are the one who lied and misrepresented yourself to me?"

Put that way, it did sound bad, he thought. "I want you to give us a chance to work this out and come to a reasonable solution." As he had planned all along.

Charlotte shook her head in abject misery and wiped the tears from her eyes before they slid down her cheeks. She went back to sealing her envelope. "As if I could ever trust you one whit after this!" she murmured.

Brett watched her roll the mailing invoice into the typewriter. "Charlotte, please—" Desperation edged his voice.

Her attention focused on her work, Charlotte began to type. "You're afraid I'm going to tell someone what I know, aren't you?"

Brett sat on the edge of her desk. "I'm afraid you're going to do something stupid that you will regret while you're still in a temper, yes."

Still typing rhythmically, Charlotte shook her head in silent regret. "What a joke our relationship has turned out to be," she muttered contemptuously.

"I never thought of it that way."

"Then what was it to you, Brett?" Charlotte ripped the finished invoice out of the typewriter with a flourish. "A bad novel? One of those B-movies, where everyone knows the truth but the guy's wife? Or, in our case, I guess I should say ex-lover. Emphasis on the *ex!*"

"You're wrong about that," Brett said quietly, watching as Charlotte stuffed the invoice inside an envelope.

When she was done, he clamped a hand on her shoulder and leaned in. "It isn't over between us, no matter how much you want right now to think it is. Furthermore, the fact I told you who I was, when I clearly didn't have to, should speak volumes about my intentions."

"You knew I had found the novel."

Brett shrugged, knowing he could have easily talked his way out of that sticky situation had he chosen to. "You had no proof I wrote what you saw," he said casually. "Hell, for all you knew it could have been a bad imitation, or a bootleg copy from Sterling's publishers. There were any number of possible explanations for that. I'm a novelist. I deal with fantasy daily, and I could easily have come up with any number of plausible explanations on the spot. And yet I still told you the truth," Brett persisted.

For a second, he thought he got through to her. Then her expression stiffened suspiciously once again. Slipping from beneath his hand, she moved to prowl the room. "Who else knows the truth?"

"Only my immediate family and my lawyer, Franklin Dunn, Jr. And even his office staff has never seen what I really look like because I always gray my hair and add a fake goatee, cane and horn-rimmed eyeglasses before I go into his office."

Charlotte whirled on him, her back to the overflowing floor-to-ceiling bookcases. "You still should have told me, before we made love."

"I was going to tell you," Brett insisted.

Pink color flowed into Charlotte's face. Her glance turned skeptical. "Oh, really. When?"

"Tonight."

"Sure you were." Charlotte strode back to her desk and picked up her purse and the just-sealed envelope from her desk. She looked at Brett determinedly, the depth of her hurt obvious. "I was right all along." Her hands shook as she withdrew her car keys from her pocket. "There is no such thing as romance in real life. I can watch it on television and read it in a book... but I'll never live it because the kind of man I want—the larger-than-life, dashing Rhett Butler of my dreams—just doesn't exist."

Belongings clasped to her chest, she turned on her heel and fled.

Brett caught up with her as she reached her car. He watched her open the door. Charlotte could think it was over all she wanted; that didn't make it so. "Where are you going?" Brett asked.

Charlotte tossed her purse and the Federal Express envelope onto the seat. She stood and looked at him over the top of the open car door. She glanced at her watch. Brett knew what she was thinking. She had just enough time to get into town before the last pickup of packages for the day. "I have to go into Poplar Springs."

"Fine. I'll go with you."

Charlotte looked like she wanted to argue.

"We can take two cars or one," Brett said. "Your choice. Either way, I'm going."

"Fine—go with me." Charlotte glared at him resentfully. "Maybe it's better this way, anyway. Maybe you need to see firsthand just how far I intend to go to sever the ties between us and, in the process, save Camellia Lane."

As Charlotte got in behind the wheel, Brett slipped lazily into the passenger seat. His glance fell on the package between them. She was sending it to *Personalities* magazine.

Charlotte followed his glance. "Aren't you going to try and make me promise not to tell anyone what I've discovered about you?" she taunted impatiently.

"Nope." Brett settled comfortably in the passenger seat and fastened his seat belt. He stretched his left arm along the back of the seat, his hand resting just short of her shoulder.

Charlotte stared straight ahead of her and delayed starting the car. "You expect me to believe that?" she said skeptically.

"Yes." His answer was short, matter-of-fact and very smug.

Charlotte's temper rose another notch. "You're not the only one who can be ruthless, Brett." She fitted her key into the ignition. "I could radically change your life, you know."

"I know." The silence that fell between them was laced with passion. "In more ways than you perhaps want to admit right now," he finished softly, then paused. He gave her a look, deliberately reminding her of everything they had shared. "I'm trusting you to do the right thing, Charlotte," he said.

The right thing, she thought. And what was that?

Should she be the fool that her father was and believe in a fraud just because he had a genial personality and a compelling argument? Or should she get back to the business of living her life and saving Camellia Lane?

Hands clenching the steering wheel, Charlotte turned her attention to backing out of the drive. It was just like Brett to try and use their romance to sway her into doing what he wanted, she thought miserably.

It would serve him right if she did expose him for the lying fraud that he was. There was even a sort of frontier justice in the idea of mailing the article she had just written right under his nose.

Certainly if she did send it, it would solve all her problems. It would end her romance with Brett, give her the money she needed and enhance her professional reputation. So why did that make her feel like crying? Why did she feel like her life was over, before it had really even begun?

They drove the rest of the way to Poplar Springs in mood silence.

Charlotte pulled up in front of the Federal Express dro box next to the bank. She consulted her watch. Fiftee minutes until the last pickup of the day.

She took the package and got out of the car.

Brett made no move to follow her.

If he had...if he'd told her he was sorry for what he' done...but he just sat there with that smug, angry, know ing look on his face.

Charlotte's temper took off like a rocket.

Shoulders back, head up, she strode confidently towar the drop box. She grabbed the handle and opened the ma slot, still expecting him to leap out of the car at any mo ment.

She waited to hear the words she longed for.

He stayed where he was. Feeling more miserable than sh ever had in her life, Charlotte adjusted her grip on th package and put it in the slot.

Again, she waited for Brett to prove she was wrong abou him, to somehow make everything right. Again, he di nothing.

Heart pounding, she stared down at the package. *It re ally is over,* she thought sadly, as the last of her hope fade *He really doesn't love me.*

Charlotte closed her eyes in abject misery. She'd been fool to think they might've had something that could las she thought sadly. Then she closed the box.

BRETT KNEW WHAT SHE was mailing. And that knowledg filled him with dread. He had been so sure she couldn't d it. He had been positive she loved him. Apparently, he wa wrong. Dead wrong.

He got out of the car, his lazy movements belying th deep, roiling fury he felt inside. He had never been be trayed the way Charlotte had just betrayed him.

"I guess we've made our choices," Brett said.

Charlotte tilted her head at him. "I guess we have."

There was nothing more to say. Brett turned and slowly walked away.

CHARLOTTE STARTED to leave town, then circled back. Without even thinking about it, she ended up in the parking lot next to the bank. She slid into a space and cut the motor on her car. She was still staring at the Federal Express drop box when the van pulled up. A guy in dark blue shorts and white shirt got out.

Charlotte beat him to the box. "Hi, I'm so glad you're here," she said breathlessly.

The uniformed courier quirked a brow. "You are?"

"Yes. I just put a package in the drop box a few minutes ago. I've changed my mind about sending it and I need it back."

"I don't know, Ms.—"

"Langston, Charlotte Langston."

"This is highly irregular."

Charlotte fumbled around in her purse. "Look. Here's my driver's license, my FedEx account card with my number on it.... You can see from the return address typed on the envelope that I'm the person who dropped it off. Please help me out here. It's absolutely critical that package *not be sent*."

"I CAN'T BELIEVE THEY'RE coming out to foreclose the day after tomorrow," Charlotte said to Paige and Isabella later that same evening. She still couldn't accept that Brett was Stephen Sterling and that she had passed up the opportunity to write the story of the decade and gain a bonus all in one fell swoop. And it was all because of Brett.

He had changed her. Before, she'd cared only about her work, her sisters and Camellia Lane. Now she knew there was more. Much more.

But not with him, she thought, and her heart broke y‹ again.

Paige studied the distressed look on Charlotte's fac‹ "You did your best to find the money to save Camelli Lane," Paige soothed.

"We all did," Isabella agreed.

Charlotte knew that was true. Unfortunately, that didn make her feel any better. She hated failing... and the ide of losing the only man she had ever loved. But what choic had she had? Brett hadn't told her the truth about himsel even after he'd made love to her, and without trust, the‹ could be no love. Not the lasting kind, anyway. She close her eyes as the future she had hoped to have with him witl ered away.

"Are you okay?" Isabella asked Charlotte softly.

Charlotte realized there was a tear on her cheek. Hastil she wiped it away. "Yes." Making the effort to pull herse. together, for her sisters' sakes as much as her own, sl squared her shoulders. "I think I just need to get busy," sl said with forced efficiency, "so I'll stop feeling so mauc lin."

Desperate to find something that would get her mind o. Brett, Charlotte looked at the shelves in the library. The tas of sorting through her father's collection of research bool was a daunting one. "Father must have two thousand bool in here," Charlotte murmured.

"Yes, and ninety-nine percent of them are about the Civ War," Paige said.

"What are we going to do with them?" Charlotte aske her sisters.

"I think we should box them up until we have time to g‹ through them," Isabella said. "I'm sure there are some we' want to save."

Paige went out into the front hall and returned with stack of unassembled moving boxes. Isabella got out th scissors and tape.

Charlotte pulled the ladder over to one end of the floor-to-ceiling bookcases. She climbed up while Paige taped the bottom of a moving carton. Isabella took the books Charlotte lifted down.

Charlotte blew off a layer of dust an inch thick. "Some of these books up here on the very top shelves are really old," she said.

"How old?" Isabella asked.

"I don't know." Charlotte sighed and opened the book to the copyright page in the front. She blew off another layer of dust. It didn't look as if they'd been touched for years and years. Certainly, she and her sisters had never really had any interest in her father's staggering collection of books. "Nineteen thirty-one on this one." She opened another book. It was as dusty as the first, the print slightly smudged, the papers fragile and yellowed with age. "Nineteen oh-nine on this one."

The three sisters looked at each other. Nineteen hundred and nine! They gasped collectively. "I don't believe it," Isabella murmured in shock. She looked at Paige and Charlotte. "I never knew father had any rare editions! These books are very valuable. I wonder why he never told us."

Paige shrugged. "Maybe he didn't realize they were really worth anything, except for the detailed information they contained on the Civil War. You know, he'd been collecting them all his life, and he bought a lot of them at estate sales and used bookshops. Perhaps the people he bought these from didn't realize their value, either."

Charlotte shook her head in mute disbelief. "I don't believe it," she whispered in awe. "Here we've been looking high and low for a solution, and the answer to our problems was here all along!"

"I ONLY *THOUGHT* OUR troubles were over," Charlotte said as she slammed in the house around suppertime the next evening. She was so furious she wanted to scream.

"Hiram wouldn't accept payment?" Isabella asked.

"Worse. He *couldn't* accept payment," Charlotte cor rected, her high heels clicking on the parquet floor as sh paced back and forth. "And you want to know why? Be cause the bank sold the balloon note and the mortgage t Camellia Lane. And you want to know who the bank sol them to?"

"From the look on your face," Paige drawled, "I'r afraid to ask."

"Brett Forrest, that's who!"

"Brett!" Isabella exclaimed, looking all the more cor fused. "But how could he, a poor student, possibly a ford—?"

"Never you mind," Charlotte said, abruptly cutting of Isabella's question, though why she was still protectin Brett, she didn't know. "Where is he? Did he move ou yet?"

Isabella and Paige exchanged peculiarly nervous look Finally, Isabella offered reluctantly, "Actually, Charlotte I think he's entertaining tonight."

"Entertaining!" Charlotte fumed. Did the man's audac ity know no bounds?

Paige nodded. "I saw him in a tux, too."

Well, that just figured, Charlotte thought. Now that th jig as caretaker was up, Brett would probably go back to h normal ways, whatever the heck they were. Maybe he live more like Matt Justice than she would ever have guessec "Where is he?" Charlotte demanded. When she found hir she was going to give him a piece of her mind.

"He's down at the cottage," Paige said.

"Hold it right there, Charlotte!" Isabella blocked th front door. "You can't talk to anyone when you're this up set, particularly Brett. Camellia Lane is at stake. You've g to be calm first."

Paige wrapped a comforting arm around Charlotte' shoulder. "Isabella's right, honey. What you need is a h bath and a glass of wine. Once you have a long soak and pu on something pretty, you'll be in command of yourself once more."

Charlotte looked at both her sisters. As much as she hated to admit it, they were right. She did not want to lose her temper with Brett again. She didn't want him to think he could still tap into her passions, even though he most defiitely could... and this fierce anger she felt was proof of that.

"You know what? I think we should all get gussied up and celebrate tonight," Paige suggested with a soothing smile. "After Charlotte squares things with Brett financially, the three of us will drive into Jackson and have ourselves an evening to remember."

Isabella propelled Charlotte toward the stairs. "You just go soak, and prepare yourself for the meeting with Brett. Paige and I will take care of everything else!"

After half an hour in the tub, Charlotte had to admit she did feel better. More relaxed and in control of herself. She opened the connecting door between bedroom and bath and saw a beautiful white organdy dress on the bed. Still clad only in a towel, Charlotte opened her door and called out into the hall. "Paige, where did this come from?"

"It's one of mine," her sister called back. "I wore it to the cosmetics company sales banquet last year."

"It's a formal!" With a very long slit up the side.

Paige walked into the room, looking very glamorous in a red, floor-length dress. "Let this be a lesson to you, Charlotte," Paige said as she fastened a gold bracelet on her wrist. "When the Langston women celebrate, we don't fool around. Besides, don't you want Brett to think you have somewhere important to go as soon as you've made the balloon payment to him?"

Paige had a point. Charlotte did want him to take one look at her and eat his heart out. She wanted him to know firsthand all he had lost, betraying her the way he had. "Fine. But as soon as I talk to him, we're getting out of here!" Charlotte said.

"Agreed. Do you want Isabella and I to come with you
when you talk to him?" Paige asked.

"No," Charlotte said firmly. There was no telling what
Brett might say or do. "I'll do this alone."

Charlotte took extra care getting ready for her meeting
with Brett. She swept her dark curls up on the back of her
neck, carefully applied her makeup and spritzed herself with
lilac perfume before stepping into the strapless white organdy dress and silver evening sandals.

Deciding she looked every bit as lovely as she had the
night of the Confederate costume ball, Charlotte picked up
the check and folded it into the snug-fitting bodice of her
dress. When she handed the check to Brett, it would be
scented with her signature perfume and warmed by her skin.
Another reminder of all he could have had and had given
up....

Charlotte swept downstairs.

Her heart pounding with anticipation of the fireworks to
come, she set off to find Brett. No sooner had she stepped
off the veranda and into the formal gardens, however, than
she had the strong feeling she was being watched.

Scanning the moonlit area swiftly, she could detect nothing unusual. Still, goose bumps rose on her arms. Picking
up her pace, she hurried to the cottage. She was almost there
when Brett stepped out of the shadows.

He was dressed in a tux. He looked darkly handsome.
And very determined. Just the way she supposed Matt
Justice would look when confronting a female nemesis.
Knowing Matt Justice never lost a battle with a lover,
Charlotte struggled to maintain her outward cool. It wasn't
easy when he was looking at her like he meant to make her
his again, no holds barred this time.

"I hear you and your sisters had quite a day today," Brett
drawled as he closed the distance between them.

Charlotte swallowed. She had seen him in many situations, under many circumstances, but he had never looked
this determined or hell-bent on having his own way. There

was a decidedly rapacious gleam in his eyes, an anticipatory curve to his sensual mouth.

Charlotte felt her heart do a flip-flop. *This guy just deceived you,* she reminded herself firmly. *Don't be a fool and let him do it again.*

"Yes, we did," she said matter-of-factly, digging in where she stood. She tried to act as if his presence there were no big deal as Brett strolled farther into the moonlit formal gardens. "We sold my father's books on the Civil War to a collector in New Orleans. He drove over this morning to inspect them, gave us a cashier's check and took the rare editions with him. The rest will be shipped tomorrow. Then, as you may also have heard, I went over to the bank to pay off the balloon note on our loan."

"And found out it had been sold."

"I also found out it can still be paid off." Charlotte withdrew the cashier's check she had tucked into the bodice of her dress. Stiffly, she handed it over.

Brett accepted it wordlessly, his eyes steady on hers. Then he tucked the check right back where she'd gotten it, the backs of his fingers brushing her breasts evocatively in the process.

Charlotte's mouth fell open; a little gasp was wrung from her.

Brett continued to smile down at her in that all-consuming way. "Money's not what I want from you, Charlotte. Never was, never will be," he said softly, his heated gaze roving her upturned face.

Of course, thought Charlotte, breathing in deeply, how could she have been so stupid? Brett was and always had been truly concerned about only one thing: keeping Sterling's identity a secret. Feeling for the first time she was a little out of her league—at least when he was looking at her in such an unabashedly ardent way—she stiffened her shoulders and continued to hold herself aloof from him. "If you're worried that I told someone about who you are, you needn't be," she said, tilting her chin at him defiantly. "Not even my sisters know."

Again, Brett didn't look the least bit surprised at the way she had protected him. He did, however, look grateful. "Thank you," he said softly. "That means a lot to me. But—" he shrugged his broad shoulders eloquently "—the way things have turned out, you didn't even have to do that."

Once again, Charlotte was stunned. She felt caught off guard, like she might not ever get her equilibrium back where he was concerned.

"Oh, really? And why was that?" she asked coolly.

"Because I've decided that keeping my identity a secret is a lost cause, and I plan to give up the ruse—immediately. A plan to which my publishers and attorney have agreed."

"But, Brett—why?"

He looked at her thoughtfully. "To understand, you'd have to go way back to when the secrecy started."

Once again, Charlotte was caught up in the need to know absolutely everything about him. "I'm listening," she said cautiously.

"Okay, but if I'm telling this story, we're getting comfortable first." Before she could move to evade him, Brett swept her up into his arms and started toward the house. His strides were long and lazy, his expression implacable and arrogant as hell. Worse, he was behaving exactly the way Matt Justice would when confronted with a contrary woman he desired.

Getting over her brief moment of shock, Charlotte began to squirm with all her might. "Put me down!"

Brett paused, eyed her thoughtfully and tightened his grip on her. "Kick your legs like that one more time, Miss Charlotte, and you're gonna be hoisted over my shoulder," he warned silkily.

And he meant it.

Charlotte stopped kicking and went stiff as a board in his arms instead. "Pay attention here, Brett. I am not amused."

"Somehow, I figured you wouldn't be." He grinned, all bad boy again.

As Charlotte continued to fume, Brett continued to stride, looking no more winded than had he been carrying a sack of potato chips. He hit the veranda and marched through the back door, Charlotte still in his arms. Through the kitchen, down the hall...where Paige and Isabella were, looking not the least surprised as Brett strode by.

"Are we having fun yet?" Paige quipped.

"You were both part of this, weren't you?" Charlotte accused, glaring at her elegantly clad sisters over Brett's shoulder.

"What are sisters for?" Paige teased.

"Besides, you were being so all-fired stubborn and difficult that Brett needed some help. However, since it looks as if he's doing fine now," Isabella said with a wink at Brett, "Paige and I'll just be leaving for our evening out in Jackson, as planned."

"Traitors!" Charlotte called over her shoulder.

"You'll thank us in the morning!" Paige predicted. Both she and Isabella laughed. The door slammed behind them.

"You can put me down anytime now," Charlotte said through her teeth.

Brett bent and brushed his mouth lightly, teasingly across hers. "Not until we get to the third floor."

"Oh, no," Charlotte groaned, beginning to get an idea where all this was going.

His blue eyes sparkling, Brett grinned down at her. "Oh, yes. Some things were just meant to be. Tonight is one of them," he promised. He strode into the ballroom. Charlotte took in champagne on ice, fresh flowers and silver chafing dishes. A table for two had been set up next to the windows. Soft music played in the background. It was perfect for a romantic evening for two. Judging by the happy grin on his face, Brett was counting on having a fabulous time.

"You really are presuming far too much," Charlotte said.

"We'll see." Brett set her down on the velvet window seat. He propped a foot on the seat next to her and rested his forearm across his thigh. "Now, where were we?" he asked cheerfully.

Charlotte sat back and folded her arms in front of her. "You were going to tell me why you'd changed your mind about revealing your identity to the world," she said.

Brett nodded, his expression becoming abruptly thoughtful. "It goes back to the way things were when my career was first getting started. I knew I wanted to be a novelist from the time I entered college, but I also had to support myself."

He sat down beside her and took her hand in his.

"My first job was teaching freshman English for a college in Rhode Island. There was a lot of pressure on me to publish, but I was expected to write literary fiction. I knew if I told anyone I was working on a commercial novel, I'd take a lot of flak for it. So I told no one. When the first book came out, I was still working at the college to pay the bills. I published under a pen name, for privacy, never dreaming that the book would become a runaway bestseller."

"But it did," Charlotte reflected softly.

"Yes, and suddenly there was a lot of pressure from my publisher to get out there and promote my book." Brett's mouth twisted in a rueful grin. "You may have noticed I don't like to be told what to do."

"Just a little," Charlotte quipped.

"So I resisted, through my attorney, Franklin Dunn. Finally, when I thought about giving in and doing some promoting, the public relations department of my publisher insisted I keep up the mystery because it sold my books better than any PR campaign ever could. And so, ever since the first book, that's been a part of my contract. Only now that's backfiring, too, because you aren't the only journalist hot on my trail, Charlotte. So we've decided jointly that I will go public with my identity, and soon."

"I see," Charlotte said slowly. She disengaged her hand from his and stood. "So I gave up the scoop on you for nothing?" she asked, feeling both hurt and incredulous.

"No. We all agree you should write the story, Charlotte. So anytime you're ready, I'll cooperate."

Despite her anger with him, she had to admit it was a generous offer, one she hadn't expected to receive. "I don't know what to say," Charlotte said slowly as his warm palms slid across her shoulders and down to her forearms, before sliding back up to her shoulders again.

"How about you forgive me?" he asked.

Charlotte saw the desire in his eyes. The shiver inside her intensified. Aware how close she was to surrendering herself to him on any terms, she stepped back half a pace, her mouth dry. "I don't think so," she said breathlessly.

Brett's strong fingers twined with hers. "Why not?" he asked gently.

Charlotte watched as Brett's head tilted and dipped toward her mouth. Knowing if she closed her eyes and yielded to his kiss, she'd be lost forever, she jerked away from him, then whirled to confront him. "Because there's still a lot we have to work out," she said irascibly.

Brett waited, no less determined, no less patient. "Such as?"

Charlotte drew a tremulous breath. "Why did you buy the mortgage and the balloon note?" Was it possible Brett had wanted Camellia Lane, and not her? Charlotte exhaled shakily as Brett closed the distance between them.

"I did that because I wanted to help you and I still do. Not just with the bank," Brett said as he took her hands in his. He bent forward to kiss the tip of her nose. "But with the cotton crop, too."

Wanting desperately not to be taken in again, she studied Brett's face. "What else do you want?"

"You."

Just like that. As if nothing had ever happened, Charlotte thought angrily. "That's impossible," she said.

But Brett didn't think so.

He rubbed her lower lip with the pad of his thumb. "Tell me that after I've kissed you again and I'll believe you," he said.

She had resolved to make him pay for humiliating her, but this was fading fast under the evocative tenderness of his caress. Charlotte twisted out of his grip. She didn't want to be made a fool of again. She stood glowering at him, her arms folded tightly beneath her breasts. "If you think we're going right back to being lovers just because you now hold the mortgage to Camellia Lane, you have another think coming, Brett Forrest."

Brett looked down at her for a long moment, his look one of complete fascination. The ends of his mustache turned up as he began to grin that sexy, boyish grin she loved so much. "How about if we go back to being lovers because we want it that way and we belong together, then?" he proposed.

Charlotte stiffened. She was not going to let herself fall for that Rhett Butler charm of his again. No matter what. "You're still out of luck," she said archly.

Brett shook his head at her, his expression rueful. "I thought it might come to this," he admitted solemnly. He reached into his jacket pocket and withdrew a long white envelope. "That's why I had my attorney transfer the deed for Camellia Lane to you and your sisters again. It's yours again, Charlotte, free and clear, so forget the idea that the plantation might stand between us, 'cause it's just not gonna happen. Now, any more objections?"

"Why are you doing this?" Charlotte asked. She could tell by the way he was looking at her that he wanted something from her. He wanted a lot. Was it more than she could give? Charlotte wondered as a shiver started deep inside her. Or just enough?

"Because we have unfinished business between us, Charlotte."

Her heart began a slow, heavy beat. "Such as?"

"Such as this." Brett reached inside his blazer and pulled out a small jeweler's box. He handed it to Charlotte. "Go ahead. Open it."

She did. Inside were her mother's pendant and earrings. Tears sprang to her eyes as all the love she had felt for Brett came rushing to the fore. For a moment, she was so overcome with emotion she didn't know what to say. She only knew all the things that had separated them suddenly seemed very inconsequential. "You bought these back for me?" she whispered, stunned that he knew how much she cherished her mother's jewelry.

He nodded as he pulled her into his arms. "I didn't want anyone else to get them first."

"Oh, Brett," Charlotte said softly, the tenderness of his actions wrapping around her heart, drawing them close. "You really do understand me."

Brett grinned. "I'm sure as hell trying," he said.

The next thing she knew, they were kissing. Warm, wonderful, heartfelt kisses. Finally, when she was breathless and aching, he lifted his head. Charlotte was shaking as they drew apart. Brett wrapped one arm snugly around her waist. With his other hand, he lifted her chin. "Now on to the truly important matters. I want you to be mine, Charlotte, heart and soul," he said in a soft, urgent voice filled with love. "And I want you to wear your mother's jewelry on our wedding day."

Charlotte's heart pounded. For a moment, she was sure she hadn't heard right. She blinked. "Our wedding day?"

Brett grinned his most wicked grin. "I really think every Rhett ought to have his Scarlett, don't you, Charlotte?" He took her hand in his and got down on one knee. "Marry me, Charlotte."

Charlotte got down on her knees, too. She wrapped her arms about him exuberantly and hugged him tightly. He felt so good. So warm and strong and solid, like always. "Oh, Brett," she whispered joyously. He did love her after all!

"I take it that's a yes?" he asked tenderly.

"Absolutely," she said, with tears of happiness sparkling in her eyes. Then he kissed her again, the way he had when everything was still good, the way she had wanted him to even when they were fighting. And everything in the world felt right once again.

Brett drew her to her feet. As he took her into his arms and held her close, Charlotte felt like she had come home at last. "How would you feel about making our home here at Camellia Lane?" he asked.

Her heart pounding, Charlotte looked at Brett. She had been thinking along the same lines. "You wouldn't mind?"

"I can't think of a better place to begin our life together, or raise a family," he said.

"I can't, either," Charlotte whispered back, and then his mouth lowered to take hers in a masterfully possessive kiss.

Long moments later, he lifted his head. As he gazed down at her, his eyes were a vivid blue. "I love you, Miss Charlotte," he said tenderly. Then, apparently unable to resist, he added teasingly, "And unlike Rhett Butler, I really do give a damn."

Charlotte laughed softly, aware as always that Camellia Lane evoked all the romantic fantasy and elegance of an era gone by... but not forgotten.

Knowing that, in Brett, she really had found her Rhett, she wreathed her arms around his neck. She had never felt happier, nor more content.

"And I love you, Brett Forrest," she said softly. "So very, very much."

Fifty red-blooded, white-hot, true-blue hunks
from every State in the Union!

Look for MEN MADE IN AMERICA! Written by some
of our most popular authors, these stories feature some
of the strongest, sexiest men, each from a different state
in the union!

Two titles available every month at your favorite
retail outlet.

In January, look for:

WITHIN REACH by Marilyn Pappano (New Mexico)
IN GOOD FAITH by Judith McWilliams (New York)

In February, look for:

THE SECURITY MAN by Dixie Browning
(North Carolina)
A CLASS ACT by Kathleen Eagle
(North Dakota)

You won't be able to resist MEN MADE IN AMERICA!